Seeds of Doubt

by

James Parr

To my wife, Liz

and to my children

Clare, Jonty and Emily

Prologue

Friday, 6th April 2012

Susan Linton runs her eye along her collection of DVDs. Raiders of the Lost Ark.....Rain Man... Return of the Jedi. Where is it? Has Kate hidden it to spite her? No, there it is, hiding between Rear Window and Room with a View. Easing the disc off its spindle, she wheels herself over to the television and inserts it into the player. Then, swinging her wheelchair round, reverses to the end of the sofa.

As the opening credits roll, her mind wanders. Kate will be at the Cumberland by now. She can just picture them as they making their entrances, hugging and kissing like the close friends they never were. And how is poor Susan, they will want to know? Oh dear, and there was even the chance she might have walked again, if only she had put in more effort. But how is everyone? It's been ages. So much catching up to do...

As the credits end she clicks on SCENE SELECTION. She won't watch the whole movie tonight. Just her opening scene where she comes through the revolving doors and trips, straight into the arms of darling Richard Gere. What a lovely man. He was so kind and solicitous when he learned of the accident, telephoning every day and sending that wonderful bouquet. And what a time she had making that film. The thrill of it, just to be in Hollywood, meeting and mixing with the stars. The New York critics were in raptures about her. Another Vivien Leigh, they said - a star in the making.

There is the creak of a floorboard, a slight draught as the door is opened, but she is too engrossed to notice either. Nor does she hear the soft pad of approaching footsteps. It is only when he is right behind her that she turns to catch a glimpse as his arm sweeps down and plunges the knife deep into the soft flesh below her right shoulder blade. For a split second she feels nothing, but then a startling, searing pain shoots through her body, down even to the atrophied nerves of her lower limbs. Screaming, she grabs at his hair, his face, his neck, holding on as she tumbles out of her wheelchair to the floor. But already the strength is going out of her...she feels faint... dizzy...sick... and the light is fading...fading to darkness.

Gasping from his exertions, he kneels astride her to check her breathing. Is she dead? Best to make sure. He plunges the knife into her stomach. Then again and twice more. Enough. Rising to his feet he stands over her, barely believing what he has done. But he had no choice. She made him do it.

Chapter One

i.

Detective Inspector Steve Straker padded through to the lounge in his dressing gown and slippers and slumped on the sofa. Three days break, his first weekend off in months. But to do what?. He could mow the lawn, he supposed, though it didn't look as if it needed it yet. Or clear out the garage. He yawned. Beside him on the coffee table was the paperback still nestling in its packaging. Read something, Emily said. Anything. It will take you out of yourself. Picking it up he turned it over to read the blurb. *Stockholm, winter. A serial killer is terrorising the city and Detective Inspector Ulf Bjorkquist is charged with tracking him down. But Bjorkquist has problems of his own. His alcoholic half sister....* Tossing the book aside he slumped down again and closed his eyes.

'Is there anything we need?' Emily stood in the doorway, fastening her coat. 'We've got chicken for tomorrow's lunch... and if we're going out tonight?'

'Yes. I'll reserve a table.'

'That's if you want to go out. We needn't if you don't feel like it.'

'I've said already. I want to go out.' His tone was sharper than he intended and he had to check himself before continuing. 'I'll ring them now. Not that there'll be anyone there this early.'

She looked at him patiently for a few seconds, then turned to go. 'Okay. I won't be long.'

Stretching out again Straker sighed. Emily said he should see a doctor, but what good would that do? Depression was hardly an illness when he had every reason to be depressed. The phone rang in the hall. He sat up and listened. Who was she talking to? Not him, surely. He wouldn't be stupid enough to ring her on a Saturday.

Emily came back into the lounge. 'It's for you. It's Mary Chandos.,

'Mary Chandos?' He took the handset from her. What did she want? This was supposed to be his weekend off. 'Hi Mary. What can I do for you?'

'Sorry to trouble you, Steve, but the Chief wants to know if you've got plans for today.'

He glanced at Emily who was slowly shaking her head. 'No. Nothing in particular. Why?'

'Something's come up. I don't know what it is yet, but Jerry is keen for you to come in.'

He hesitated, but only for a moment. 'Tell him I'm on my way.'

ii.

Within the hour Straker arrived at Thames Valley Police Headquarters in Kidlington and made his way upstairs to the office of Detective Chief Superintendent Jerry Rawlings. The Chief's PA, Mary Chandos greeted him with a smile.

'Don't pump me about this Steve. He's pretty keen to tell you himself.'

Straker sat down opposite her and listened to the soft mumble of the Chief's voice behind the closed door. He liked Mary, a plump, motherly woman who took no nonsense from anybody. 'We're not short staffed this weekend are we, Mary?'

'No, there's a full team. How's Emily, by the way? I haven't seen a lot of her recently.'

'Emily? Yes, she's good.'

'We've got tickets for your play, Steve. You're a dark horse. I didn't realise you were in it too.'

Tickets for the play? He had expressly asked Emily to tell nobody connected with work. 'Oh that. No, it's only a walk on part. I'm just standing in for someone who broke his leg. Anyway, who told you I was in it?'

'Dan. Dan Masterson.'

Straker stiffened. 'You know Dan Masterson?'

'Yes, I know Dan. He was our neighbour before he moved out your way. I saw him yesterday in the town and he said he's playing the male lead opposite Emily.' She smiled. 'You had better watch out, Steve. He's quite a heartthrob.'

Straker turned and gazed out of the window. He didn't care for Dan Masterson. Recently divorced, his arrival in the village just before Christmas had caused quite a stir, especially among the women. Like Emily he had gone to the first audition saying he was happy to take any role, even a small one. But it was evident before he had read even a page that he was a natural. Anton, the director, was completely besotted and immediately offered him the male lead. Only later did Masterson let slip that he had once worked in repertory theatre, until the need to support a young family put paid to an acting career.

5

'I'd rather you didn't put it about that I'm in a play, Mary. I don't think amateur dramatics is good for my image.'

'Oh dear. And I've already mentioned it to Jerry, though I'm sure he didn't take it in.' She paused and listened 'That's him finishing now.' Picking up the phone she pressed the button. 'Steve is here to see you, Jerry.'

A moment later the door opened and out came the Chief, a bear of a man, with a shock of frizzy white hair. 'Good morning, Steve. Thanks for coming in at short notice. I appreciate it.'

'No problem.' Straker gave Mary a wink as he passed her desk into Rawlings' office.

iii.

Directing him to a seat, Rawlings eyed him through his bushy eyebrows. 'Not long to your play, eh? I told Grace we had a budding thespian in the team and we thought we might come along. Actually, I was thinking of getting up a party of the lads. Give you moral support.'

Straker felt himself growing hot. 'I'd prefer it if you didn't, Jerry. Acting's not my forte. I'm only doing it to help out.'

Thankfully Rawlings appeared to forget the play as he leaned forward, hands clasped. 'The name Susan Linton ring any bells?'

'Susan Linton? Yes. Film actress. She had a riding accident a few years back that left her paralysed. She lives somewhere over my way, I'm told.'

6

'That's right, she does. Or did. Elleswood. Near Princes Risborough. She's been murdered. Found by her housekeeper around 8.30am this morning. Stabbed several times in the chest and stomach. The local police got there soon after 9.00am and the Scene of Crime boys arrived about fifteen minutes later. Jack Meredith is there too with some of his Forensics team. He called me just now with an update.'

'What have they found so far?'

'The whole house was turned over. Cupboards and drawers pulled open, contents tipped out, that sort of thing. On the face of it, a burglary that got out of hand. Drug related, maybe. But why kill a helpless woman in a wheelchair? I know some of these drug heads are pretty crazy, but she could hardly have posed much of a threat.'

'Was she sexually assaulted?

'Jack thinks not. She was fully clothed and there was no obvious sign of interference.'

'Do they know how her attacker, or attackers got in?'

'Through a door at the back apparently. A glass panel was broken and the key taken from the inside. Though Jack thinks whoever did it left by the front door. When the housekeeper arrived this morning it was wide open.'

'And who's leading the investigation, Jerry?' said Straker, sensing where the conversation might be leading.

Rawlings leaned back in his chair. 'I want you to lead it, Steve. I thought it would be right up your street, what with you being a bit of a thespian yourself.' He smiled. 'No, I'm serious. This is a Category A murder. There'll be a lot of media interest. You know, televised news conferences, Crimewatch probably. I need someone with a bit of presence to head it up. Care to take it on?'

Straker hesitated, but only momentarily. 'Glad to.'

Rawlings picked up a typed sheet and handed it to him. 'We haven't got much to go on so far. We're trying to locate the lady's next of kin and I've arranged to pull in all the local suspects and registered drug addicts for questioning. We've also put calls through to the mental health clinics and secure units to see if anyone has gone missing.'

Straker ran his eyes down the sheet. 'Didn't she have a husband who went to prison?'

'She did. George Mannering, also an actor, working mainly in TV soaps. Married him in 2001 and they divorced five years later, shortly after her riding accident. He's just done time for sex crimes. Internet grooming, that sort of thing. Came out a few weeks ago'

'That's right. I read about it. Hasn't he just been charged with more offences?'

'He has. More of the same, I think. He's currently on bail, living in a halfway house in Manchester. We've just put in a call, but the warden says he's not there. Hasn't been seen since yesterday morning. It's a lead, Steve, something to work on.' Rawlings sat back. 'What else can we do to get things on their way for you?

'CCTV, speed cameras?

'Yes. I doubt if there's much, but it's worth a look.'

'Okay.' Straker stood up. 'I'll get straight over.'

'Elleswood House, Steve, two miles outside Wendover. I've checked it on Google. Big pile, stands on its own. The housekeeper's address is there too. Kate Bellingham. She has a small cottage just up the road from the house. There's a Community Support Officer with her now. I suggest you base yourself at

Aylesbury. I've phoned and they are arranging to allocate you an incident room and an office.' He paused. 'And I was thinking, Steve, that you might take DS Wakeman as your number two.

Straker looked steadily at Rawlings. He didn't care for Kevyn Wakeman. 'Fine. I'm sure Wakeman and I will work well together.'

'We can allocate more as you need them, but I suggest you keep a tight team. There's bound to be a lot of media interest and we can't afford any leaks.'

Rawlings smiled. 'I know Wakeman has some rough edges, Steve, but he's a good man. I thought you would be just the person to smooth him out.'

iv.

Fifteen minutes later Straker and Detective Sergeant Kevyn Wakeman were on their way to the village of Elleswood. Wakeman drove aggressively, paying scant attention to speed limits or other road users. Straker decided to keep his cool. He wanted to get the relationship off to a good start and there seemed little point in creating friction before the investigation had even begun. But he was annoyed at being saddled with Wakeman. The two of them held the same rank until six months ago and he had sensed Wakeman's resentment ever since his promotion. Of similar age, their backgrounds could hardly be more different. Straker had joined the police at twenty eight but, as a graduate, quickly gained a place on the High Potential Development Scheme and had risen to his present rank of inspector in just eight years. Wakeman, by contrast, left school with no academic

9

qualifications and spent six years in the army before joining the police at twenty three. So, with six more years service, it was hardly surprising that he resented Straker's promotion ahead of him.

'Had you heard of this actress woman then, Steve?' said Wakeman, chewing gum ferociously as he manoeuvred the car in and out of the line of traffic and using every opportunity to overtake.

'Susan Linton? Yes. Had you?'

'No. Don't go to films much. A looker, was she?'

Straker could feel his irritation rising already. 'She wasn't glamorous, if that's what you mean.'

'Good looking, glamorous. Same thing isn't it, when it comes to women?'

'She was mainly on stage, but she did a few films. I expect you've seen her in something'

'I wouldn't know.' Wakeman turned towards him and grinned. 'A little bird tells me you're a budding actor yourself.'

Straker sighed inwardly. Did Jerry keep nothing to himself? 'No, it's my wife who's into amateur dramatics. I just lend a hand behind the scenes.'

'Not what I heard? I heard you were playing a detective.'

'Yes, well... it's only a small part. I'm just doing it to help out.'

'And your good lady? What part is she playing?'

Thankfully Straker didn't have to answer as Wakeman's attention was now focused on the elderly driver in front who was resolutely occupying the crown of the road while staying obediently within the speed limit. Unaware of Wakeman's aggressive tailgating, he was signalling to turn right, even though the turn off was still a good three hundred yards ahead. Suddenly, with a muttered curse, Wakeman swung the steering wheel and with an angry burst of speed, overtook on the inside.

Straker gave a weary sigh 'Susan Linton is dead, Kevyn. I don't think an extra five minutes will make any difference.'

'No, but he shouldn't be driving at his age, should he? Did you see him? He must have been eighty at least. I'd make everyone take another test once they get to seventy. That would get a lot of them off the road.'

Straker didn't respond. They were passing now through Stoke Mandeville, close to the hospital where Susan Linton was treated after the riding accident that ended her career. He remembered his shock when he heard it on the news. At first everyone thought she would end up like Christopher Reeve, the Superman actor, with little or no function from the neck down. Then the prognosis began to look more optimistic. Some feeling and movement returned to her arms and one of her legs. But it was evident that her career was over and she quickly faded from the news.

Wakeman slowed a little as they arrived at Elleswood with its long line of houses facing the sweep of fields that rose to the ridge of the Ridgeway escarpment. Ahead of them, blocking the road was a police car, parked at forty five degrees and a police officer directing traffic. Wakeman wound down the window and flashed his identity badge as they turned between two tall brick columns into the drive. There were three cars parked already in the large gravelled area in front of the house. one of which Straker recognised as belonging to Head of Forensics, Jack Meredith. In their white overalls, two members of the Scene of Crime team were working within an area enclosed by red and white plastic tape that stretched

11

down the side of the property. Two more crouched in the porch, presumably looking for footprints.

Straker looked up at the house. Though probably Victorian, it was built in a mock Tudor style with a half timbered black and white facade and tall elaborate chimneys. It looked in a poor state of repair, with rotting sills and window frames and large areas of bare woodwork where the paint had flaked away. Ivy had spread its tentacles across several of the windows and up on to the moss covered roof. To the right of the house stood a prefabricated double garage, its concrete side panels green with mould. Tall weeds grew in front of the padlocked doors indicating that they were rarely opened. The grounds, about an acre in total, had evidently not been tended in years. What might once have been elegant lawn had turned to field grass, thick with nettles, thistles, and self seeded saplings.

'Good morning, Steve. Good morning, Kevyn,'

They turned to see the burly figure of Jack Meredith, coming round from the back of the house to greet them. 'So Jerry nobbled you did he, Steve? He said you were just the man for the job.'

'I don't think I had much choice,' said Straker as they shook hands. 'How's it going?'

'Slow, but we're making progress.' Meredith nodded in the direction of the large window to the left of the door. 'The body's in there.'

Straker peered through the window. 'I gather her attacker came in through the back door.'

'It looks that way. And made his exit via the front door, it seems. The housekeeper found it wide open when she arrived this morning.'

The three men walked round the side of the house. Through the large bay window Straker could see more of the Scene of Crime team at work. 'Have you spoken to the housekeeper?'

'Briefly. I called on her at her cottage once I'd done a walk through the house. She was in quite a state, so I only stayed a minute or two.'

After examining the back door with its broken glass panel, they returned to the large gravelled area at the front of the house.

'Any footprints or tyre marks?'

Not that we've found so far. As you see we're checking the pavement and road in both directions, as well as the drive. Meredith opened the small briefcase he was carrying and took out an Ipad, which he placed on the bonnet of his car. 'You'll appreciate I can't let you into the house just yet, gentlemen. But I can give you a quick video tour.'

The tour began with a wide angle shot of the lounge, showing books and papers strewn all over the floor. It panned then across to a cupboard with the doors flung open and a chest with the drawers pulled out, before zooming in on Susan Linton's body. The actress was stretched out on the floor, close to her wheelchair, in front of a large old fashioned television. She was lying on her back. One arm covered her face, the other reached out towards the fireplace. Her bloodstained blouse was in tatters.

How many times was she stabbed?' said Straker

'Four times at least to her chest and stomach. But to her back as well, judging by the blood that has seeped out from under her. We haven't moved her yet. We think she was watching a film when it happened. The DVD was in the player and the television was still on, set to the DVD channel."

The video tour moved out of the sitting room and into the hall, pausing at the far end to show the staircase and a chairlift fitted against the wall.

Crossing the hall it passed into the dining room, furnished with a large central dining table and an elegant Victorian dresser. Again cupboard doors were wide open and drawers pulled out, although here none of the contents appeared to have been disturbed.

'What about that filing cabinet?' said Straker as the camera panned to the right to reveal a grey metal cabinet beside another door.

'Not touched. It's still locked and there's no sign of any attempt to open it. According to the housekeeper, it contains the actress's fan mail. I asked for the key but she said she hasn't seen it in years. Apparently Miss Linton became quite possessive about her fan mail following her accident. We'll find it before the day is out. Otherwise we'll force it open.'

The tour passed through the kitchen and other downstairs rooms, before going upstairs to the bedrooms and bathrooms. Although untidy, these rooms looked in better order, suggesting that by this time, either the intruder had found what he was looking for, or concluded that there was nothing else worth taking.

'Okay,' said Straker. 'We'll go and talk to the housekeeper. How soon before you can let us into the house?

'Give me an hour Steve. By that time we should be able to clear you a way through.

v.

Straker and Wakeman drew up outside a small white cottage on the narrow switchback road leading to the upmarket village of Wendover.

'We need to handle her gently, Kevyn,' said Straker, sensing Wakeman's impatience to get the investigation moving. 'She's had a nasty shock this morning.'

'No problem, boss. It's your call.' Wakeman strolled round the car to join him on the pavement. 'But you're going to need a lead or two before you go on TV this afternoon.'

'I know that.' Straker felt a small shiver. He had never done a televised press conference. 'We'll get from her what we can.'

The door was opened by a female community support officer who stepped aside to allow them to enter the narrow hall. She pointed to a door on the right. 'She's in there. She's had some tea. Would you like some?'

'We're fine, thanks,' said Straker opening the door to a tiny sitting room where Susan Linton's housekeeper rose diffidently to greet them. Far from being the middle aged or elderly woman he was expecting, Kate Bellingham was tall and elegant with high cheekbones and long dark hair swept back in a pony tail. He guessed her to be somewhere between forty five and fifty.

'Miss Bellingham, good morning. Detective Inspector Steve Straker, Thames Valley CID and my colleague, Detective Sergeant Kevyn Wakeman.'

She looked nervous. 'Good morning gentlemen. I'm sorry. I'm afraid it's rather cramped in here.'

'We're sorry to trouble you, Miss Bellingham. This is a distressing time for you.'

She gestured for them to sit down. 'I'm afraid the sofa might not be big enough for both of you.'

Wakeman stepped aside. 'Go ahead boss. I'm happy to stand.'

As Straker sat down opposite Kate Bellingham he was acutely conscious of Wakeman hovering over him behind the sofa. He felt nervous. He wasn't comfortable with women, especially elegant, attractive women.

'You will appreciate, Miss Bellingham that we need to ask a lot of questions. If you feel like taking a break, please say so.'

'Thank you, Inspector, but I hope that won't be necessary.' She took an embroidered handkerchief from her sleeve and wrapped it tightly round her fingers.

'Can I begin by asking you to describe what you saw when you arrived at the house this morning?'

Kate Bellingham described how she had arrived at about 8.15am, which was a little later than normal because she had been in London the previous evening and stayed overnight in a hotel. Catching an early morning train back to Wendover, she drove home to change, before walking down to the house.

'The first thing that struck me, Inspector was that the door was open. I don't mean just unlocked. It was wide open. Two or three years ago that wouldn't have surprised me. In the early days following her accident, Susan would sometimes get up early and practise walking outside on her walking frame. But she hadn't done that in a long time. In fact, over the past year or more, she was usually still in bed when I arrived. So I called out as I entered, but there was no answer.'

She seemed on the verge of tears now as she continued twisting the handkerchief between her fingers.

'Please take your time, Miss Bellingham,' said Straker gently.

'I'm sorry,' she said, her eyes brimming with tears. 'This has all been such a shock. Anyway, as I came

16

into the hall I was aware of an unfamiliar smell. I can't describe it, but it wasn't a nice smell and I sensed that something wasn't right. Then I looked in the drawing room. The door was half open, which was unusual as Susan was in the habit of closing all the doors before she went to bed. I didn't see her at first because the room was such a mess. There were things all over the floor, drawers pulled out, books, papers, all over the place. I thought, my God, we've had burglars. Then I thought, dreadful as it was, perhaps Susan wasn't even aware that there had been a break in. She often took sleeping pills, you see, and I even had to wake her sometimes. But then I noticed her wheel chair parked at an odd angle at the far end of the sofa, right up against the television. I thought, why is that there? She always leaves it at the bottom of the stairs when she goes up to bed on the chair lift. Her voice faltered and she paused a few moments. 'Then I saw her. I hadn't seen her at first because the sofa was in the way, but there she was lying on the carpet, covered in blood. It was such a shock...She was my friend, Inspector, my closest friend...'

Straker looked away as she dabbed her eyes with her handkerchief. After a few moments she shook her head as if to get a grip on herself. 'I knew she was dead. I knew there was nothing I could do for her.'

'Was that when you called the police?'

'No, not then. At first I just stood there. It was as if I was glued to the ground. But then I came to my senses. Only a madman could have done this, I thought. What if he was still in the house, in another room perhaps, or upstairs searching the house? At any moment he might come and find me. In a panic, I just turned and ran out of the house, down to the crossroads and round the corner to the first house I came to. Fortunately Mr Carter was at home and he

17

made me sit down while I told him what had happened. He called the police immediately and then he made me a cup of tea. I stayed with him until your young officer arrived and she brought me home.' She paused, looking anxiously at Straker. 'I'm sorry. I'm not being very coherent, am I.'

Straker gave her an encouraging smile. 'On the contrary, you're being most helpful. May, I ask how long you've known Miss Linton?'

'A very long time. We met at drama school. I was an actress too, you see.'

They listened as Kate Bellingham described her long friendship with the actress, from their first meeting at drama school, through their early years of flat sharing when they were both working in repertory, to the time when Susan Linton began to make a name for herself on the London stage. Her big break came with the offer of a supporting role in a Hollywood film which led to a short spell on American television. This was followed by two more Hollywood films, both in larger roles.

'She could have made a fortune, Inspector but, in the end, she decided she didn't care for the Los Angeles lifestyle. She made those two films, then insisted on being released from her contract. They weren't very good films and they didn't have much success at the box office, but she won good notices. Perhaps you remember them.'

Straker was listening with such rapt attention that it took him a moment to realise that a response was required 'Yes, I think I remember seeing one of them, at least.'

Wakeman came round the sofa and perched himself on the arm. 'You say you were in London last night, Miss Bellingham. What you were doing there?'

Disconcerted by his sharp tone, Kate Bellingham hesitated. 'I... I was at a reunion of some old friends. Fellow actors. Susan and I used meet up with them from time to time. But that was before the accident.'

Straker shifted uneasily. He wished he had made it clear to Wakeman beforehand how he wanted to conduct the interview.

'Then, a few days ago, I happened to be talking to one of them and we decided it would be nice to have a get together in London, even though Susan was unable to join us. Some of them are getting on a bit now, so we didn't want to leave it too long.'

'And where did you meet?' continued Wakeman.

'At the Cumberland Hotel. There were five of us. We met in the bar before going on to a restaurant in the Edgware Road.'

'What time did you get to the hotel?'

Now she began to get flustered. 'I don't know... At about 7.00pm I think. I caught the 5.47pm train from Wendover and walked there from Marylebone.'

'And you came back this morning, you say.'

'Yes. The others all live in London, so they went home. But, as I said, I decided to treat myself and stay at the hotel overnight.'

'So you went to London, stayed overnight, and then came back this morning to find your employer murdered. You do this often, do you?'

She gave Wakeman a puzzled look. 'Do what often?'

'Go to London and stay in a hotel overnight.'

'No, no...hardly at all. In fact this was the first time in years.'

'I see. So, was it a spur of the moment decision, or...?'

'No, it wasn't a spur of the moment decision,' she replied, tears welling. 'I booked in advance.'

As Kate Bellingham put her handkerchief to her eyes, Straker signalled to Wakeman to desist from further questioning. 'I'm sorry Miss Bellingham. I know this is painful for you. Why don't we leave you for a few minutes.'

She began to rise to her feet, but he raised a hand. 'No, please don't get up. We'll go outside.'

vi.

Straker walked out on to the narrow footpath, followed closely by Wakeman. Only when they were several paces from the cottage did he turn to face his colleague. 'Kevyn, I know you served in Iraq and Afghanistan, but this is a witness we're dealing with, not a suspected terrorist.'

Wakeman returned a puzzled frown. 'But it's the golden hour, Steve. I was only testing the woman's alibi.'

'Why? Are you suggesting she might be involved in some way?'

'We don't know yet, do we? We don't know anything at this stage.'

Straker hesitated. He was right. No one could be ruled out at this stage. 'Okay, but try being a bit gentler in the way you put your questions. In fact you can leave the questioning to me from now on. When I want your input, I'll let you know.'

Wakeman shrugged dismissively. 'Fine. You're the boss.'

When they returned to the cottage, Kate Bellingham seemed more composed. She had powdered her face and attended to her make-up, but her eyes were still red.

Wakeman resumed his position behind the sofa as Straker sat down opposite her. 'I'm sorry if we've upset you, Miss Bellingham,' he said, acutely conscious that their knees were almost touching. 'Are you ready to continue?

Holding his gaze, she smiled. 'I'm perfectly all right now, Inspector, thank you.'

He looked away. But for the circumstances he could almost believe she was flirting with him. 'Would you say there was much in the way of money or valuables around the house?'

'No, Inspector. Susan had nothing. And I mean nothing. She was living mainly on benefits these last two or three years. In fact, things had reached the point recently where she couldn't even pay my wages. If the intruder thought he was going to find a treasure trove of money or jewellery, he must have been very disappointed.'

'But she earned a great deal when she was working, didn't she?'

'Not as much as you might think, what with agent's fees and so forth. And the accident was seven years ago, remember. She earned virtually nothing after that. Added to which she wasn't very lucky with her investments.'

'Did she manage those herself?'

'No, her agent looked after them for her. Michael Bristow. He's retired now. He has an office in Wembley. I can give you his address and telephone number.'

'Yes, we'd be grateful for that. What about friends? Did she have many friends?"

Kate Bellingham shook her head. 'Before the accident Susan had many friends, but they dwindled

21

away one by one. Not that I blame them. She had become quite a recluse in recent years, never wanting to go anywhere or see anyone. I would sometimes take her for a drive in the country, but even then she would always wear dark glasses. She didn't like people to see her the way she was.'

'Would you say she had any worries, things that were troubling her?'

'I would say she was worried mostly about money. Just trying to make ends meet.'

'Anything else?'

She frowned. 'Sometimes recently I did think there might be something else troubling her. There was a time when Susan used to confide in me about everything, but in these last few months she became more and more withdrawn. Secretive even. Yes, secretive is the word I would use. And sad. She spent a lot of her time going through her old fan mail. I suppose it was a comfort to her.'

'You didn't help her with that at all.'

'No. I did in the old days. But since the accident she insisted on opening all the mail herself. Not just fan mail, everything. Even bills and junk mail. She would hand bills and the like back to me, but all her personal mail she kept locked in a filing cabinet in the dining room. Not that she received much fan mail any more. A letter a month at most.'

'And did she answer the letters?'

'I don't think so. She never gave me anything to post.'

'Miss Bellingham.' Wakeman came round the sofa and perched once more on the arm. 'Can you think of anyone with a reason for wanting Susan Linton dead?'

'A reason?'

'Yes. A reason, a motive, a grudge maybe.'

Kate Bellingham looked startled. 'I don't think so. Why? Are you suggesting that she might have known her killer?'

'It has to be a possibility,' said Straker, looking sharply at Wakeman. 'We need to explore all possibilities.'

'Yes, I see that now, of course. But your colleague down at the house said a glass panel in the back door had been broken to get hold of the key.'

'Yes, it may have been burglars,' said Straker. 'But burglars aren't usually murderers. Usually they just want to get in and out again as quickly as possible. We're only saying we can't discount the possibility that the murderer was someone Miss Linton knew. Is there anyone you can think of who might have done this? Someone with a grudge perhaps?'

'Like her ex husband, for example,' said Wakeman.

Her eyes widened. 'Oh, you mean George?'

Yes, George Mannering. He's a pretty nasty piece of work, isn't he?'

She looked sternly at Wakeman. 'I agree that George could be unpleasant. And the way he treated Susan was appalling at times. But...'

'Was he ever violent towards her?' said Wakeman impatiently.

'Yes, he could be violent when he was drunk. Not that I ever saw him hitting Susan, but she used to tell me about his drunken rages and more than once I've seen the bruises he gave her.' She turned back to Straker. 'George Mannering is rotten, through and through, Inspector, but I really don't think...'

'He was released from prison a few weeks ago,' said Wakeman. 'You know that, don't you?'

'Yes, I know that. After serving only half his sentence. I thought it was a disgrace letting him out so soon.'

'Were he and Miss Linton on good terms?' said Straker. 'I mean after the separation.'

'I would say so, yes. Susan did her best to stay on good terms with George. She gave him £200,000 in settlement following the divorce, which was more than generous in my opinion. We could have done with that money.'

'And do you know if he has made contact with Miss Linton since his release from prison?'

She hesitated. 'I know he tried a couple of times, because I took the calls. The first time was about six weeks ago, a day or so after his release. The second call was about three weeks ago.'

'Did he say why he wanted to speak to Miss Linton?'

'He said he needed money to tide him over until he found work. Of course, he might have telephoned her at other times too, when I wasn't there.'

'Wouldn't she have told you if he had?'

'Possibly not. As I said, Susan had become more distant recently. I can't explain why.'

'Was his manner aggressive when you spoke to him?'

'Very. But George never liked me. He was very belligerent the second time he rang, mostly I think, because I wouldn't let him speak to Susan.'

'But did he have any sort of grudge against Miss Linton that you can think of? Any reason to want her dead?'

She hesitated. 'No. George isn't a nice man, but I can't think of him as a murderer.'

'We're all capable of murder, Miss Bellingham' said Wakeman, 'Believe me, I've seen what supposedly civilised people are capable of doing to one another....'

'All right Kevyn,' said Straker. 'I'm sure Miss Bellingham gets your point.' He closed his notebook and stood up. 'Thank you. We'll leave it there for now. Perhaps we can resume tomorrow when you're feeling a little better.'

'Of course.' Her eyes glistened with tears as she too stood up. 'I'll be better tomorrow, I'm sure.'

Do you know if Miss Linton made a will, Miss Bellingham?' said Wakeman, who remained seated on the arm of the sofa.

Straker tried to catch Wakeman's eye but they remained fixed on Kate Bellingham.

'Yes, she made a will. It's with her solicitor.'

'And do you know who the beneficiaries are?'

'As a matter of fact I do. She left her estate to me. She made her will shortly after the accident. There isn't much money left now of course. And I doubt if the house will fetch much in its present state.' She turned to Straker who was standing at the door. 'I'm sorry, Inspector, you wanted some names and addresses. It will take me a few minutes to write them out for you.'

'This afternoon will do,' said Straker. 'Just a list of people that Miss Linton had dealings with. Her solicitor, friends, relatives, anyone she was in contact with.'

'Including the people you say you were with last night,' said Wakeman.

'Yes, including them. And perhaps we could call again tomorrow morning. There may be are a few more things we need to go through by then.'

As Straker put out his hand, she gripped it firmly. 'Of course, Inspector. I'll be better tomorrow.'

He felt himself blushing. 'I'm sorry if you found some of our questions intrusive or upsetting. We'll try and manage it better next time. In the meantime, if anything comes to mind, however trivial or seemingly unimportant...' He took a card from his pocket. 'My mobile number is here. Please don't hesitate to call me.'

vii.

Back in the car Straker decided to assert his authority before things got out of hand. 'Kevyn, you and I are in danger of falling out.'

Wakeman stared insolently back at him. 'About what?'

'Didn't it register with you just now that I was bringing the interview to a close?'

'I was only asking about the will.'

'A bit insensitive, don't you think, in the circumstances?'

'Not at all. Follow the money. Isn't that what they say?'

'True. But that woman had just had just been through the trauma of discovering her close friend murdered. You were quizzing her as though she was your prime suspect.'

'Okay, boss. Message understood.' Wakeman switched on the ignition and checked his mirrors. 'But I think she had more to tell us about Mannering, if you'd let her.'

'Maybe, but all in good time.'

We can't afford to hang about, Steve. In a few hours they'll be quizzing you on television. Anyway the woman's a dyke, isn't she?'

26

Straker closed his eyes in exasperation. 'And what has that got to do with anything?'

'It's obvious isn't it. Not married. Loyal companion for twenty odd years.'

'Even if she is a dyke, as you describe her, which I doubt, I can't see what relevance it has to the investigation.'

Wakeman didn't speak again until they turned once more into the drive of Elleswood House. 'Anyway, I've already ruled Bellingham out as a suspect.'

'Oh, you have? That was a quick turnabout.'

'Yes, since she's the main beneficiary of the will. Unless she's in a hurry for the money, of course, though that seems unlikely. Not many of us can afford to stay in posh London hotels just when we feel like it.'

Straker climbed out of the car. 'Okay, I'll ask her about George Mannering tomorrow, if you think she had something to tell us. But cool it, will you. You're a policeman now, not a squaddie.'

As they approached the front door, Jack Meredith came out to meet them. 'Come in gentlemen. We've cleared a path for you now.'

'Any prints, Jack?'

'Plenty. Though I suspect most of them belong to the ladies themselves. We've taken prints from the body. Do you think the housekeeper will mind us calling on her later?'

'She'll be fine. She was very cooperative just now.'

Meredith turned towards the house. 'Okay, ready for the tour?'

Straker and Wakeman followed Meredith into the drawing room.

'Don't go too near,' said Meredith. 'The carpet around her is soaked. Not just blood. There's urine from her catheter bag. The tube must have come away in the struggle.'

They crossed the hall into the dining room. Along the top of the sideboard were several framed photographs of well known actors. In one Straker was able to pick out a younger Kate Bellingham standing arm in arm with Susan Linton. Was she a lesbian? He knew it shouldn't matter, but it did.

'The entire house wasn't done over,' said Meredith as they climbed the stairs. 'In fact the upstairs was hardly touched.'

They walked from room to room, taking care not to touch anything. The fitted carpets everywhere were stained and threadbare and the furniture and furnishings were depressingly dark and old fashioned. Everywhere looked shabby and uncared for.

'I've still to put my full team together Jack,' said Straker, 'but I'm having a meeting at 4.00pm to review what we have so far. Will you be able to join us?'

'I'll be there,' said Meredith. 'Maybe I'll have something more for you by then.'

viii.

It was mid afternoon by the time Straker rang home. 'Hi Emily. Sorry not to have rung sooner.'

'That's okay. How's it going?'

She sounded low. 'It's a big one Em. I knew it would be or I wouldn't have gone in.'

'I know. It was on the news. Susan Linton's been murdered. So, Jerry's put you in charge, has he?'

'I couldn't say no. It's high profile and there's going to be a lot of media interest. I'm doing a televised press conference at 5.00pm.'

'Good for you. I'll be watching.'

'I'm not sure exactly what time I'll be home.' She didn't answer. 'I haven't called the restaurant yet. Do you think you could do it?'

No, we'll stay in tonight. I'll get something out of the freezer. We can always celebrate another night.'

'Are you sure?'

'Yes, it's fine. I'll see you when I see you. Good luck with the press conference. I'll be looking out for you.'

Straker relaxed a little as he put down the phone. He was sorry they weren't going out. He knew he hadn't been good company these last few weeks and it would have been a good time to make a fresh start. He dialled Rawlings' number.

'Jerry. It's Steve Straker. Just calling to update you.'

After delivering his report he listened as Rawlings briefed him on the progress made by the team at HQ. Susan Linton's next of kin, an older brother living in Swansea, had provided a list of all relatives and friends that he was aware of. Footage was being gathered from all operational CCTV and speed cameras within a five mile radius of Elleswood House. A list was being compiled of all persons in the local community whose criminal record or medical history indicated a violent disposition. George Mannering had still not turned up at his Manchester hostel. A full support team would move across to Aylesbury in the morning.

As Straker put down the phone there was a knock on his door. It was DC Becky Reedman, a member of the Major Crime Unit at Oxford.

'Hi Becky. I thought you were on holiday this week.'

'I am. But I live this way. I thought I would just pop in to see if I could be of any help. I don't mind giving up my holiday. I mean, this would be good experience for me.'

Straker had already given thought to the personnel he wanted on the team, but he had completely overlooked Becky who hadn't made much of an impression since arriving from Hertfordshire, Western Division a year ago. Although conscientious and hard working she was a quiet, diffident girl, with a pretty face, largely hidden behind thick framed glasses. The general view was that she needed to develop more confidence if she was to progress.

'Certainly, Becky. In fact I'm having a review meeting in ten minutes, prior to the press conference. Can you stay for that?'

Her face lit up. 'Great. Thank you sir.'

'I'm warning you though. There won't be much leave until we crack this case.'

'That's fine by me,' she said, standing up and retreating. 'I'll wait outside.'

As Becky left, Jack Meredith put his head round the door. 'Got a moment, Steve?' He came in and sat down. 'We're analysing all the fingerprints we've managed to collect. So far we've found only a couple that don't belong to one or other of the two ladies. I was hoping to find prints at the point of entry and on the door to the drawing room and the front door. But no such luck. They're as clean as a whistle. Either the person we're looking for was wearing gloves or he cleaned up after him.'

'A pity.' said Straker 'I was hoping by now for something to tell the media. I guess I'm just going to have to play a straight bat.'

'I wouldn't worry about the first news conference, Steve. They won't be expecting much just yet. And they'll have plenty to be going on with just dealing with the lady's career. Here, I've got this for you.' Meredith handed him an A5 size envelope. 'From Miss Bellingham. She said she hopes it's of some use.'

Opening the envelope Straker took out a typed sheet listing the addresses and phone numbers of Susan Linton's solicitor, her former agent and the four friends she had met in London the previous evening. Also enclosed, neatly stapled to a sheet of A4 paper, were the credit card receipts for her overnight stay at the Cumberland Hotel and her share of the meal at the restaurant.

Now Wakeman appeared at the door. 'Everyone's ready for the briefing, Steve.'

Straker got up from his desk. 'Good. Who do we have so far?'

'Eight, including you and me. Two researchers from Oxford HQ, plus Becky Reedman whom you know about and DC Mark Taverner from Crime Support. We've also got two lads they've spared us from the local CID. The Chief's on his way over. Should be here any moment.'

'Good. Let's go.'

The meeting began with a few words from Rawlings about the high profile nature of the investigation and the need to ensure that the police were always presented in a positive light. With this in mind, all enquiries by the media should be referred to the Press Office. On no account should any member of the team talk directly to journalists. Then, between them, Straker and Meredith set out what was known so far. Based on the condition of the body and temperature readings, death was estimated to have occurred sometime between 5.30pm and 9.00pm the previous evening. The victim had sustained four stab wounds to the chest and stomach, plus one to her back, below the right shoulder blade. Two sets of fingerprints had been discovered that belonged neither to the deceased nor her housekeeper, but neither had shown up on the National Fingerprint Database. Unlike other doors in the house, the front door, the door to the lounge and the door to the small upstairs sitting room were all clean of prints, suggesting that the murderer had taken the precaution of cleaning up before leaving. No murder weapon had been found.

'So that is where we are at present, Ladies and Gentlemen. I'll take questions. Then we'll allocate tasks.'

ix.

At half past midnight Straker slid under the bedclothes, taking care not to disturb Emily who was curled up on the other side of the bed, apparently asleep. Normally by now one of them would have given way. But not tonight. The televised press conference had gone well. Jerry Rawlings complimented him on his assured performance and even Kevyn Wakeman gave him a thumbs up sign as he stepped away from the cameras. But he arrived home to find the house empty and a note from Emily to say that she had gone round to Dan's to rehearse. Frustrated and angry, he spent the next hour pacing backwards and forwards, listening for her car. When she finally turned up at just before 7.30pm, she was full of apologies. They had watched him on the

6.00pm news, she said, or most of it. Dan's clock was a few minutes slow so they only caught the end of it. Never mind, she was sure he did brilliantly and they could watch it again together on the News channel.

By this time, he was feeling too sorry for himself to respond with good grace and his sullen mood soured the rest of the evening. They ate the meal she had prepared largely in silence and at 10pm Emily went off to bed, telling him again she was sorry, but if her apology wasn't good enough, there wasn't much she could do about it.

Moving his leg to her side of the bed, Straker ran his foot down the smooth, warmth of her calf, but she didn't respond. He turned on his side, facing away. So, she had been with Dan Masterson again. This was getting to be a habit. Last week he had come home early to find Masterson's car parked in the drive. By the time he came in, the two of them were sitting at opposite ends of the sofa, books in hand. Where they were and what they were doing until they heard his car, he didn't care to think about, but both seemed flushed and embarrassed as they got up to greet him. Were they having an affair? The thought had crossed his mind more than once recently.

'I'm afraid the problem lies with you Mr Straker.'

It was the shock of it as much as anything. For years Emily had been having tests and investigations and he hadn't really got involved, beyond listening to the range of possible reasons for her failure to get pregnant. When the latest consultant suggested that he be tested too, at first he baulked at the idea. But eventually he agreed to go through with the humiliating procedure and, a couple of weeks later, he and Emily attended the clinic to get the result. Donaldson didn't mince his words.

33

You have an extremely low sperm count, Mr Straker. So low, in fact, that even with the aid of In Vitro Fertilisation, I'm afraid the chances of your being able to fertilise an egg are miniscule.

So that was why all those investigations came to nothing. The problem wasn't with Emily, it was with him. All these years he had been firing blanks.

Turning the clock radio towards him he looked at the time. 12.45am. No point in just lying there. Creeping out of bed he went downstairs and switched on the television. Yes, it had crossed his mind quite a lot since the consultation that she might be weighing her options. After all, it wasn't as if they ever had that much in common, and if he couldn't give her the child she was so desperate for, what was there to hold them together?

Getting up and going over to the sideboard Straker poured himself a whisky. Perhaps he had been too trusting. In their twelve years together there must have been many times that Emily wondered whether she was hitched to the right man. She always used to say that she liked the strong, silent type, but could she now be having second thoughts? The strong, silent type was all very well in a two hour action movie, but might be tedious company after twelve years of marriage. Especially when it turned out that he was unable to father the child she wanted so badly.

'How long have you been down here?'

Emily, barely awake, stood in the doorway, her dressing gown clasped tightly around her.

'About half an hour. I couldn't sleep.'

She came over to him. 'Well, it's not surprising. You must have a lot on your mind right now.'

He nodded, but didn't look up.

She put a hand on his shoulder. 'I'm sorry about tonight, but I don't know what else I can say.'

'It's okay.'

'It's just that Anton doesn't want to see any books from Monday and Dan's part is even bigger than mine.'

'Monday? You mean Anton's called a rehearsal on Easter Monday?'

'He's had to, Steve. It's only ten days now to curtain up. It won't be a long one, he's promised.'

Straker turned away with a weary shake of his head.

She knelt so that her face was level with his. 'Steve, I know I should never have dragged you into this, but please don't back out now. You're almost there with your lines. And I can rehearse you at home if need be.'

Still he didn't look at her.

'Are you listening to me?'

'Yes.' He took her hand and squeezed it. 'I won't back out.'

She held on to it tightly. 'You'll get cold sitting down here. Come back to bed.'

Chapter Two

Sunday, 8th April 2012

Huddled in a blanket he watches the dawn. Through the gap in the curtains he can see the three caravans that share the site. All is quiet now, but it won't be long before they are up and about. Maybe he should he leave now, move on before they wake. Although he knows it is only prolonging the agony because they will catch up with him sooner or later.

Unless he kills himself first. He has often thought of it these last few years, but never had the courage. Attach some hose to the exhaust and run it into the van. They say you just get drowsy and go to sleep, but he finds that hard to believe. He would panic surely, as he choked on the fumes and reach for the door handle to throw himself out. Taking an overdose is another option, but that isn't so easy when you're on the run. It takes time to gather enough pills and even then, there is no guarantee it will work. Step in front of a train? Yes, he might do that. Keep his mind blank until the last moment, until the noise of the train is so deafening that it crowds out everything else. Then step out.

He climbs over to the driver's seat. Yesterday it was on the radio all day. George Mannering has gone missing from his hostel. The police want to interview him urgently. Today, nothing. The murder isn't even mentioned. Maybe he should go out and get the newspapers. Because it is certain to be in the papers by now. Everything. His name, a description of the van, the registration number, even a photograph.

The door of one of the caravans opens. Time to move on.

i.

Kevyn Wakeman gave the coffee machine an angry kick as it rejected his coin a second time. He had skipped breakfast and driven in early so as to be seen at his desk when Straker arrived. The ploy hadn't worked. Arriving just after 8.00am, he was dismayed to find him already in his office, talking on the telephone. He'd put his head round the door, but he just went on talking as if he wasn't there. Why was Straker promoted ahead of him, even though he had far less service and experience. The only reason he could think of was that Straker was a graduate and he wasn't. As if having a degree meant anything. In his judgement, graduates were no better than anyone else and often a good deal worse.

As he searched his pocket for another coin, he noticed Becky Reedman arriving at her work station. She had her hair up this morning and was wearing a slim fitting jumper and pencil skirt that showed off her trim figure and nice legs. Pity about the glasses because she had quite a pretty face, though he doubted she was aware of it. Returning to his desk he gave her wink and was rewarded by a shy smile.

Sitting down, he ran his eyes down the action plan and was pleased to see that tracking down George Mannering was listed as top priority. People who are murdered in their own homes usually know their attacker and he was confident it would prove so in Susan Linton's case. And where better to start than with her former husband - a paedophile, an alcoholic and, if the housekeeper was to be believed, a man easily provoked to violence. The housekeeper didn't seem to think he bore her a grudge, but his own researches suggested differently. Susan Linton testified against him at his first trial and might do so again when the new case came to court. Moreover, Mannering hadn't been seen since the morning of the murder.

Wakeman glanced across the room at Straker's still closed door. What was he up to in there? Whatever it was, he had no right to shut him out like this. Getting up he strolled over, catching Becky's eye again as he passed her desk. She held his gaze for a moment, then looked away, blushing. With a perfunctory tap on Straker's door, he went in.

'Morning, Steve. You appear to be a busy man this morning.'

Straker looked up distractedly. 'Ah, good morning, Kevyn. Sorry about earlier. I was talking to the Chief. Have you seen the papers?'

'I've had a quick glance.' Wakeman, dragged a chair across and sat down opposite him. 'Watched you again on the box last night. I have to hand it to you. You did well.'

'Thanks.'

'Looks like this amateur dramatics you go in for has stood you in good stead.'

Straker gave him a suspicious glance, but didn't respond

' And this morning you're all over the front pages. How does it feel to be famous?'

'Roughly the same as before,' said Straker, closing the newspaper and returning it to the pile. 'Which ones have you looked at?'

'Only *The Herald.* Their money's on George Mannering.' Wakeman drew the newspaper from the pile and opened it out . "Listen to this. 'LINTON MURDER - POLICE SEEK PAEDOPHILE EX-HUSBAND.' And that's just the headline." He read on. *'Police investigating Susan Linton's murder are keen to trace her former husband, TV soap actor George Mannering, Released from prison in February following a three year sentence for underage sexual grooming, Mannering is now thought to be on the run...'*

'Here, let me see.' said Straker, turning the newspaper round to face him. He scanned the report before pushing it to one side. 'Just their usual sensationalism. I doubt if Mannering had anything to do with it.'

'Why not? He didn't come back to his hostel again last night. That's two nights he's been missing, and he hasn't played truant before. Surely that's suspicious in itself?'

But what has he got to gain from killing his ex wife, apart from another much longer spell in prison? He must know she was practically broke. And he knows too that he's one of the first people we would want to interview.'

'People don't always behave rationally, Steve. She testified against him at his trial, remember. Maybe he killed her in a fit of rage and now he's lying low. It would explain why he hasn't been seen since Friday morning.'

Straker looked at him in surprise. 'She testified against him at his trial?' Are you sure of that?'

'Absolutely. 'I read up on the case last night.'

40

'I see. Then that certainly makes a difference.' Straker pulled the pile of newspapers towards him. 'Remind me what you're doing today.'

'First I'm interviewing a couple of the local nutters and hard cases they've brought in for questioning. After that I'm off to see Susan Linton's former agent, Michael Bristow.'

'What about her solicitor?'

'On holiday. We've made contact with one of the partners and they're trying to track him down.'

'And this afternoon?'

'I thought I'd drive over to Grendon Underwood where Mannering served the last part of his sentence. Have a chat with the warders and some of the inmates to get a feel for Mannering's state of mind while he was inside.'

'Good. Sounds like you've got plenty on your plate.' Straker lifted the next newspaper off the pile. 'Don't let me hold you up.'

Wakeman remained seated. 'And how about you, Steve? What are you up to today?'

Straker gave him a wary glance. 'If you want to know, I'm going to see Kate Bellingham again. Continue where we left off yesterday.'

'By yourself?'

'Probably. We don't have manpower to spare right now.'

Wakeman gave him a sly grin. 'I would take someone with you, Steve. If you ask me, that woman's got designs on you. And I saw the randy look in your eye yesterday.'

Straker looked angrily at Wakeman. 'I don't know what you're talking about.'

'Only joking, Boss. Just don't let her get her claws into you, that's all I'm saying.'

41

'You know, you're not being exactly consistent. Yesterday you were telling me she was a lesbian. Now it seems the woman's a nymphomaniac.' Straker looked at his watch. 'Anyway, enough of this. Thank you, Kevyn. I've got work to do, even if you haven't.'

Wakeman rose from his chair. 'If Mannering doesn't show up soon, I think I should drive to Manchester and see what they're doing up there.'

'Fine, you do that,' said Straker, taking another newspaper from the pile.

'I thought I might take Becky Reedman with me. It will be good experience for her.'

Getting up, Straker crossed purposely to the door and opened it. 'Thank you Kevyn. Let me know before you set off to see Bristow. If I'm free, I'll join you.'

ii.

Returning to his desk Straker sat down with a sigh. Wakeman was proving more of a trial than he was expecting.   Yet, for all his crassness and over familiarity, there was no denying his antennae were in good order. That remark about Kate Bellingham having designs on him. Had he really noticed something about the way she reacted to him? He knew it shouldn't matter one way or the other, but it did. Because, for reasons he couldn't explain, that woman stirred up feelings in him yesterday that he had forgotten he was capable of. It made no sense. She was ten years his senior at least and although she had a good figure for her age, she wasn't exactly what one might call beautiful. Maybe it had something

42

to do with the way she presented herself, the way she spoke, the way she smiled. Actresses were taught that kind of thing; how to make themselves alluring and seductive.

He looked at his watch. 8.35am. Was it too early to ring her? Wakeman said not to go on his own, but why shouldn't he see her on his own? The full team wasn't yet in place and he doubted the local force would have personnel to spare on Easter Sunday morning. He picked up the phone and dialled her number.

'Kate Bellingham?'

'Good morning, Miss Bellingham.' He could feel his heart pounding already. 'Steve Straker, Thames Valley Police. I called on you yesterday.'

Oh, good morning, Inspector. I was hoping it might be you.'

'I was just wondering if you had had any more thoughts about the things we discussed yesterday. For example, if you could think of anyone who might have fallen out with Miss Linton, or had reason to bear her a grudge.'

'Well, yes, Inspector, I thought a lot about that after you left. Actually, there is one person who might have had reason to bear Susan a grudge. Though hardly enough to want her dead.'

'And who was that?'

'George. George Mannering - her former husband...'

Within fifteen minutes Straker was parking his car outside Kate Bellingham's small terrace cottage and walking up the short garden path to the door. Yes, she said. She would be delighted for him to call round immediately, or at any time to suit his schedule. But would he be coming on his own? She would prefer it if he could come on his own, as she found the detective he was with yesterday rather intimidating.

The door was opened by a smiling Kate Bellingham. 'Inspector, good morning. Do come in.'

She was wearing a grey cowl neck jumper and slim fitting jeans. Her hair hung loose. Straker took her hand and held it firmly. 'Thank you for seeing me again at such short notice.'

She smiled warmly. 'It's the least I can do. When you came yesterday, I was in such a state that I'm afraid I wasn't much help.'

He coughed nervously as she led him into the small sitting room. 'And thank you for being so prompt with those names and addresses you sent over.'

'Well, I knew you would want to see them as soon as possible,' she said, as he sat down. 'Everyone has to be checked, don't they? Including me.' She sat down opposite him, her knees neatly together.

'I wouldn't put it quite like that.' He tried to hold her gaze, but found himself looking away. 'But we do need to talk to as many people as possible who knew the deceased. I have a team calling on Miss Linton's neighbours this morning. And another calling on the friends you met on Friday evening. I think you said they were Miss Linton's friends as well as yours.'

She sighed. 'Yes, but I'm afraid we had both rather lost touch with them in recent times. Susan was...'

She looked down and, for a moment, Straker thought she was about to cry.

'I saw you on the news last night,' she said, recovering herself and dabbing her eyes with a handkerchief. 'I thought you handled the questions with great assurance.'

Straker blushed. 'Thank you. Although there wasn't very much I could tell the media yesterday.'

44

'Even so, you spoke with authority.' She fixed her dark brown eyes on him. 'You have presence, Inspector. Did you know that? Not many people have presence.'

'Really?'

'You know, with your good looks, you might have done well on the stage.'

'Oh, I'm no actor,' said Straker. He could feel himself relaxing at last That's my wife's department. She's rehearsing a play at the moment with our local drama group We both are actually. I'm only filling in for someone who had to drop out, but she's playing the lead.'

'Really, where is this? I'd love to come and see it.'

'Oh, I don't think so. We would all forget our lines immediately knowing there's a professional actress in the audience.'

Kate Bellingham laughed. 'Then, I might have to come without telling you...But I'm sorry. I'm distracting you from what you came to see me about.'

'Yes... this shouldn't take long.' said Straker, disappointed that their light conversation had ended so soon. He opened his notebook.

'Before we begin, may I offer you some coffee?'

Should he? He really needed to get back. 'Thank you. Coffee would be nice.'

As she went out to the kitchen, Straker felt a quiver of excitement. Last night he looked her up on Google and, sure enough, there she was in Wikipedia. Born in 1964, she graduated from the Central School of Speech and Drama in 1986. The entry included several photos, plus a string of credits – theatre, television, even a couple of films. But no information about her private life.

He looked around him. The room was furnished in a modern style, with candles on the small dresser and fresh flowers on the table in the window, in pleasing contrast to the depressing gloom of Elleswood House. On the mantelpiece was another framed photograph of her and Susan Linton standing arm in arm as they smiled at the camera. Perhaps Wakeman was right after all. He hoped not.

'Milk and no sugar. Have I guessed correctly?' she said, returning with a cafetiere and crockery on a tray which she set down on the coffee table. In her slim fitting jeans her legs were long and slender.

'Yes, no sugar. Thank you.'

'Are you married, Inspector? ' she said, drawing the coffee table towards them. 'Or shouldn't I be asking such personal questions?'

That smile again. Warm, intimate. It made him want to reach out and touch her. 'Yes, I'm married.'

'Children?'

'Sadly, no.'

'I'm sorry...Does your wife work?'

'Yes, she's a teacher. In a primary school...'

As they sat drinking coffee, Straker found himself talking more freely than he had in years. In response to her gentle probing he told her about growing up as the only child of parents who divorced when he was sixteen. Then of his three years at Durham, where he and Emily met for the first time. He even found himself telling her of his devastation on learning of his father's death, just as he was about to sit his finals.

'After that...' Straker stared down at the table, 'for a long time I just drifted. Then one day on a fruit farm in Australia I met up again with Emily and she rescued me.'

Kate Bellingham reached across and rested her hand lightly on his. 'You must love her very much. But then, she was lucky too.'   .

'In what way?

'In finding you, of course. I envy her.'

Straker suddenly felt tears in his eyes. 'To tell you the truth, Emily and I are not getting on very well right now...' He stopped abruptly, conscious that he was being indiscreet as well as disloyal. 'I'm sorry. Here am I talking about myself when I'm supposed to be asking you questions.'

'You must blame me for that, Inspector. Forgive me. But you're a very interesting man.'

Opening his notebook Straker could feel his heart thumping again. 'You said on the phone that George Mannering may have had reason to bear Miss Linton a grudge.'

For a few seconds she hesitated. 'Yes, George may have borne Susan a grudge. Although hardly to the extent of wanting her dead. George was no friend of mine, but I can't believe him capable of murder.'

'Miss Linton testified against him at his trial. Is that what you're referring to?

'Not only that. This was more recent. When George moved in with Susan he had a laptop computer, but then he bought a new computer and the laptop went into a cupboard. Five years later, when they divorced and he moved out, he took all his belongings with him. But he had obviously forgotten about his laptop because, last year, I came across it as I was sorting out some cupboards. I didn't think about it again until just before Christmas when Susan had a visit from the police. They said they were investigating George following some new allegations and they wanted to know if we had any old computers, disks or memory sticks, belonging to him. Susan said we didn't, but then I remembered the laptop. So I fetched it and we handed it over.'

'Would he have known you did this?'

'I assume so. Wouldn't the police would have told him about it when he was re-arrested?'

'Not necessarily. They would have to release the information before the trial, but they may not have done so yet.'

Kate Bellingham was silent for a few moments. 'In which case, he might have remembered it and come back on Friday night, hoping to retrieve it.'

'It's a possibility,' said Straker. 'It would certainly explain why the house was turned over.'

'Yes. And why the glass in the back door was smashed. Susan would never have let him in if he'd come to the front door.' She shook her head.' No. It's impossible. I never cared for George, but I can't think of him as a murderer.'

'Even so,' said Straker, rising to his feet. 'The information may turn out to be important. If George Mannering doesn't yet know that the police have it, he may well have come back to retrieve it '

'Really?' Now she rose too, standing so close that they were almost touching. ' So I was right to tell you, was I?' She took his hand and gave it a small squeeze. 'You will come and see me again, Inspector, won't you.'

iii.

'So, George Mannering is our prime suspect, is he?' said Straker, breaking the silence that had lasted since he and Wakeman set off from Aylesbury

'Absolutely. All the more so after what you told me about the laptop.'

'But he would have to be mad, surely, to believe he could get away with it.'

On his return from calling on Kate Bellingham, Straker had made further enquiries about George Mannering's recent arrest and learned that he was now facing possible charges relating to a paedophile ring. The officer he spoke to thought it unlikely that Mannering had yet been told that the laptop was in police possession.

'It's my guess he'd forgotten all about it until his re-arrest,' said Wakeman.

'So, he came all the way down from Manchester last Friday night to retrieve it, did he? And murdered Linton when she refused to tell him where it was hidden. Is that your hypothesis?'

Wakeman nodded. 'Something like that.'

Straker sat back. Until now Wakeman had been driving well inside the speed limit, probably in response to his rebuke of yesterday. But now, as they approached the North Circular slip road, instead of joining the long line of cars waiting to go up the ramp, he continued in the middle lane until he was within twenty yards of the turn off. Then, taking advantage of a driver who was a little slow off the mark, he cut in sharply and accelerated up to the roundabout.

'If Mannering doesn't show up by tonight, Boss, I reckon I should go to Manchester and shake them up a bit.'

'I agree,' said Straker. A couple of days without Wakeman seemed an increasingly attractive prospect.

'You married then, are you, Steve?'

'Yes, I'm married. Are you?'

'I was. Not any more though. You got kids?'

'No.'

'I've got one. A boy. He's nine now. Lives in Aldershot with his mum. Don't see much of them these days. She prefers it that way. You know what they say, Steve. Marriage is the price men pay for sex....'

'Yes. And sex is the price women pay for marriage,' said Straker wearily. 'A bit simplistic, wouldn't you say?'

'No. I believe it. It's just kids that women want really. Procreation of the species. That's what they're here for. To them, sex is just a means to an end.'

'A bit of a generalisation, wouldn't you say?'

'Well, I can't say I've met that many nymphos in my time, in spite of what you read in magazines.' Wakeman accelerated hard, swerving out to overtake the lorry, before returning to the inside lane. 'As far as I'm concerned, Steve, women want men for two reasons. First, to get them pregnant. And then, to support them while they raise the family. Otherwise, they wouldn't give us the time of day.'

Straker gazed gloomily ahead. No doubt he would be hearing more homespun opinions from Wakeman before the investigation was completed. 'Okay Kevyn,' he said briskly. 'You lead today. Let's see what we make of Michael Bristow.'

Wakeman took the chewing gum out of his mouth and pressed it into the ashtray. 'Yes. Maybe Mannering had nothing to do with it and Bristow's our man. Maybe he's been robbing Linton blind all these years and had to kill her when she found out about it.'

Pulling into a service road in front of a line of shops they drove slowly along until they spotted a grey metal plaque on a door between two shop fronts. It read *Michael Bristow and Associates, Theatrical Agents* in heavy black lettering. Looking up, they were just in time to catch a glimpse of a face retreating

50

from a window and a few moments later, the door was opened by a short, balding man of about sixty.

'Good morning gentlemen. Police officers, I assume.'

'We are sir,' said Wakeman, stepping out of the car and holding out his identity badge. 'Detective Sergeant Kevyn Wakeman and my colleague Detective Inspector Steve Straker. Sorry to be late. Gridlock all the way back to Denham.'

iv.

Bristow's office, was large and sparsely furnished with badly worn carpeting. There were a couple of tired looking sofas at one end of the room and a cluttered mahogany desk surrounded by an assortment of chairs at the other. Framed black and white photographs, complete with penned dedications, filled the walls.

'Now then, gentlemen. What can I do for you?'

Straker studied Susan Linton's former agent. He had chewed down fingernails and there was dandruff on the shoulders of his jacket. His thinning hair was combed elaborately to mask his baldness.

'Good of you to come in on a Sunday morning sir,' said Wakeman, taking out his notebook. 'I'm sure you've got better things to do with your weekend.'

'No, I was here anyway. I often come in on a Sunday. The weekends tend to pass a little slowly for me since my wife died.'

After a brief exchange in which he spoke of his shock at learning of Susan Linton's murder, Bristow described the history of his relationship with the actress, going back to her time at the drama school, which he had also attended some years earlier to study stage management.

'Susan was a wonderful person, a remarkable actress as well as a dear friend. Her accident was a great tragedy. It came just as her career was really taking off.'

'I gather you also looked after her investments.' said Wakeman.

'I did until quite recently. Susan wasn't what you might call financially literate. And since I managed the business side of her career, it made sense to give her a hand with her investment portfolio as well.'

'But you don't have her portfolio now.'

'No. The work was getting a bit much for me to tell the truth. I went to see Susan in January and we agreed that I should pass it on. The investments are with Horizon Woldwide now, based in Mayfair.'

As Wakeman quizzed Bristow about Susan Linton's finances, Straker found his thoughts returning to Kate Bellingham. Since the consultation in January, he had had lost all interest in sex. Yet last night, in bed, he was aroused just thinking about her. He wouldn't see her again. At least, not on his own. If it was necessary to interview her a third time, he would send Wakeman.

'For the record Mr Bristow, can you tell us where you were last Friday evening?'

'Yes I went to the cinema in Wembley. It was the new Bond film, Skyfall.'

'What time was this?'

'About 6.30pm. It was the early evening showing.' Bristow took out his wallet. 'I think I still have my receipt. Yes, here it is.'

Wakeman examined the receipt for a few moments before handing it back. 'Thank you Mr Bristow, I think that will do for now. Unless my colleague has further questions.'

Straker shook his head.

'Do you have a copy of Miss Linton's portfolio by any chance?'

Bristow pulled open a drawer in his desk. 'I do for what it's worth. Though it only shows transactions until January this year. You'll have to talk to Horizon if you want the up to date picture.'

'Even so, we'll take it away with us if we may.'

Bristow frowned. 'Why? I don't see what relevance it has to a murder investigation.'

'I'm sure it hasn't,' said Wakeman, 'But we need to explore all avenues.'

'I assure you I was always scrupulous in my dealings with Miss Linton.'

'Just for a few days, sir, that's all.'

Fifteen minutes later they were back on the A40 heading back towards Aylesbury. Wakeman was in cheerful mood and was driving at a normal speed. Either he had forgotten about Straker's chastisements of yesterday, or decided he had sulked long enough.

v.

Detective Constable Becky Reedman sat at road works in a queue of ten cars. Beside her sat Detective Constable Mark Taverner, recently arrived from the Met. They had barely spoken on the drive into London, which suited her well enough because she was in no mood for talking. She tapped the steering wheel in frustration. The lights had been red for so long that it was possible there was a fault, but there was no point in getting stressed about it. Okay, someone had to interview the four friends Kate Bellingham spent the evening with on Friday. But she felt Straker could have given her an assignment more fitting to her seven years experience. The lights changed at last and she followed the traffic in the direction of Swiss Cottage.

First on the list had been Roland Frobisher, a diminutive, slightly effeminate man of around sixty. He was still going for the odd part, he said, but was no longer dependent on acting because his partner had a menswear shop that kept them in reasonable comfort. Confirming Kate Bellingham's account of the events of Friday evening, he said he was surprised to get the invite as he hadn't seen any of the group in the six years since Susan's riding accident. Asked about her ex husband, George Mannering, he said he had worked a little with him in the early days before either of them knew Susan. A bit of a drinker, as he recalled. As to whether he was of a violent disposition, he really had no idea.

As for Kate Bellingham, Frobisher said that she and Susan had lived together since drama school. Until she married George Mannering it was generally assumed that the two of them were an item. Certainly Kate's nose was put out by the marriage, because Mannering made it clear when he moved into Elleswood House that she would have to move out. Fortunately Michael Bristow, came to her rescue with the offer of a receptionist/book keeping role. Then came the riding accident and Susan's divorce from George. At least the two events brought Kate and Susan back together.

'Do you like music?'

Becky turned and looked at her companion almost for the first time. He had said so little since they set out that she had almost forgotten he was there. What was he - twenty four, twenty five? He had a nice head of dark hair that folded over his slightly protruding ears and enviably long eyelashes. 'Yes, I like music.'

'What kind?'

'I don't know. All kinds, I suppose. Except jazz. I don't like jazz.'

'Classical?'

This was getting tricky. She did like classical music and listened to it a lot on Classic FM, but her knowledge was sketchy. 'She decided to put the ball back in his court. 'What about you?'

'I like all kinds.'

The conversation lapsed as the sat nav informed her that she had missed the turn. Continue to the next roundabout, it said, then take the fourth exit to bring them back down the road they were on already.

'You are watching out for the streets, aren't you,' said Becky, embarrassed at her mistake.

Mark sat up straight. 'Sorry, I wasn't concentrating.'

Swinging the car round the roundabout, she drove back the way they had come. Next on the list was Mary Whatton. Answering the door in a pink jump suit, with matching trainers, she might have been Barbara Cartland's younger sister. Ushering the two of them into a lavishly over furnished sitting room, she immediately launched into a long tribute to her dear friend Susan. How anyone could do such a terrible thing to such a darling creature was completely beyond her comprehension. Unless it was some madman, of course, because there were so many about these days, far more than there ever used to be and they didn't live in lunatic asylums any more, did they, but right here among us in the community, because it was government policy, whichever party

55

was in power. Anything to save money, with no thought to the danger they were putting us all in.

Questioned about the Friday night reunion she confirmed the sequence of events described in Straker's account of the interview with Kate Bellingham. Kate's call came right out of the blue, she said, but she was delighted because she didn't get out much these days. Kate asked her to call the others because she had rather lost contact with them, preoccupied as she was with the daily demands of looking after Susan. Asked about George Mannering, she said none of them cared for him. He was a handsome man and something of a charmer in his younger days, but the drink got to him and before long, there wasn't a director who would work with him. As for his conviction for internet grooming, no one was surprised. There was always something a bit unsavoury about George. The surprise was that Susan married him in the first place.

Ever been to the Proms?

Becky glanced again at her companion. She supposed he was quite good looking in a boyish sort of way. 'Only once. My dad took me when I was about twelve.'

'I've just got tickets for the Venezuelan Youth Orchestra's concert at the Festival Hall. I struck lucky. They're like gold dust.'

'Sounds good,' said Becky. She hadn't heard of the Venezuelan Youth Orchestra.

'I saw them at the Proms a few years ago. Julian Lloyd Webber said it was the best Prom he'd ever been to. I agree. They were fantastic.'

Becky was about to ask if Julian Lloyd Webber was any relation to Andrew Lloyd Webber when her mobile rang. Glancing at the screen, she breathed a weary sigh. Her mother again. She pressed the off button. She would have to break her habit of telephoning at all hours of the day with enquiries about what she was doing with herself and whether she had met any nice young men recently. How could she convince her that she was perfectly contented with her single existence and that finding a man wasn't at the top of her list of priorities right now? Not that she was ruling it out permanently, but she had no illusions about herself. She knew she wasn't most men's idea of the perfect date.

In three hundred yards turn left into Gayton Road

Although things had been looking up recently. Kevyn Wakeman, of all people seemed suddenly to be taking an interest in her. Some of the girls didn't like him, saying he was too brash and confident for his own good, but she liked confidence in a man.

In fifty yards turn left into Gayton Road

His broad, slightly flattened nose gave his face that rugged, lived in look. Not much hair, but that didn't matter because he had a nice shaped head and a great physique.

38 Gayton Road is one hundred yards on right

Yes she liked DS Kevyn Wakeman, in spite of what people said about him. He was particularly kind to her the day she heard the news about Dad, even offering to drive her over to the hospital. Mum thought he was charming.

You have arrived at your destination

They pulled up outside the home of the last two on their list, a married couple, both actors. It was just after 3.00pm. Maybe they would be back for the 5.00pm review meeting after all, though she doubted she would be making much of a contribution.

It was 4.00pm as Kevyn Wakeman came out through the gates of Grendon Underwood Prison and made his way back to his car. He might as well get home early. With little progress to report, there would be no press release today and, with the full team not yet assembled, Straker had decided to cancel the 5.00pm review meeting. In the circumstances he had suggested that Straker might like to join him this afternoon. George Mannering had served most of his sentence at Grendon Underwood and it was possible they would learn something from the inmates and staff about his current state of mind. But Straker declined, saying he needed to work on getting his team in place.

As things turned out, the visit wasn't very productive. None of the inmates he interviewed told him anything to support the theory that Mannering was involved in the murder of his ex wife. They said he had adapted well to prison life and was generally cheerful. Nor did it seem that he was nursing a grudge against Susan Linton. His main concern, they said, was what he would do for money following his release. Returning to the stage or television was not an option and finding a job at all would be difficult now he was on the sex offenders register.

Wakeman drove back down the A41 in despondent mood. By now they should, at the very least, have some leads to pursue, if not a list of possible suspects. What had they got? Virtually nothing. For six years Susan Linton seemed to have led the life of a recluse. She had no relatives, apart from a brother who claimed not to have seen or spoken to her in years. And since her riding accident she seemed also to have lost touch with all her former friends and acquaintances. As for the neighbours, these were mainly elderly and appeared to know very little about the occupant of Elleswood House.

Nor had they gleaned much from the interviews carried out so far. The actress's housekeeper/companion, Kate Bellingham hinted at a strained relationship with her employer in recent times, but appeared to be genuinely distraught at the murder of her friend. And as sole beneficiary in the actress's will she would surely have little reason to want her dead. Unless, of course, she wanted to get her hands on Elleswood House sooner rather than later. Or had reason to believe her employer was having second thoughts about whom she wished to inherit her estate. On the other hand, her alibi for the night of the murder was watertight, which meant she would need an accomplice prepared to do the dirty work on her behalf.

Someone like Michael Bristow, perhaps, though he seemed, on the face of it, an unlikely assassin. True, he and Kate Bellingham had known one another for many years, but what did Bristow have to gain from the murder of Susan Linton? If he really had been milking the actress of her wealth, he would surely have done better to steal quietly away rather than come under the spotlight of a murder investigation.

Which left only two possibilities. Either Susan Linton was the victim of a random intruder, a possibility he wasn't yet prepared to countenance, or she was murdered by her former husband. Did George Mannering have a motive? If the missing laptop contained deeply incriminating material, he may have had good reason for wanting to retrieve it before the police could get their hands on it. But did he need to murder his ex wife in the process? Maybe she was uncooperative, throwing him into a rage by refusing to tell him where the laptop was? Or, by admitting that she had already handed it over to the police?

As he pondered these questions, Wakeman cruised past a pleasant looking pub that he hadn't noticed before. Slowing down and reversing into a side road he turned the car round. Never too early for a pint and he might get a bite to eat. Save cooking when he got home. Driving into the empty car park he switched off the ignition.

Yes, it was a plausible scenario. Breaking in via the back door Mannering finds her in the lounge watching television. She tells him she hasn't seen his laptop, so he goes hunting for it, but without success. His frustration and anger growing, he goes in search again, still without success. Returning via the kitchen, he picks up a knife and threatens her. Terrified, she thrashes out at him and both are thrown off balance. As she tips out of her wheelchair and they fall together to the floor, by accident, he stabs her. Dismayed at the situation he finds himself in, he considers his options. If she recovers enough to give evidence he will face a new charge even more serious than the ones he currently faces. In a panic he goes through the house, emptying cupboards. pulling out drawers to make it look like the work of some drug crazed random intruder. His mobile rang.

'Yes? Who is this?'

'Hi Kevyn. It's Gary.'

Gary? 'Hi. What can I do for you?

'A little bird tells me your working on the Linton murder?

'I might be.' Now he remembered.

'Come on mate. You can tell me that surely. Are you on the team?

'I am actually. Second in command.'

'What, and you still a detective sergeant?'

'Yes, Gary. Still a detective sergeant.'

'And second in command?'

'You heard me the first time.'

'Then you're just the man I need to talk to. What leads are you working on right now?'

'Give us a chance mate, we've only been at it since yesterday morning.'

'Come on, that's all of thirty six hours. Have you talked to her ex husband yet?'

'Not yet. He hasn't been seen at his hostel since Friday morning.'

'That's interesting. Is he in the habit of going AWOL?'

Wakeman hesitated. He was in danger of saying more than he should. The first time Gary called him was about a year ago. He'd asked him who was working for, but Gary wasn't giving much away. He was a free lance journalist, he said, who paid good money for good information. And Kevyn wasn't to worry, because he knew how to be discreet. So he had fed him one or two fairly innocuous little snippets, just to test him and, to his surprise, was promptly rewarded. Small amounts, not more than a hundred pounds each, paid online into his bank account. He hadn't heard from him since.

'Still there, are you Kevyn?'

'Yes, I'm here.'

'I was asking if Mannering was in the habit of going AWOL. That's not a sensitive question, is it? I know where he's living, so I can always find out by calling the hostel direct.'

'No. It's the first time.'

'Then, I would think that makes him a serious suspect, wouldn't you say?

'Everyone's a suspect at this stage Gary. You know that.'

'Yes, but you know what I'm saying. Does Mannering have a motive? Come on. All I need is a head start and I'll make it worth your while. Don't worry, I've worked on your side of the fence too, so I know how to play it. Is Mannering a serious suspect?'

'What's in it for me, Gary?

'Depends. Feed me with exclusives and I'm willing to pay good money. I just need to stay ahead of the pack, that's all.'

vii.

Straker sat on the garden bench, brooding on last night's upset with Emily. With the warm, dry weather of the last few weeks he had got into the habit of coming outside after supper and sitting there until the sun went down. To be fair, Emily was more cheerful when he got home than she had been at breakfast. She was wearing a dress, for once, rather than her usual scruffy jeans. Was that to please him, he wondered? Or had she spent another afternoon with Dan Masterson and got home too late to change? She welcomed him with the usual hug, but he sensed she was still cool towards him. Though, when he thought about it, she hadn't been her usual self for weeks. Not since the end of January, in fact, and the consultation. Watching television, she was often restless and would leave him half way through a programme to go and tidy up in the kitchen or retire to another room with the newspaper.

He waited until the sun sank below the thick line of cloud along the horizon, then rose from the bench and made his way indoors. She was in the kitchen writing a children's birthday card.

'Who is that to?'

She didn't look up. 'It's for Zoe, Dan's daughter. It's her birthday on Tuesday and she's invited me to her party.'

Crossing to the dresser Straker flicked through yesterday's still unopened mail.

'And when did you meet Zoe?'

'Yesterday. I went to Dan's to rehearse. Such a pretty girl. I quite fell for her.'

'And are you going to her birthday party?'

'I thought I might. There are going to be at least six children. Too much for Dan to manage on his own.'

Straker returned to the sitting room and sat down. He clicked the TV remote and ran down the menu on the screen. So, she was helping with his daughter's party. He could hardly object. The trouble was that he didn't trust Dan Masterson. And he wasn't all that sure about Emily.

His mobile rang. As he went to answer it, he glanced at the screen. It wasn't a number he recognised. 'Steve Straker.'

'Inspector. It's Kate Bellingham.'

He caught his breath. 'Oh...good evening Miss Bellingham.'

I'm sorry to trouble you at home. Is this an inconvenient time?'

'No, not at all.' He lowered his voice. 'Is everything all right?'

'Perfectly, thank you. It's just that you said yesterday that if I remembered anything unusual, I was to tell you. Well I did remember something after you left this morning and I've spent the day agonising

over whether it was important enough to call you. I really don't want to waste your time.'

'You are not wasting my time, I assure you. But where are you speaking from?'

'I'm at home... Oh dear. This is a mistake to call you now. I'm sure it can wait until the morning.'

'Is it something we can discuss on the telephone, or would you like me to...' Straker paused as Emily came in from the kitchen and sat down opposite him. '...I mean, I could call on you tomorrow morning on my way to work. I virtually pass your door.'

'Really? Would you? I would so much prefer to talk to you in person, if it's not too much trouble.'

'What time? I tend to go in rather early.'

'Inspector, please. I'm available to you at any time.'

'Would 8.30am be okay?'

'8.30am would be perfect.'

Ending the call, Straker returned the handset somewhat clumsily to its cradle.

'Who was that?' said Emily, picking up her copy of the play.

'Just Susan Linton's housekeeper. She said she's remembered something that may be important. Probably nothing, but you never know.'

'What's she like?'

Straker shrugged. 'Pleasant enough, I suppose.'

Emily picked up a copy of the play and handed it to him. 'I thought we might go through your lines, if you're not too tired. Anton said he doesn't want to see any books from tomorrow night.'

Straker groaned.

'He said it won't be a long rehearsal. Come on Steve. Let's see if you can go right through the scene without any prompts.'

Chapter Three

He wakes to the sound of rooks squawking in the trees and a tractor on the lane. He has slept so soundly that for a moment he isn't even sure that it wasn't just a terrible dream. But as he lifts the curtain and is dazzled by the low morning sun he knows it was no dream. The memory is as real as that blackbird sitting on the fence. What time is it, what day is it even? Rubbing his eyes he reaches for his watch. Last night, driving in late to take the pitch in the far corner, he was glad to be on his own. Now he isn't so sure. Maybe he should move on again, this time to a busy site where he is less likely to be noticed.

He switches on the radio in time to catch the 7.00am news. Michael Gove making a speech about education; another British soldier killed in Afghanistan; gloomy forecasts for the economy... But no mention of the murder. Has the investigation stalled, or are the police just being cagey? They must have checked the house by now, examined it for fingerprints, found the letters. Why wait for the inevitable? He should drive to the railway line now. Stand against the side of the bridge until the sound is deafening. Then step out...

Standing at the door of Kate Bellingham's cottage Straker felt a queasy thrill of anticipation as he heard her coming to the door.

'Good morning, Inspector. This is so kind of you.'

Her hair, dark and shining, her lipstick newly applied, she looked radiant.

'I... hope I'm not too early for you.'

'Not at all.' He moved past her and into her small sitting room. 'I'm glad to see you looking so much better today.'

She smiled. 'Thank you. Although I think you're saying that just to flatter me, because I barely slept a wink again last night. Can I offer you some coffee?'

He shook his head. 'I won't. But don't let me stop you.'

'No, I'll wait. I drink far too much coffee as it is.' She sat down opposite him.

Taking out his notebook, Straker coughed to cover his nerves. 'You were saying when we spoke last night...'

'Yes, Inspector. I just hope I haven't called you on a fool's errand.'

'I'm sure you haven't'

'This probably means nothing at all.'

'Tell me anyway.'

'Well, it was a few weeks ago. I happened to be driving past Susan's house one evening on my way to my book group. As I came down the hill I noticed a rather scruffy camper van parked ten or twenty yards beyond the house. It was dark, but I saw the driver get out of the van, cross the road and walk towards the house. He was in my headlights so I got a good look at him. He was carrying something, an envelope,

I think. Anyway I drove on past but, as I glanced in my rear view mirror, I formed the distinct impression that he was making directly for Susan's mailbox which is on one of the columns at the entrance. Of course he might not have been going there at all, but there was something about the man's appearance and the state of his vehicle that made me suspicious. So I drove on a little, looking for a place where I could turn round and then I drove back. By this time the camper van had gone, but I decided to take a look in the mailbox. Sure enough there was an envelope, just a small brown envelope, the sort that bills come in. So I took it out and looked at it, using the torch on my car keys.

'Was it addressed?'

'No. The envelope was sealed but there was no address or name.'

'What did you do?'

'I put it back in the mailbox and made a mental note to ask Susan about it when I brought the mail in next morning. But here's the strange thing. When I arrived at the house the next day, the mailbox was empty. Which was odd because the postman always arrives before I do and there is usually something. Now, Susan does fetch the mail occasionally herself, particularly in the summer months when it's warm outside. She has two walking frames - one at the top of the stairs which she uses to get from the chair lift to her bedroom, the other downstairs by the front door.'

'So, you think, on this occasion, she may have fetched the mail herself?'

'Yes. I asked her and she said she had.'

'Did she say she was expecting something?'

'No. She said that since it was a nice morning she decided to go out and fetch the mail. But there was nothing important - just some junk mail, which she put straight in the bin.'

'Did you say anything about the man you saw?'

'No. I assumed he must have been some local trader distributing leaflets.'

'And did you check the bin?'

'I didn't. To tell you the truth, I didn't think any more about it.' She hesitated. 'But that's not the end of the story, Inspector. About two weeks later I saw the same man again. This time he was standing at the mail box as I came down the hill, so I didn't get a look at his face. But it was the same man, I'm sure of it, and the same camper van.'

'And was this at about the same time as on the previous occasion?'

'Yes, just after 8.00pm. I know the time because my book group starts at 8.00pm and I was running a few minutes late.'

So you didn't go back on this occasion to look in the mailbox.'

'Not then, but I did stop on the return journey at around 10.00pm.'

'And what did you find?'

'Nothing. The mailbox was empty.'

Straker gave her a reassuring smile. 'Well, as you say, Miss Linton could walk a little. Presumably she went out during the evening to retrieve what he'd left there?'

Kate Bellingham studied him intently. 'But why would she have done that? The post arrives in the morning, not the evening. She must have been expecting something, or why would she venture out in the dark?'

With a jolt Straker realised that what she was telling him could be significant after all. 'So you think Miss Linton might have been communicating with someone via her mailbox?'

'Exactly. He was a strange looking man, Inspector. Not at all the kind of person we usually see in these parts.'

'Did you mention any of this to Miss Linton?'

'No. I decided not to probe. As I mentioned on Saturday, Susan and I hadn't been getting on well recently. She was quite withdrawn, as if there was something on her mind, something troubling her. But whenever I asked her if she was all right, she would jump down my throat.' She looked down. 'She used to be such easy company and I was so fond of her....' 'I'm sorry. I shouldn't have called you. I'm wasting your time. '

'Not at all,' said Straker, conscious that they were sitting so close to one another that he could touch her. 'What you've just told me may be important. You said yesterday that Miss Linton didn't get much personal mail.'

'Not usually, no. Although, early last year there was a feature about her on Breakfast News and she received a dozen or so letters of sympathy. But since then, only a letter a month at the most. Her fan mail didn't come directly. It came to her via Michael, her agent. He would post it on or, if I was seeing him for any reason, he would give it to me.'

'If Miss Linton was secretly communicating with someone, surely it would have been simpler to use the telephone.'

'I know. But Susan never phoned anyone. I don't know why we had a phone at the house because I rarely used it either.'

'And she didn't have a mobile?'

Kate Bellingham laughed. 'No. Susan wasn't into the new technology. She could barely work the television.'

Straker paused. 'Can you describe the man you saw at the mailbox?'

'I would say he was about fifty. Not tall. Five feet seven or eight at most, but very overweight. Eighteen stone, I would say, at least.'

'And his facial features?'

'Yes, his face was very distinctive. He was bald, but with thick sideburns and a large, drooping moustache.' She hesitated. 'Are you sure this is important? I could be describing a perfectly innocent person.'

'Then it is just as important to identify him so that we can eliminate him from our enquiries. Can you describe the van?'

She hesitated. 'It wasn't a big van, more the size of a car or small delivery van. Quite old looking and very scruffy. If I saw some pictures I might be able to describe it better.'

Straker closed his notebook. 'Do you think you could help us build an artist's impression of the man you saw?'

'You mean a Photo Fit?'

'Yes, though it's called an E-Fit these days. It's a specialist area, so I'll need to make some phone calls. But if I can arrange it for later today, perhaps you could come in to the police station. I can send a car for you.'

'There's no need for that. I can drive in to Aylesbury.'

'No, I insist. Someone will come and collect you.'

'Then I'll wait for someone to telephone me, shall I?

'Yes, I'll call you as soon as I've arranged something.' 'Straker rose to his feet. 'Thank you Miss Bellingham. You've been a great help.'

She rose too, smiling, as she put out her hand. 'I do hate it when people call me Miss Bellingham. It makes me sound like a dreadful old spinster, doesn't it?'

As they stood facing one another she reached out and brushed a piece of fluff from his lapel. 'Was your wife with you when I rang last night?'

'She was actually.' His throat was suddenly dry.

'I thought so.'

'Why do you say that?'

'You sounded different, that's all. More distant I suppose. As if you were a little bit cross with me.'

'I wasn't cross.'

'Then I'm glad. You're a very nice man. Do you know that?'

Straker looked away. 'I'm not sure my wife would agree with you about that.'

'Then she should.' She looked up at him, holding his gaze. 'I suppose it wouldn't be appropriate for you to call me Kate.'

His throat was so dry that his voice was husky. 'Maybe, in due course, when this is all over.'

Moving gently past him, she led him to the door. 'Then I hope I won't have too long to wait.'

ii.

Kevyn Wakeman watched as Straker strode through the Incident Room to the spacious office that had been allocated to him. Where had he been until now? Could it be that he had he had actually overslept on this bright, sunny morning? Or had there been a development? Something he had yet to be told about.

71

Whatever it was, it was annoying, because he had come in early a second time, all to no avail. His relationship with Straker had got off to a bad start, and he knew he was doing himself no favours by deliberately antagonising the man. The trouble was, it was hard to resist. The way he behaved with the housekeeper on Saturday, for example, stammering and tripping over his words like a teenager on his first date, She could have told him anything and he would have been happy to believe it. Okay, she was in pretty good nick for a woman her age, but she wasn't that hot.

He continued watching Straker through the half opened door as he sat down at his desk and picked up the phone. The question was why was the man so smitten? He'd seen his missus at the Christmas party and she was quite a looker. Lively too. Laughing and joking with everyone, while Straker stood stiffly at the bar. Maybe that was it. Maybe she was bored and had started putting herself around.

He waited until Straker ended the call, then got up and strolled over, giving the usual perfunctory tap on the door as he entered. As he looked up his face was flushed and excited, as if he had some news to impart.

'Good morning, Kevyn. And how are you today?'

'I'm good,' said Wakeman, sitting down to face him. 'So what happened to you this morning? Here I was at 8.00am, raring to go, but no sign of our leader.'

'That's because I had things to do,' said Straker tartly.

'Have you seen today's Herald?'

'Not yet. No'

'There's a double page spread about George Mannering. They must have been in touch with his hostel, because they know he's been missing since Friday morning. With that sort of coverage, they must be counting on an early arrest.'

But Straker wasn't listening. 'There's been a development, Kevyn. I had a call from Kate Bellingham last night.'

'Wakeman grinned. 'What's this? Something she forgot to tell you in her previous two interviews?'

'Not exactly. When we saw her on Saturday, you remember I asked her to think back over recent weeks and call me if anything unusual came to mind.'

'So, she came up with something, did she? I thought she might.'

'I called on her on my way in. I think what she told me may be significant.'

Wakeman listened impatiently as Straker told him about the man Kate Bellingham had seen outside Susan Linton's house and of his plan to issue an E-Fit picture. Did the man realise what he was letting the team in for? Once the picture hit the media, there would be dozens of sightings, every one of which would need to be followed up. Meanwhile George Mannering was still at large. He had telephoned the hostel warden again this morning and still he hadn't shown up. Added to which, a report from Fingerprints confirmed that Mannering's prints had been found in the house. Most probably dated back to the time he lived there, but it was possible that some were fresh.

Back at his desk, Wakeman looked around him. Over by the window, Becky Reedman was tapping away at her computer. Strange. A year ago he wouldn't have given her a second glance, yet now he felt quite drawn to her. It must be his age. Maybe the time had come to be looking for someone to settle down with. Someone he could talk to, have a conversation with. She looked up and glanced in his direction, then looked away. Getting up, he strolled over. 'Hi Becks. I hear you had a crap day yesterday.'

'It was okay.'

'Fancy a drink tonight when we finish?'

'Thanks, but I said I would go round to my Mum's tonight.'

'I only meant after work. Though, on second thoughts we could make an evening of it. Why not call her and say something's come up.'

For a few seconds she seemed to waver. 'Sorry, no. She's expecting me. I always try to go on Mondays since....' Her voice trailed away.

He remembered now. Her dad died just before Christmas. 'Tomorrow then. Unless you're already booked for tomorrow.'

'No. I don't think I'm doing anything tomorrow night...'

The conversation was interrupted by the ring of his mobile. Giving Becky a thumbs up, he turned away and put the phone to his ear. 'Wakeman speaking.'

'Hi, DS Wakeman? Geoff Hunt, Greater Manchester Police. We've found your man.'

'Mannering? You've found him? Where ?

'In a bar in the city centre. We had a tip off.'

'Great. Can you can hang on to him until the morning? I'll travel up today.'

Ending the call he turned again to Becky. 'George Mannering's been picked up. I'm going to have to drive up and question him.' He smiled. 'Maybe you could come too and keep me company. Don't worry. I'll square it with the boss.'

For the third time in the space of an hour Straker looked in at the interview suite where E-fit specialist Simon Winchester was working with Kate Bellingham. It was now mid afternoon and he was keen to get the news release out in time for the early evening news bulletins.

'Are we there yet, Simon?'

Winchester, a spare, bearded man turned to Kate Bellingham who sat beside him in front of the monitor. 'I think so. You're happy with this now, are you, Miss Bellingham?'

She nodded. 'I know it looks like a caricature, but he was such an unusual looking man. Yes, I think you've caught him well.'

The three of them studied the 'E- fit image, depicting a bald headed middle aged man with long sideburns and a drooping walrus moustache .

'Good. Thanks for coming in at short notice, Simon,' said Straker. 'And thank you, Miss Bellingham. You've been a great help.'

After seeing Kate Bellingham into her car, Straker returned to the Incident Room where the team was assembling for the briefing meeting. As the investigation was gaining momentum, so the investigating team was growing. Two researchers had arrived from Oxford that morning, bringing the total complement to ten. One would provide general support, while the other would take responsibility for HOLMES2, the police information technology system used to record all information gathered from witnesses, enquiry officers and members of the public..

Jack Meredith began the meeting by summarising the reports from Forensics and Fingerprints and the findings of the post mortem. The search of Elleswood House had also come up with two sets of fingerprints, other than those belonging to Susan Linton and Kate Bellingham. One set was identified as belonging to George Mannering, the other to a person unknown. These had been checked with the National Fingerprints Database with negative results. The post mortem (to Straker's satisfaction) appeared to contradict Wakeman's theory of an attack delivered in a frenzy of rage. It concluded that the actress's death was caused by a single stab wound beneath the left shoulder blade that pierced her heart. Moreover, the relatively small amount of bleeding from the four wounds to the chest and stomach suggested that the actress was already dying or dead by the time they were delivered. He could, of course, have telephoned Wakeman, who was now on his way to Manchester, but decided against it. Someone had to interview Mannering, so it might as well be Wakeman. It was just a pity that he couldn't find him something else to do to keep him up there. But his request that Becky Reedman be allowed to accompany him, he had turned down flat.

Straker brought the E-fit up on the monitor screen 'This, ladies and gentlemen, is the likeness of a man seen by Miss Bellingham on two occasions in recent weeks delivering something to the Elleswood House mail box. He paused until he had everyone's full attention. 'She saw him first on the 22nd February at around 8.00pm and again on the 7th of March at around the same time. Miss Bellingham was clear about the dates because she went to a book group on those two evenings. The man may, of course, have been perfectly innocent - a local tradesman perhaps delivering circulars, although Miss Bellingham doesn't think so for reasons I will come to...'

As Straker delivered the account Kate Bellingham gave him earlier in the day, he studied the expressions on the faces of the team. What were they thinking? That this was a significant lead, or a time wasting blind alley. He was beginning to wonder himself.

'So, we have two possibilities. Either Miss Bellingham was mistaken on this second occasion and the man made no delivery to Miss Linton's mailbox. Or that he did and Miss Linton retrieved it sometime between 8.00pm and 10.00pm.'

'By which time it would have been dark,' said Meredith.

'Exactly. It is one thing to take exercise on a bright sunny morning but would Miss Linton have gone out to the mailbox in the dark on a cold winter evening, unless she was expecting something?'

For several seconds no one spoke.

'So, there you have it. Maybe something, maybe nothing. Any questions?'

Becky Reedman raised a hand. 'How do you think the tabloids will treat that E-fit, sir? Isn't there the danger of an innocent man being demonised?'

'I take your point, Becky. But I don't see we have a choice.'

'I mean, you know the kind of headlines they'll come up with. *Hunt on for Walrus Man,* or something stupid like that. As you say, he may be just some local tradesman going about his business.'

Straker shrugged. 'I understand what you're saying, Becky. But this is a murder we're dealing with. We need the media onside if we're going to solve this case.'

Mark Taverner raised a hand. 'So, you think, sir that Miss Linton may have been conducting some private correspondence with this man?.

'It's a possibility, that's all. Unfortunately Miss Bellingham didn't confront Miss Linton with what she had seen. Apparently the actress was quite withdrawn in the last three or four months, as if something was worrying her. She said she didn't want to antagonise her by seeming to probe.'

'And the camper van,' said Jack Meredith. 'Did she get a good look at it?'

'She did. Miss Bellingham described it as light coloured, probably white, and very scruffy. Based on different makes we've shown her, we think it might have been a Renault or Volkswagen.' He paused. 'So there we have it. A distinctive vehicle and, I think you'll agree, a very distinctive looking person. I plan to get this E-fit out as a news release in the next half hour and hopefully, it will be featured on the early evening news bulletins. Okay, thank you, we'll end it there.'

iv.

Returning to her desk, Becky sat gazing disconsolately at her monitor screen. She should have followed Dad's advice. *Only speak up when you really have something to say but, otherwise, keep your own counsel.* Straker had put her in her place just now and she deserved it. Of course they had to release the E-fit to the media. How else were they to make progress? She wouldn't make that mistake again. But making her presence felt was easier said than done. She had six years service behind her now,

78

four of them in Serious Crime, yet there was still no hint of promotion was coming her way. She was even beginning to regret giving up her Easter weekend for all she had been given to do so far. Meanwhile Kevyn Wakeman was on his way to Manchester and, but for Straker's intransigence, she would have been accompanying him. Too valuable to be spared, said Straker, though what he had in mind for her over the next couple of days, he hadn't revealed. Probably helping to field the hundreds of calls they would get as soon as that E-Fit picture hit the media.

Not that she was naive enough to think she would be doing anything more useful in Manchester. But it would have been an adventure, and an adventure was what she needed right now. Her social life had been in the doldrums for months and the prospect of an overnight stay in the company of Kevyn Wakeman filled her with excitement and apprehension in equal measure.

To tell the truth she had spent much of the morning imagining how it would be; starting with the leisurely drive up the motorway and maybe stopping off for a snack somewhere en route. Then booking into the hotel and arranging to meet in the bar for a drink before dinner. But what about after dinner? What if he suggested coffee or a nightcap in his room, or hers? Would she say yes? Probably. In spite of everything she had heard about Kevyn Wakeman, the fact was he was nearly thirty two and it was a year since she last had a regular boyfriend. When Kevyn came over to tell her that Straker had vetoed his proposal she was so disappointed that she almost burst into tears.

Over by the window, Mark Taverner and the two research staff from Oxford were working through Susan Linton's fan mail. No key had been found to the filing cabinet so it had been brought to the incident room and forced open. Evidently Susan Linton wasn't a very organised person, because inside they found all four drawers crammed to overflowing with fan mail. These had now been emptied out on to a long table to be sorted first by correspondent and then by date. It would to take days.

Turning back to her monitor, she ran the cursor to her report on the reunion interviews. Had Straker even bothered to read it? She supposed he had, although he barely referred to it at the meeting. After seeing Roland Frobisher and Mary Whatton yesterday morning, they had called on Simon and Julie Pettifer, a married couple who made up the rest of the reunion gathering. Neither was able to suggest a possible motive for the murder, or suggest anyone who might have borne her a grudge. Asked about Kate Bellingham, they said she was a talented actress in her time, but they never cared for her. She had a reputation for being highly promiscuous in those early days, and there were even rumours that she was in a relationship with their agent, Michael Bristow, long before his wife died.

'I thought you might like this to keep you going.'

She looked up to find Mark Taverner standing by her desk with two cups of coffee. 'Oh, thank you, Mark. That's kind of you. But I'm not staying. I was just setting off.'

'Well, you might as well drink it before you go,' he said, parking himself on the end of the adjacent desk. 'So, you didn't get to go to Manchester after all.'

'Seems not.'

'Any plans for tonight then?' He sipped his coffee, not quite meeting her eye.

'I go and see my mother on Monday evenings.'

'Can I buy you a drink before you set off?'

She looked at him in surprise. Two invitations in one day. Maybe things were looking up. 'Thanks, Mark, but I'd better not. If I get there early, I can leave early and not be too late home.'

Taking her paper cup Mark slotted it inside his own. 'Then maybe you would like to come with me Wednesday night. We're playing in Hemel Hempstead.'

'Playing? Playing what?'

'In a band'

'You mean, you play in a band?'

He smiled. 'Yes. It's called moonlighting,'

'Whose band is it?'

'Mine actually. You can find us on You Tube. We could go straight from here and maybe get something to eat on the way. That's if you're not doing anything.'

Becky gathered her things. 'Well, thank you Mark. I might just do that.' Getting up from her desk she looked over at the long pile of letters down the centre of the table. 'You're leaving too aren't you?'

He shrugged. 'No. I think I'll give it a couple more hours. Until I get bored.'

'Then don't stay too long. See you tomorrow.'

Becky made her way downstairs and across the parking area to her car. So Mark Taverner played in a band. Maybe there was more to him than met the eye.

v.

'Kiss me.'

'Not here.'

'Why? No one's going to come. Kiss me.'

'Wait. What was that?'

'Nothing.'

'No. I heard something,'
'Come on. We're safe here. One last kiss before I go.'

As Dan Masterson drew Emily into that now all too familiar embrace, Straker got up from his seat and made his way out to the entrance lobby. When was the last time Em had gazed into his eyes with such passion? Or kissed him with such abandon? All right, it was only acting, but you don't get to give a performance like that unless you've actually been there.

Walking out on to the steps he felt the cool breeze on his face. Today they completed the last interviews of local criminals and mental health patients. Some of their alibis were a bit dicey, but he was confident that Susan Linton's murderer wasn't some random intruder high on drugs any more than it was her ex husband, George Mannering. His hopes rested now on identifying the man Kate Bellingham saw delivering something to Susan Linton's mailbox. If he turned out to be innocent, they were back to square one.

He walked down between the cars to the railings. Were Emily and Masterson having an affair? This morning at breakfast she was distant and preoccupied. It was the same this evening when he came home for a quick sandwich before the rehearsal. Okay, the news that they couldn't have a child was upsetting, but what more could he do? Given his *'virtually non-existent sperm count'*, as Donaldson chose to describe it, In Vitro Fertilisation wasn't even an option. Adoption too seemed fraught with difficulties. A trip to Peru or China seemed to offer a better prospect of success than going to an adoption agency. As for employing the services of a sperm bank, he wasn't prepared to go down that route. Fortunately, Emily hadn't suggested it.

Work/life balance. It had been her mantra for months, ever since they came down from Shropshire. A fresh start, she'd said, then maybe things would happen for them. But he would have to change too. It was no good if he just carried on in the same old way, putting in twelve hours a day and coming home too tired to do anything except sit in front of the television flicking channels. And so he'd agreed. No more hanging around at HQ when there was really nothing to keep him there. No more calls at the pub for a quick one on the way home. And they would find some outside interests, things they could do together.

He looked up at the poster occupying on the Community Centre notice board. *Murder by Candlelight, 7.30 pm, Wednesday 18th April to Saturday 21st April.* He supposed that for her the play had filled a gap. She hadn't acted since university, so it was with some trepidation that she went to those first auditions. But she needn't have worried. She came home that evening thrilled with the news that she had been offered the female lead. And suddenly she was a different person. She had a new focus, something to distract her from her miseries.

But joining the drama group with her was a big mistake. He only agreed in a moment of weakness, and then on the strict understanding that he would be a behind the scenes man. Fine, said Anton when rehearsals began just after New Year, the limelight isn't for everybody. Then Geoff Pike broke his leg skiing and Anton pleaded with him to take on the minor role of the detective. Come on Steve darling. It's what you do for your day job anyway. Give it a go and help us out.

'Steve, you're on.'

It was Clare, one of set designers. 'They're nearly finished and Anton says he wants to do your scene next.'

With a wave, Straker made his way slowly back into the hall. Emily and Masterson were still up on stage, holding hands as Anton addressed them from the centre of the auditorium.

'Lovely darlings, both of you. But Dan, I think a little more passion in the embrace wouldn't come amiss. The two of you have just spent the best part of the night together, remember'.

They weren't just holding hands. Their fingers were intertwined. Did casual friends intertwine fingers?

'But, I'm quibbling. Wonderful, both of you'

Anton strutted up the steps and on to the stage.

'All right, on to scene six. No - on second thoughts, we'll do scene 3 first and the finding of the body. Beginners please...

Still holding hands, Emily and Masterson came down the steps and up the aisle to where Straker was sitting.

'We're free for half an hour, Steve, so Dan thought we might pop over the road for a quick one.' She smiled. 'How about it? '

Straker looked at them suspiciously. 'You mean, me included?'

'Of course, you fool. Come on.'

Two minutes later he and Emily were sitting at a small table at the King and Queen while Masterson was at the bar ordering drinks.

She put a hand on his knee. 'Try and be nice to Dan. He's had a terrible year, what with the divorce and losing the children and then having to move house. For my sake. You don't have to like him if you don't want to.'

'I don't dislike him. I have no opinion of him one way or the other.'

'Yes, you do. He's acutely conscious of your hostility and it's affecting his performance. Which means mine is affected too.'

Arriving at the table, Masterson set down the drinks tray.

'Here we are. Dry wine for Emily and a lager shandy for you, Steve.' He sat down. 'I really am grateful for Em's offer to give me a hand with the kid's party. I wasn't sure how well I was going to cope with half a dozen five year olds.'

'Glad she can be of help,' said Straker, raising his glass to his lips.

'Well, cheers everyone.'

Masterson and Emily clinked glasses and he raised his own belatedly to join them.

'So, how's it going with the investigation, Steve? Or, shouldn't I be asking such a leading question?'

'It's going okay.' Straker took another sip of his drink.

'Well, it's great that you're finding the time to do the play. We would have been stuck without you.'

'I hardly think so.' Was he serious? Or was he just trying to flatter him? 'I think anyone could have made a better stab at the part than me.'

'Oh, I don't agree. There isn't a lot for you to get your teeth into but I think you're doing really well. Isn't he, Em?'

Emily leaned towards him. 'Of course you are, Steve. Dan was saying only yesterday, what stage presence you have. Once you've mastered the script, you'll be fine.'

Straker snorted. 'Oh, well that's all right then. Good to hear I get the Dan Masterson seal of approval.'

Emily looked at him sharply. 'Dan was paying you a compliment, Steve. At least accept it with good grace...'

vi.

Straker came out of the bathroom into the bedroom. Emily was already in bed, reading. Catching her eye he gave her a tentative smile.

'Why were you so horrible tonight?' she said, without looking up from her book?

'When?'

'In the pub. Why were you so rude to Dan? He made several attempts to engage you in friendly conversation and you stonewalled him every time.'

Straker walked round to his side of the bed and climbed in. 'Well, if I did, you certainly made up for it.'

She looked at him. 'And what's that supposed to mean?'

'Actually, I was a bit surprised when Anton told you put more passion into it. It looked to me as if the two of you were already going at it hammer and tongs.'

She gave a bitter laugh. 'I don't know what's eating you, Steve, but you're not a very nice person to be around these days. Do you know that?'

'I see. So, maybe you'd prefer it if I wasn't around. Is that what you're saying?'

'There's no need to put words in my mouth.'

'You like him, don't you?'

'If you mean Dan, yes I do. He's good company.'

'A bit odd then, if he's such good company, that his wife decided to walk out on him.'

Emily put her book down. 'Dan was the innocent party, Steve. It was she who broke up the marriage, not him?'

'Oh really? In what way?'

'By having an affair. Not just one. Several. She couldn't leave men alone.'

'Really. Well I don't go along with this idea of the guilt being all one sided. As far as I'm concerned, it takes two to tango.'

'What's that supposed to mean?.'

'Well, maybe she had good reason to go off with other men. Maybe he was neglecting her, taking her for granted...'

'You mean, like someone else I could name?'

Straker lay back and was silent for a few moments. 'Sorry. I rather walked into that one.'

She lay back too and reached for his hand. 'You've been awful these last few weeks, Steve. All right, you've had a blow to your self esteem and I'm sorry. But I've just as much reason to be depressed as you.'

'Have you?'

'Yes. Because I wanted us to have a child.' Now she started to cry. 'And I thought you did too. Don't you understand what that means to me?'

'Of course I understand.'

'No you don't. You pretend you do, but you've never cared about starting a family as much as I have. All those years, Steve... all those years when you made me stay on the pill. And now I know it's never going to happen.'

'So, maybe you'd like to be out of it. Is that what you're trying to tell me? Get a real man next time and start over'

For several seconds she was silent. 'No.' she said quietly. 'Of course I don't want that. And I never want you to think it either.' She drew him to her and buried her head against his chest. 'Hold me Steve. I hate it when we're not friends.'

vii.

Leaving her mother's small semi detached house in Ruislip at just after 10.00pm, Becky was still musing on the irony of the day's events. It had been a pleasant enough evening, but she knew it was time to start making a social life for herself, instead of pretending that she needed to keep going home for her mother's sake. Because she didn't. It was over six months now since her father's death and her mother was going out more and more these days. There had even been occasions when it was necessary to change the day of her visits to fit in with her mother's social engagements.

Cruising along the A40 she drove carefully, constantly having to remind herself that there was a fifty mile speed limit stretching almost to Uxbridge. But, at last, the de-restriction sign came into view and she was able to put her foot down. Then her mobile rang. Cursing under her breath, she switched on the speaker. Probably her mother to tell her she had left something behind. 'Hi, is that you Mum?'

'No, it's Mark.'

She laughed in surprise. 'Mark? What are you doing ringing me at this time of night? I might have been in bed. Where are you?'

'I'm still at work.'

'What? You don't mean to tell me you've been there all evening.'

'I have actually. Listen, I've found something. Something in the fan mail. Where are you right now?'

'On the A40 actually, going past Uxbridge.

'I've found two letters from someone called Paul. Both typed on a typewriter rather than a computer, judging by the look of them, with lots of spelling mistakes and not much punctuation. But listen to this. This one's dated the 8th August 2011.

Dear Susan, Thank you for your letter. I have been waiting for it every day. I can't believe that you also have fantasies about me. When do you have them Susan? Is it when you are lying in bed, or in the daytime..... He goes on like that a bit, before signing himself off with three little kisses.'

Becky moved to the inside lane and slowed down. She needed to concentrate. 'So, what are you telling me Mark? That some of Susan Linton's fans had fantasies about her?'

'Becky, this letter was written recently, last year in fact.'

'I still don't understand why....'

'Don't you see? *I can't believe you are also having fantasies about me.* This letter has to be in answer to a letter from her. It's telling us that as late as last year, Susan Linton was in intimate correspondence with at least one of her fans.'

Pulling into a lay-by Becky switched off the engine. 'Okay, so she was writing intimate letters to one of her fans.....'

'Bear with me, Becky. This one's dated the 28th December 2011, that's just four months ago. *Dear Susan, I want to help you with the money but I haven't got £5,000. I think I can get some money from my mother's account, but I can only get small amounts or she might notice it's gone. If I got you £1000 do you think that would be enough to make him go away?*

89

How can I get it to you, Susan I don't want to post it to you in case it gets lost. I will wait to hear from you.'

Now he had Becky's full attention. 'You're sure it's from the same person?'

'As sure as I can be. Same poor spelling and punctuation. Same uneven typeface. Definitely the same signature.'

'And he signs himself as Paul. No second name?'

'No. Just Paul, plus three little kisses.'

'Mark, stay where you are. I'll be with you as soon as I can.'

Chapter Four

Spreading the newspaper out on the steering wheel, he stares at the picture. Mr Walrus. That's the name they have given him, though it looks nothing like him. Except for the moustache.. His real name is Paul, they say, but they don't give his second name. A description of the camper van too, Possibly an old Renault or Volkswagen, but they don't give the registration number.

Folding the newspaper he puts it down on the seat. Someone must have called the police. Not Mother. She would never have called them. But David, maybe. Though, if it were David, the police would have everything - his name, his address, the registration number of the van, even a photograph.

Mother must be sick with worry. He left his mobile in the flat. By now it will be full of messages, begging him to call her and say he had nothing to do with Susan Linton's murder. Did he murder her? That's the trouble. He isn't sure. Since Friday night he isn't even sure of his sanity. But the police will know. If he did murder her, they will have evidence to prove it. If not, they will know that too.

He looks at his face in the driving mirror. He should change his appearance. Shave off his moustache and sideburns. Wear a hat or a hood when he goes out.

Maybe he will give himself up. He hasn't decided yet. He hasn't decided anything.

i.

'Is that you Steve?'

Straker came into the bedroom. 'Yes. Sorry if I woke you.'

Emily switched on the bedside light. 'What time is it?'

'6.40am.'

'You look exhausted. Are you coming to bed?'

'No. I'll just shower, grab some breakfast and get back. There's been a breakthrough, Em. I'm sorry, but I have to be there.'

'You mean, you know who did the murder?'

'Not for certain, but we have a promising new lead.'

Emily got out of bed and reached for her dressing gown. 'I suppose you'll be late again tonight then.'

'Probably.'

'There's a rehearsal. You know that, don't you?'

'Yes, I know. I'll try to be there.'

She put her arms round him. 'It's important, Steve. Only a week now to curtain up.'

'I'll be there, Em, okay? It's only a play, for God's sake. I'm trying to solve a real murder.'

By 7.30am, Straker was on his way back to Aylesbury. Becky's call came just as he was going to bed. But by the time she had read him three of the letters, he knew he had to join them. For the next five hours he, Becky and DC Taverner worked through the large pile of fan mail, looking for more letters from this man signing himself as Paul. By 5.45am they had found eighteen letters, all conscientiously dated by day, month and year. Seven belonged to the period prior to 2007, the year of Susan Linton's accident, each letter signed with his full name, Paul Priestley. Of greater interest were the other eleven letters, all of which were dated within the past twelve months and all sent from the same Croydon address. Before going home these eleven letters were photocopied, then secured in separate transparent protective sleeves in readiness for fingerprint analysis.

Arriving at his desk, Straker sat down to read through the photocopied letters again. It was the breakthrough they had been waiting for. Because now they had Paul's full name and address and with that, they would shortly have the make and registration of his vehicle. Taking the first letter he read it again in its entirety.

30 July 2011

Dear Susan

Thank you for writing to me I never dreemed you would send me a personnel letter I will tresure it allways. I have seen all your films and on the stage too. I met you once but you wont rmember that. I have a lot of fantasees about you Susan, tho I dont think I should really be telling you this !!?? You ask me about myself so I will tell you I come from a very respectible family in Melrose. My father was a big noise in the city and my mother was a maggistrate. As for me I was not so lucky becaus I had problems which meant I coud not go to a proper school like my brother but had to go

93

away. Dont get me wrong when I say I
have sufferd from mental problums in my
life which got me in trouble somtimes but
now with the drugs I take am quite stable.
It does not mean I am not rite in the head
becaus I am just as good as evreeone
else. I dont have much money rite now only
what I get on benifit but not for long becos
my Mother is old and she will die soon
Then my brother and me will inherrit her
house and I will be rich.. That is all for now
Please write me soon.

That Paul Priestley was completely obsessed with Susan Linton was evident from the sheer number of letters he had written to the actress over the years. But this letter told them a good deal more. That he had a history of mental illness, for example, and was unemployed and living on benefit. Also, surprisingly, that he came from a wealthy background, and stood to inherit a substantial sum when his mother died.

Judging by the content of Paul's next three letters, the last piece of information was not lost on Susan Linton. Determined to get her hands on some of that wealth, she appears none too scrupulous as to the method she will use achieve her goal.

8 Aug 2011

...I cant beleeve that you also have
fantasees about me! When do you have
them Susan? Is it when you are lyin in bed,
or durin the day. I have them all the time
!!!??. You ask about my truble . Yes it is

94

true I did sumthin crazy when I was young and they took me away. I wont go into the detale becaus I am alrite now... I dont think I can send you any money Susan. The money I sent you was what my mother gave me on my birthday I am not sure about asking her for more rite now becaus she will think I am in truble and will tell my brother to find out what is going on...

20th August, 2011

...I remember when you marrid George Mannering and I was jealos, in fact I was glad you got divorcd becaus I olways new he was no good for you and I was not surprizd that he went to prison. I hope they give him a rouf time. And I should know Susan because I have done time myself but not in prison actualy...I am sorry you dont have much money and I wish I culd help you but I cant. Maybe when my mother dies I will be able to but she is quite old so she may die soon...

1st September, 2011

...I don't think I can send you any money Susan. The cheque for £1,000 I send you was what my mother gave me on my birthday I am not sur about askin her for more rite now becaus she will think I am in truble and will tell my brother to find out

*what is goin on. Maybe I can send you a
few pounds when I get paid...*

Now a gap in the correspondence of over four
months...

13 Jan 2012

*...I was very happy to get your letter as I
thort you had given me up becaus I coud
not send you any money. I am sorry about
the truble you are in Susan. I allways knew
George Mannering was up to no good but
you must not let him blackmale you Susan.
If you give him money he will only cum
back for more. Shall I deel with him for you.
If you tell me where he lives I will go and
stop him once and for all. He wont threten
you again I promis....*

So, Susan Linton is being blackmailed by her
former husband. Or so she says...

20 Jan 2012

*...I want to help you with the money but I
have not got £5000!! If I send you £2000
do you think that woud make him go away.
But how do I get it to you Susan. I dont
want to post it to you in case it gets lost.
Tell me what I have to do...*

True or not, her appeals are finally
bearing fruit...

27 Jan 2012

...I have got the money out of my Mothers account. Phewwwww!! I had to go to the cashpoint seven times!! and I hope my Mother does not check her statment, I will put the money into a brown envlope and put it in your malebox like you said at 8oclock next Tuesday and I hope it will be enouf to stop Mannering bothring you, If it is not enouf you should let me deal with him Susan he wud never bother you again!!! I will finish him off once and for all if that is what you want...

10 Feb 2012

...I have got another £1,000 for you but you must not ask me again... I will deliver it on Friday at 8oclock but that must be the end of it Susan. Why don't you let me deal with Mannering. Just tell me where he is and I will pay him a visit!!

By now, Paul has delivered £3,000 to Susan Linton's mailbox, yet still she wants more. He is starting to get angry and frustrated...

22 Feb 2012

...I cant give you more money... Just tell me where Mannering is living Susan and I will kill him like you kill a rat becaus that is what he is no better than vermin just as he

is thretening you. Give me his adress and I promis you will never hear from him again...

9 Mar 2012

I cant help you any more. If you wont let me deal with Mannering you must go to the police. He will never stop blackmaleing you Susan. I have alredy given you so much money, does that mean nothink to you. I don't like the way you are treeting me Susan. You are not being nice to me!...

...until finally, he loses patience altogether....

17 Mar 2012

How can you be so kruel after all I have done for you and the money I have given you. I reelize I have been a fool all these years to love you. You have been using me Susan, thats what I think. Well you will not get your money whatever you do and I don't care what he does to you becaus you deserve it. And I give you a big warnin now Susan not to telefone my mother. Anyway she wont listen to you. But if you do I am warnin you it will be the worse for you!!! And if I am not good enugh for you then my money isnt good enugh for you either and I want it back. And all my letters as well. I will give you a week to get my money or I am tellin you Susan I will be paying you a big visit!!!....

'Morning, Steve, how's it going?'

Straker looked up to see Chief Superintendent Jerry Rawlins at his office door. 'Good morning, Jerry. You've arrived at a good moment. Take a look at these.' Rawlings came in and sat down. 'Eleven letters to Susan Linton. All from one devoted fan and all written within the past year. See what you make of them.'

Passing him the sheaf of photocopies, Straker sat back and watched as the Chief read them one by one.

'My God, Steve!' he said, handing the letters back to Straker. 'Where did you find these?"

'In the locked filing cabinet we brought over from the house. Mixed in with thousands of other letters from Susan Linton's fans. DC Taverner came across the first two or three at around 10.00pm last night. He was joined by DC Reedman and later by me. It took us most of the night to find them all. Some go back twenty years or more, but these eleven were written in the past twelve months. In fact, right up to within a few days of the murder.'

'So, Paul could also be our man with a van?'

'The letters seem to point to it.'

'And Susan Linton's murderer. Do we have a second name?'

'Yes. And his address. Paul Priestley. Lives in Croydon. I'm about to ask the local CID to go round, though I doubt if they'll find him at home. But now we have his identity it won't take long to get the make and registration number of his vehicle.'

Rawlings, picked up the final letter and browsed through it again. 'So, George Mannering's mixed up in this too. A blackmailer as well as a paedophile. I gather he's back in custody.'

'He is. Kevyn Wakeman drove up to Manchester yesterday afternoon. He'll be interviewing him this morning.'

Rawlings rose to his feet. 'Well, congratulations Steve. Looks like we're on our way.'

ii.

Switching off the Breakfast News, David Priestley felt so close to fainting that he had to sit down.The shaven head, the sideburns the large drooping moustache – it was Paul. his brother; it couldn't be anyone else. The description too. A middle aged man of short, stocky build, seen on two occasions recently outside Susan Linton's house. And as if that wasn't enough to identify him, the police had reason to believe that he was the owner of a light coloured camper van. Thankfully, there was no suggestion that Paul was under suspicion. Only that they wanted to interview him so they could eliminate him from their enquiries.

He had learned of Susan Linton's murder only last night as he was returning from a long weekend in Brussels. Reading about it in the evening newspaper, he was so shocked that it even occurred to him to telephone Paul there and then. Because Susan Linton was the love of Paul's life. He had seen all her films and watched her countless times on the West End stage from cheap balcony seats. On his rare visits to his brother's succession of rented flats around London, the book of press cuttings was always there

100

on the cluttered kitchen table he used as a desk. He had even met the actress once. Following her return from Hollywood, she appeared in a West End play and Paul waited at the stage door for her autograph. She made quite a fuss of him, signing his programme for him and planting a kiss on his cheek as she thanked him for his loyalty.

Yes, Paul idolised Susan Linton. Would he ever forget the way he went on about her on that long drive up to Melrose for Father's funeral? Why did she marry that man Mannering in the first place? Only a complete swine would walk out on his wife within months of her being left paralysed and confined to a wheelchair. Hunched beside him in the car, his fat fingers tugging irritably at the seat belt, Paul seemed more preoccupied with Susan Linton's broken marriage than their father's death.

Picking up the telephone, the bleeping tone told him that he had three new messages. Mother probably. She would have learned about the murder over the weekend and would be worrying about how Paul had taken the news. Had he been to see him? Or spoken to him, at least? It wasn't right that Paul was living all by himself in that awful flat. He should go and see him and make sure he was all right.

Tapping in Paul's number again, he listened, but the number rang on, not even going to voicemail. He needed to think. A man with a light coloured camper van seen outside Susan Linton's house. Seen when? The police hadn't said. He reached for the telephone again. If he would just answer he would know, because his voice would betray him. Was he there even now, staring at the telephone, too terrified to answer? Or was he in hiding? Yes, that was more likely. He had driven off in his camper van and parked in some field or lay-by until he was approached and recognised. Or until the money ran out.

David Priestley rose from his desk and crossed to the window. No, he was overreacting. Here he was, already labelling Paul a murderer, when the police simply wanted to interview him so they could eliminate him from their enquiries. His brother was odd in many ways, but he wasn't violent. He wouldn't hurt a fly. Remember how he nursed that baby bird he found under the beech tree, feeding it every day. And how he cried himself to sleep when Father drowned the kittens.

Yet there was no denying that Paul also had a morbid interest in violence. What about that time he caught a glimpse of him lifting a floorboard and hiding something as he was passing his bedroom. He crept in later to take a look. Magazines, dozens of them, full the most horrific pictures he had ever seen. He never mentioned it to Paul, or to anyone, but he remembered gazing at his brother in silent awe as they ate supper that night under Mother's watchful eye.

Mother. He picked up the phone. She would know where he was. She had bought Paul a smart phone for Christmas and made him swear to carry it with him on all his trips, so she could keep in touch. She worried about him incessantly, loving him with a fierce protectiveness. Did he have enough money? Did he eat properly? He should never have left Scotland. How could he possibly be happy, living all by himself in London?

She answered almost immediately.

'Paul, is that you?'

'No Mother, it's David."

'Oh... hello darling. I thought it might be Paul.'

'I've been in Brussels over the weekend. I suppose you've heard the news about Susan Linton.'

'Yes. Awful business. We heard it on the news and it was in Sunday's paper.'

Mother was over eighty now and in poor health but, talking to her on the telephone, he always chose to remember the mother of their childhood when it was she, not Father, who ruled the household. She had been such a strong woman then. He recalled the time Paul came home from school with a torn shirt and a bleeding nose. She went straight round to Andrew Mackay's house, threatening to call the police if the bullying didn't stop at once. And it was she, not Father, who marched out to confront the gang of youths who gathered each day at the end of the road, so that Paul was too frightened to come home from school.

'He's going to be upset, Mother. Have you spoken to him?'

She didn't answer.

'Mother? Are you still there?'

'Yes, of course I've spoken to him darling. He was with me. We heard the news together. He was very upset of course.'

'Paul was in Melrose? With you?'

'Yes dear, since Friday evening. He came up for the weekend. Didn't he tell you he was coming to see me?'

'You mean, he arrived on Friday evening and stayed all day Saturday and Sunday?'

'Yes. He came to see me, darling. We just stayed at home and had a lovely, lazy time together.'

Priestley felt a surge of relief. 'I didn't know he was coming to see you, Mother. When did he set off home?'

'Yesterday. We had a late lunch because we went for a walk. Let me see. It must have been about four o clock. I've been trying to call him on his mobile as he may have stopped over somewhere in his van. But he's not answering. If you speak to him, do get him to ring me so I know he got home all right. Tell him it's very important he rings. I worry so much about him.'

As he put down the telephone, David felt uneasy. He keyed her number again.

'Paul?' Her voice was breaking with emotion

'No Mother, it's me again. He hasn't been with you, has he?'

Now she burst into tears. *'You must find him David. You have to find him before he does something silly. He isn't strong, you know. You're his brother. You must look after him, whatever he's done.'*

iii.

The investigation was gathering pace. The DVLA database in Swansea had confirmed Paul Priestley as the owner of a 2001 Renault Master Camper Van, registration number Y949JPP. Police officers from the local Police Station had called at his South Croydon address, but there was no reply. Nor was there any sign of his camper van. The eleven letters had been sent off for forensic analysis and while one team was employed taking calls in response to the release of the E-Fit image, another was going through the fan mail a second time to see if the actress had been in correspondence with any other of her former fans.

Straker sat at his desk with the letter photocopies laid out in front of him. Something was troubling him.

104

In his letter dated the 2nd September 2011, Paul Priestley mentioned sending Susan Linton £1,000. Presumably, this was in the form of a cheque, which would then have to be paid into a bank account. Why had Kate Bellingham never mentioned it? He picked up the phone.

'Kate Bellingham.'

'Good morning Miss Bellingham It's Steve Straker....'

'Steve who?.. Oh, Inspector. Forgive me. I didn't recognise you for a moment.'

'I'm sorry to trouble you Miss Bellingham, but I was just wondering if the name Paul Priestley rings a bell.'

'Paul Priestley?'

'One of Miss Linton's fans.'

'Actually yes, I do remember someone of that name. He sent Susan some money a while ago now. Quite a large amount actually.'

Straker's mood lifted immediately. 'Do you remember when this was?'

'About a year ago. You remember I told you there was a piece on Breakfast Television about Susan's life since the accident. She received quite a few sympathetic letters, as well as a generous gift of £1,000 from Mr Priestley.'

'Were the letters sent directly to her home address?'

'No. All personal mail went to Mr Bristow' office address and he sent it on.'

'Unopened?

'Unopened, of course. As I told you, Susan was very possessive about her fan mail.'

'Though I assume she showed you this letter.'

'Yes, of course. She had to, because it was my job to bank it.'

'Did you acknowledge the gift, or did she?'

'We did it together. Susan dictated. I typed.'

'Do you still have Mr Priestley's letter accompanying the cheque? We didn't find it among Miss Linton's fan mail.'

'I'm afraid I don't. If it wasn't in the filing cabinet, Susan must have thrown it away.'

'Do you know if Miss Linton received any more letters from Paul Priestley?'

'If she did, she never mentioned them to me.'

'And you don't remember seeing any letters in recent months that looked like personal mail.'

'There may have been two or three. As I say, any fan mail came to her via Michael.'

'Did Miss Linton ever give you any letters to post?'

'No. I don't recall her giving me any personal letters to post. At least not since her accident.'

'But she could have been writing letters and posting them herself. I mean, without your knowledge.'

'She could. Though it would have been difficult for her. There's a post box at the crossroads, but that's a hundred yards from the house. '

'What about stamps and stationery? Did she have access to those?'

'I used to keep a small supply of stamps in the kitchen drawer, with notepaper and envelopes. Although it never occurred to me that she would have gone there. Why, Inspector? Do you have reason to think she was writing to Mr Priestley?'

'Actually, we know she was. We've found eleven letters from Paul Priestley in her filing cabinet, all dated within the past twelve months. Judging by their content, they were in frequent correspondence.'

'Eleven letters?' Kate Bellingham seemed shocked.

'The most recent letter is dated the 17th March this year, just a few weeks before Miss Linton was murdered. The earlier letters were probably posted, but we have reason to think the later ones were delivered by hand to her mailbox.'

But I always collected the mail, Inspector. If there had been any personal mail, I'm sure I would have noticed it.'

'Unless she went out earlier and collected it herself. You said she could walk...'

She interrupted him. *'Inspector, are you suggesting that the man I saw could have been Mr Priestley?'*

'I am. At least, that's the assumption we're working on. But we can't be sure until we find him. We telephoned his home number this morning, but there's no answer.'

'But surely, Mr Priestley couldn't have killed Susan. Not after making her such a generous gift.'

'I know it seems unlikely. But we have to keep an open mind until we know more. Thank you Miss Bellingham. You've been most helpful.'

Well, thank you for keeping me informed, Inspector.' There was a pause. *'Is it likely I shall see you again?'*

Straker hesitated. 'I can't say at the moment. But I will let you know of any developments.'

'I am available to you at any time, Inspector. You know that, don't you.'

Ending the call, Straker felt a thrill that was almost visceral. *Available to him at any time.* Was she sending him a sexual invitation? He had barely replaced the handset when his phone rang.

'Straker.'

'Hi Steve, how's it going?'

'It's going well, Kevyn. Have you talked to Mannering yet?'

'I've had one session. So far, he's claiming amnesia. He says he spent the entire weekend on

107

one long drinking binge. Claims he doesn't remember much at all.'

'Do you believe him?'

'No. I think he's playing games. How about you? Any sightings yet?

'Several. And there's been a major development, Kevyn. Pity you weren't here. We could have done with your help.'

Wakeman listened in silence as Straker told him about the discovery of the letters and the identification of the writer as Paul Priestley, the owner of a Renault camper van.

'Good, well done, Steve. So, Mannering was blackmailing his ex wife, and this man Priestley was sending, or bringing her money to pay him off. Is that what you're telling me?'

'It appears that way?' I'll email you photocopies of the letters. See what you make of them.'

'Thanks, mate. Are you searching Priestley's flat?

'A team is going in as soon as we have the search warrant. Hopefully, we'll find the other half of the correspondence there. I'm driving over to Croydon myself shortly. See what I can learn from the neighbours.'

'Okay, Boss. Email me those photocopies. In the meantime I'll have another go at Mannering.'

iv.

David Priestley took a right turn into a large estate of mainly social housing. Why he was going to the flat, he wasn't sure. Presumably Paul wasn't going to be there, since he hadn't answered his mobile or his landline. But he had to do something. He was glad he had his sat nav to guide him, because he had visited Paul only once since he moved to Croydon and that was long ago. He was fond of his brother, of course he was, but they had so little in common. Not that Paul was unintelligent, but his interests were so narrow and specialised. He wasn't interested in watching television, or sport, or the arts, or politics. Bird watching. That was his passion. But not bird watching as most people would define it, certainly not that. Paul was interested only in certain species or sub species, usually rare and only to be found in specific places at specific times of the year. So, apart from telephoning him occasionally and sending him money from time to time, the two of them had little contact.

The sat nav directed him to turn right in three hundred feet. Yes, he remembered it now. Paul's flat was on the left, on the ground floor of a modern two storey block. Driving on, he parked at the end of a long line of cars and walked the fifty yards back to the communal entrance. With its scuffed, litter strewn floor, the lobby could hardly be more different from the entrance to his own Knightsbridge penthouse and he felt a familiar pang of guilt as he ran his eyes down the names next to the bells. It still pained him to remember that day at school when he came into the playground to find a gang of boys taunting Paul and pushing him around. Later he found him sobbing in the toilets, his face bloody from a nosebleed. Why hadn't he gone to his rescue? As junior captain of cricket, he was popular and a timely intervention could have made all the difference.

'Who are you looking for?'

Priestley looked up to see a smiling man of Asian appearance peering down from the landing.

'Paul Priestley. He still lives here doesn't he?'

'Yes. Just below me.' He came down the steps. 'Is Paul not answering? Then he must be away. I am Mr Patel, his landlord.'

'Good morning, Mr Patel. David Priestley, Paul's younger brother. I'm sorry to trouble you, but I'm trying to contact him. Do you have any idea where he might be?

'No idea whatsoever. Paul is always coming and going.' Patel went to the entrance door and looked out in both directions. 'His camper van isn't here, so I guess he must have gone on one of his trips. Mr Priestley is always going away on trips.'

David Priestley thought for a moment. 'Look, I know this is asking a bit of a favour, but it's important I contact him. I've tried his mobile as well as his landline, but I'm not getting an answer. I wonder if I could just take a quick look in his flat. I know Paul keeps a desk diary. It might give me a clue as to where he is.'

Patel looked uneasy. 'Is Paul in some kind of trouble, maybe?'

'No, not at all.' Priestley hesitated. 'It's our mother, you see. She's been taken ill.' He took out his wallet and opened it. 'Here you are. My driving licence. David Priestley. Paul's younger brother.'

Patel studied the driving licence. 'Very good. But I must come in with you, you understand. One moment, I will go and get the keys.'

Two minutes later Priestley entered his brother's flat, with Patel standing at the door. It was as squalid as he remembered it from his last visit. Papers, magazines and discarded clothes covered the floor and every available surface. In the sink and on the draining board were unwashed dishes. The empty packaging of several take-away meals littered the worktops. Not really knowing what he was looking for, he decided to start at the table by the window, where he knew Paul spent most of his time. Like everywhere else, it was covered with paraphernalia of every kind including, sure enough, the scrapbook devoted to Susan Linton, containing photographs and other memorabilia. Then something caught his eye, a pile of letters lying open next to the scrapbook. All handwritten, the top one was dated just a few weeks before and signed 'Susan'. Picking up the letters, he turned to see if Patel was watching. Fortunately he had moved out into the lobby to smoke a cigarette.

Running his eyes down the letter he was so dismayed by its content that he had read it a second time. What on earth had Paul got himself into with this woman? Stuffing the letters into his inside pocket, he crossed quickly to the door. 'Thank you, Mr Patel. No luck, I'm afraid. I'll just have to hope that he gets my message soon and calls me back.'

v.

'Okay Mr Mannering, let's have another try and see if the fog is starting to lift.'

Wakeman sat opposite George Mannering in the small interview room at Manchester's Bootle Street Police Station. 'You say you spent Friday morning at the hostel. What I need to know, is where you went after that and who with? I'm going to need some names and places pretty soon, my friend, or you might find yourself spending tonight behind bars.'

Mannering stretched languidly before taking a cigarette from the silver case in his breast pocket. 'As

111

I've said already, all I remember about Friday is that I was here until around lunchtime.' Lighting the cigarette he blew out a long plume of smoke. 'Things get a tad hazy after that.'

Wakeman eyed Susan Linton's former husband with barely concealed contempt. For his age he was still a good looking man, with an enviable mane of dark, greasy hair that hung over his collar. It seemed unfair that a man of fifty should still have such a thick mane, while his own much younger head was shaved to mask a rapidly receding hairline.

'Come on, Mannering. You're wasting my time. You don't seriously expect me to believe you can't remember where you spent Friday night.'

'That's the trouble,' said Mannering, tossing the match into the waste bin. 'You see, I always go on a bit of a bender on Fridays and sometimes it's Saturday lunchtime or even later before I start to surface. Frequently, I wake up to find I'm in a strange bed and, if I'm really lucky, there's a woman beside me.' He gave Wakeman a sardonic smile. 'Though never a man, in case you're thinking that just because I'm an actor, I'm of the other persuasion.'

Wakeman closed his notebook. Should he spring the blackmail allegation on him? No, best to wait for the photocopies of the letters. 'Okay. If you're not going to play ball, you don't give me any choice. I'm going to have to caution you and...'

Mannering raised a hand. 'Actually, I think I may be able to help you after all. I'm pretty sure now that I started out on Friday lunchtime at the Ship. It's most likely, as it's only just down the road from the hostel and usually my first port of call. If so, I would guess I was there until about 1.30pm or 2.00pm at which point I probably moved on to the Rose and Crown. Or maybe the White Hart, though it doesn't matter which was first because I would certainly have visited both. Not sure I can manage much after that.'

'Then you'll have to think a little bit harder, my friend,' said Wakeman, who was getting increasingly frustrated at the way Mannering was playing cat and mouse with him. 'Because if I arrest you on suspicion of murder, there isn't much chance of your getting bail. Not with your track record.'

Mannering slapped his hand down hard on the table. 'Suspicion of murder? Come off it. Why on earth would I murder Susan? Actually, I remember now. I stayed with a chap called Trevor Fullerton on Friday night, one of my drinking pals.'

So that's your alibi for Friday night, is it? ' said Wakeman. 'You stayed with your friend Trevor Fullerton. Respectable, is he? Someone we can trust? Or is he another paedo like yourself?'

'He could be, for all I know. Though he doesn't have a criminal record if that's what you mean.'

'And he'll vouch for you?'

Mannering snorted derisively. 'Give it up, will you, officer. You're barking up the wrong tree and you know it. Do you honestly think I would have travelled all the way down to Buckinghamshire to murder Susan, just because she happened to hand over a laptop I didn't even know she had, until you reminded me just now. And even if I had wanted to murder her, do you really think I would have taken the risk, given that I'm the first person you would want to interview?'

Wakeman looked down at his notes. Straker had said much the same only yesterday. 'Okay, you say you were with Trevor Fullerton on Friday night. What about Saturday and Sunday? Did you spend those two days with Fullerton as well?'

Mannering exhaled slowly. 'Yes, Saturday and Sunday too.'

'Why?'

'I don't know. Sheer bloody mindedness I suppose. I knew I would be the first person you buggers would come looking for. So I decided to give you a bit of a run around.'

'And why would you want to do that?'

'Because I knew exactly how your simple minds would be working. Famous actress found murdered. Former husband, a convicted criminal. Where else did you need to look?' Mannering leaned towards Wakeman. 'Actually not everyone thinks I'm a sex monster, you know. Quite a lot of people think I got a raw deal.'

Wakeman stared disdainfully back at him. 'So you stayed with Fullerton on Saturday and Sunday night.'

'That's right. And we got through quite a lot of whisky between the two of us, I can tell you. To tell you the truth, I was pretty cut up when I heard about Susan. She and I didn't get on that well towards the end, but she was pretty generous to me after the divorce and I've always had a bit of a soft spot for her.'

'Even though she handed your laptop over to the police?'

'Now, who gave you that information, I wonder? Not Susan. I'm pretty sure of that. More likely it was that bitch of a woman who claimed to be looking after her. Not that it makes a lot of difference. The police probably found my name on a lot more computers than just my laptop.'

Wakeman closed his notebook 'So you're telling me you were here in Manchester the whole weekend and Fullerton can vouch for you..'

'Absolutely.'

'Right, I'll go and have a talk with him. And let's hope he can vouch for you, or you'll definitely be spending tonight behind bars.

vi.

Straker was about to email the letter photocopies to Wakeman when the Chief put his head round the door. 'Anything to report, Steve?'

'Not really, Jerry. We've rung Priestley's landline and mobile again, but there's no answer.'

He came in and sat down. 'Well, it shouldn't take long to track him down. By the way, have you seen The Herald's front page this morning?

'Not yet, no.'

'Listen to this. *LINTON MURDER. POLICE SEEK MR WALRUS.* That's today's headline, spread across four columns. And beneath it, the E-fit image. Pity, in a way, that we didn't wait a day. By tonight we could be releasing a photograph.'

'In the meantime, the E-Fit will grab public attention. And who knows? Someone may recognise him'

Rawlings nodded. 'Though, if he's got any sense he'll have shaved that moustache off by now.' He sighed. 'Mr Walrus! You'd think they would come up with something a bit more original. Do you think you've found all Priestley's letters?'

'We haven't found the one accompanying the £1,000 cheque. Miss Bellingham thinks it must have been thrown away.'

'I see. So, what's our next move?'

'We're obtaining a warrant to search Priestley's flat. I expect to have a team in there within the hour. Meanwhile, I thought I would drive over to Croydon and talk to his landlord. He lives in the flat above and appears to know Priestley quite well.'

'Excellent.' Rawlings rose to his feet. 'Keep me posted of any developments.'

Following Rawlings to the door, Straker noticed that Becky was at her desk by the window. He went over. 'Good morning Becky. I thought, after your long night, you and DC Taverner were taking the morning off'

She looked up brightly. 'I know, but I couldn't sleep, so I thought I would come in. DC Taverner's in too. He was at his desk a moment ago.'

'Come and join me a moment.'

Becky followed him to his office

'Paul Priestley has no criminal record that we can find. Have you seen the sightings report from the E-Fit?'

'Yes, I gather we're up to thirty.'

'Including three in Scotland and two in Northern Ireland. It's a significant breakthrough, Becky, thanks to the two of you. I've arranged to see Priestley's landlord at 12.30pm. Care to come with me?'

'I'd love to.'

Half an hour later the two of them were on the M25, heading for Croydon. The traffic was moving so slowly that Straker was briefly tempted to take the M4 turnoff and drive through central London. But there was no great urgency and Becky was pleasant company. This afternoon they would release Priestley's full name and hopefully, a photograph. Then the hunt would begin in earnest. He glanced at his companion. She looked exhausted 'I should take a nap, Becky? We'll be another hour at this rate.'

116

Once past the M3, the traffic began to move more easily and Straker put his foot down. He was glad to have Becky on the team. She was intelligent as well as conscientious and certainly a lot more pleasant to work with than Kevyn Wakeman. Which reminded him. Why hadn't he heard again from Wakeman. Probably because he had drawn a blank with Mannering and was too embarrassed to admit it, Okay, Mannering may have been blackmailing his former wife, but that was about the sum of it. Still, it was nice to be rid of him for twenty four hours. He just wished it could be longer.

At last they reached the Croydon turn off. Straker turned on the sat nav and let it guide them through a large housing estate.

'I think it must be that block of flats on the left,' said Becky, coming alive as they turned into Mandela Drive.

'And this could be the very man we've come to see,' said Straker as a swarthy, middle aged man stepped out on to the road and began directing them to a parking space. He lowered the window. 'Mr Patel?'

'That is me, sir. Sajan Patel. Good afternoon and welcome?'

'Sorry to keep you waiting,' said Straker getting out of the car and showing his badge.

As they followed Patel into the entrance lobby the aroma of Indian food wafted down the stairs towards them.

'May I offer you and your lady some refreshment after your journey?

'Thank you, sir. A cup of tea would be welcome.'

Over tea, served by Patel's smiling, but totally silent wife, Patel told them that Paul Priestley had taken the tenancy of the flat downstairs about seven

117

years ago. Describing him as a quiet, shy man who was always polite when spoken to, he said he never seemed to have visitors, but would often go off in his camper van for two or three days at a time. From what he could gather he was keen on nature and wildlife, but other than that, he knew little about him. If he was in employment, it could only be intermittently, although he always paid his rent on time.

Patel picked up a copy of the Daily Mail from the coffee table and opened it at the page featuring the Photofit picture. 'I am certain Mr Priestley is your man, Inspector, but it troubles me to think he may be a murderer.'

'We have no reason to think that at the moment,' said Straker. 'We simply want to interview him so that we can eliminate him from our enquiries. You said on the telephone you've already had a visit this morning, from a man claiming to be his brother.'

'Yes, and a very respectable man he was' said Patel. 'So much so that at first I couldn't believe he was the brother of Mr Priestley. He is very wealthy I think to judge from his beautiful Bentley car.'

'And you showed him into the flat, I gather.'

'Yes, but only for a minute or two and I was with him all the time.'

'Might you show us the flat too? I have a team arriving shortly with a search warrant, but it would be helpful if we could just take a quick look round.'

Patel jumped to his feet. 'No problem. I have the key here. Please come with me.'

Straker had never been partial to the smell of Indian food, but it was infinitely preferable to the stench that greeted them as they walked through the door of Paul Priestley's flat. And judging by the state it was in, he realised it was going to take more than a cursory search to find Susan Linton's letters.

'I have the address and telephone number of Mr Priestley's brother,' said Patel. 'He asked me to contact him immediately if Paul showed up.'

'Thank you sir. That's most helpful.'

Ten minutes later Straker and Becky were back on the A215, heading this time not for the M25 but for the Knightsbridge home of David Priestley, brother of the man they were increasingly coming to regard as their prime suspect.

vii.

David Priestley went to the sideboard and poured himself another whisky. At nine o clock this morning there seemed at least a chance that it was a case of mistaken identity. But, after reading the poisonous content of Susan Linton's letters, he could come to only one conclusion. Driven beyond endurance by this cruel, manipulative woman, Paul had stabbed her to death in a frenzy of rage and humiliation. That he would be found guilty seemed beyond doubt. For what could be offered by way of mitigation? Not insanity. Paul had a history of mental health problems, but he doubted any psychiatrist could be persuaded that he didn't know the difference between right and wrong. Nor could the circumstances of the murder be construed in his favour. Had the actress been strangled of suffocated, it could be argued that the murder was unpremeditated. Hardly so with a stabbing. A stabbing required a lethal weapon, such as a knife, and law abiding people were not in the habit of carrying knives about their person. His telephone rang.

119

'David Priestley?'

'Mr Priestley. This is Detective Inspector Straker of Thames Valley CID. We'd like a word if you don't mind. It's about your brother.'

Priestley felt his insides turn to water. 'I'm sorry, I can't help you. I've been trying to contact Paul myself.'

'All the same, Mr Priestley, there are a few questions we'd like to put to you. We're in your area now. Would it be convenient if we called for a chat?'

Ten minutes later he showed the two detectives into his drawing room and the interrogation began. When was the last time he saw his brother? Did he know where he had been over the weekend, or where he might have been? Did he know the names of anyone he associated with? As David Priestley stumbled to come up with any useful information at all, he was thankful, at least, that their mother wasn't sitting in on the interview.

'How would you describe your brother, Mr Priestley?' said the inspector. The female officer sat beside him, pen poised.

'My brother is a strange man, Inspector. But he's not a murderer.'

'In what way would you describe him as strange?'

'He is what I suppose you might call a loner'

'Is he younger than you?'

'He's older than me by a couple of years. Paul is fifty one.'

'Married?'

'No.'

Asked for a brief account of the family background, Priestley described how he and Paul were raised in Melrose in relatively privileged circumstances, but both attended the local state schools at their mother's insistence, so she could keep a close eye on Paul. He himself had gone on to win a scholarship to Cambridge, but Paul who was diagnosed with unspecified mental health problems at an early age, had to be taken frequently out of school and his education suffered. He also had learning difficulties which, combined with these other problems, held him back considerably.'

When you say other problems, what do you mean?'

Priestley sighed. 'Several labels have been used to describe my brother's condition. Schizophrenia. Autism, Aspergers - the list goes on. As a child Paul didn't have friends, or seem to need them for that matter. He was a keen birdwatcher and fond of nature in general. Although his interests narrowed over time, becoming more and more specific. I can't claim to understand my brother. Although he has learning difficulties, he has a very individual mind and is not unintelligent.'

'You say he was sometimes taken out of school. Taken where?'

'I suppose it was what today you would call a secure unit.'

'You mean he was sectioned.'

'Yes, twice, but only to protect him from himself. In his teens he went through a phase of self harming. But he was never violent to others, at least not to my knowledge. Paul wouldn't hurt a fly.'

The inspector frowned. 'We have been given to understand that your brother was a devoted fan of Susan Linton. Is that compatible with what you've just told us?'

'Yes, that's true. He idolised Susan Linton. I can't explain why. I suppose he was...' He hesitated. He was about to say that Paul was obsessed with the actress, but decided against it. 'What I mean to say is that my brother was a great admirer of Susan Linton.

121

But only from afar, as I'm sure were thousands of others.'

'But he wrote to her, didn't he? Sent her fan mail?'

'Yes, he told me that he used to write to her occasionally. Whether she ever actually read his letters, I really can't say.'

The inspector paused. 'Why did you go to your brother's flat this morning, Mr Priestley?'

Priestley's stomach muscles tightened. 'Why? Because I was worried. I was looking for him.'

'You mean you saw the E-Fit image in the paper and thought it might be your brother. Was that the reason?'

'Yes. I thought it could be Paul.'

'You recognised him. Is that what you are saying?'

'I suppose so yes. Although I have to say, the image is utterly grotesque. The description too. I gather one of the tabloids has already nicknamed him, *Mr Walrus.* Inspector, Paul doesn't have too much going in his life, but I happen to know he is proud of that moustache. I wouldn't be surprised to learn that he's shaved it off by now.'

'I'm sorry if that proves to be so, sir. But to return to the visit you made this morning to your brother's flat. You asked his landlord if you could take a look inside. Is that right?'

'I did. I thought I might find something, a diary perhaps with a clue as to where he might be.'

'And did you?'

Priestley hesitated. Should he hand over Susan Linton's letters? His brother was a murderer, but not a cold blooded murderer. He was driven to it by that cruel malicious woman. No. Plenty of time for that. Let a lawyer see them first. 'No, nothing.'

'Do you happen to have a recent photograph of your brother?'

'Yes, I think I do. Give me a moment.'

As Priestley went into his study he could feel his heart pounding. Nothing would ever be the same again. Not for Paul, not for Mother, certainly not for him. From the day Paul went to trial he would be the subject of whisperings and gossip wherever he went. At least there was one consolation. With Paul behind bars, he wouldn't have to keep a watchful eye on him any more. Retrieving the photograph taken the day of their father's funeral, he returned with it to the sitting room. 'This is a group photo but I expect you can crop and enlarge it. Paul is the one over on the left, but I suppose that's obvious. Do you intend to release it to the media?'

'I'm afraid we must.'

'With his address too, I suppose.'

'No, not at this stage.'

'Look, I know things look bad for my brother, Inspector. But in this country a man is innocent until he's found guilty. You realise that once his name is released to the media, his life won't be worth living, not to mention how it is going to affect our mother. She is in her eighties and not in good health. This could kill her.'

'We fully understand your concern, sir.' The inspector stood up and his colleague followed suit. 'Let me assure you that we will take every care not to let this get out of hand. Our press release will simply state that your brother is someone we want to interview. There will be no suggestion that he is a suspect.' He put out his hand. 'Thank you for your time today, Mr Priestley. Naturally, if you hear from your brother, we would be grateful if you would contact us immediately.

'Do you believe George Mannering was blackmailing Susan Linton, sir?' Becky was at the wheel for the return journey to Aylesbury.

Straker stirred. Now he too was having trouble keeping awake.

'Or was she was just saying that to persuade Priestley to send her money? I mean, why would Mannering blackmail her? He must have known she had no money.'

Straker sat up and lowered his window. 'She did insist that Priestley delivered the money as cash. If it was for her own use, why couldn't she ask for it to be sent by cheque?'

'Maybe she didn't want her housekeeper to know what she was up to. A cheque would have shown up on her bank statement '

Straker took out his mobile and tapped in Wakeman's number. 'How's it going Kevyn?'

'Hi Steve. Yes, good. I was about to call you.'

'Is Mannering's alibi sound?

'I haven't been able to check it out as yet. But I'm beginning to come round to your view. I don't think Mannering was involved in the murder.'

'What about blackmail? You've seen the photocopies I sent you.'

'Yes. He denies it completely. He admits he rang her a couple of times prior to coming out of prison. Said he had no money and was desperate. But he was only asking for a sub, he said, to tide him over... So where have you got to, Steve? Have you been in Priestley's flat?'

124

'Briefly. The Forensics team are in there as we speak. There's too much to tell you over the phone. I assume you're coming back tonight.'

'I guess so, yes.'

'Then I'll brief you first thing in the morning.'

Straker smiled as he ended the call. Wakeman's decision to rush to Manchester on a hunch had been shown up for what it was, an expensive, time wasting digression. Perhaps he would show a little more deference in future.

It was 5.30pm by the time they got back to Aylesbury. After sending Becky home Straker spent a few minutes on the phone briefing Jerry Rawlings and discussing their next move. Rawlings was wary of releasing too much to the media. Finally, they agreed that the news release would include Priestley's full name and photograph, plus a photograph and description of the make and model of the camper van. But it would say nothing to suggest that he was a suspect. He would be described simply as a person they wished to interview in connection with their ongoing enquiries.

He was about to tidy his desk prior to setting off for home when Jack Meredith appeared at the door.

'Something of interest for you, Steve,' he said, handing him a large, highly decorated ring binder. 'Everything you ever wanted to know about Susan Linton and were afraid to ask.'

What is it, a scrapbook?'

'A book of memorabilia, I suppose you call it. Photos, newspaper articles, old theatre programmes – that kind of thing. And, best of all, several letters from the good lady herself to our friend Mr Priestley. Though, I doubt whether they actually came from her. In her glory days, she probably had a team of staff employed to deal with her fan mail.' He sat down. 'But

125

we did come across four recent letters to Mr Priestley that we thought you would be interested to see.'

'Where?' said Straker. 'In the folder?

'That's where we found them. Neatly pasted, a page to each letter. We've removed the originals and sent them off to Forensics for analysis, but we took photocopies.' He took a sheaf of A4 sheets from his briefcase and passed them to Straker. 'As you see the first letter is typed. That's the one to thank Priestley for the £1,000 cheque. It's the other three letters that I think you'll find of more interest.'

Straker picked up the letter, Dated the 7th May 2011 it thanked Priestley for his cheque for £1,000, telling him how comforting it was to know that there were such kind people in the world.

The second letter, dated the 27th July 2011 was altogether different. Although, like the first, it was addressed from Bristow's Wembley office, this letter was handwritten.

> ...I *can't tell you how grateful I was to receive your cheque a few weeks ago...went through my files and discovered that you have been writing to me for nearly twenty years... such a comfort to have someone as caring and kind to correspond with...*

Now a more intimate tone.

> ...I *want to know all about my knight in shining armour. Are you tall, dark and handsome Paul? No matter if you are not, but I would love you to tell me about yourself. Please write again soon...*

The third letter was dated the 4th August 2011.

...You sound like a really nice man. . . certainly don't think of you as 'wrong in the head' because you suffer from depression. I have suffered from depression myself.. . .You ask me about my fantasies. Yes, I have them all the time. . . Because I still have feelings Paul even though my legs don't work properly any more. . .You sound such a sweet kind person. . .I like to think of you lying beside me. But I will say no more about that because it makes me blush even as I write!.....If you were able to send me something, even just a small amount like £500 I would be so grateful...

And the final letter

24th August, 2011
...I am so short of money Paul. Are you sure you can't help me? Wouldn't your mother or your brother give you a loan?...

He looked up at Meredith. 'And to think I used to be half in love with this woman.'

Meredith nodded. 'I know what you mean. Though I can't say I remember her that well.'

'But are there more letters, Jack? This is only the beginning. Priestley's side of the correspondence goes on for another six months.'

Meredith shook his head. 'That's all we've found so far. We'll keep looking.'

ix.

Approaching the junction where the M32 joins the M6, Wakeman decided he would stop at the next service station and get himself something to eat. His expedition north had been a mistake, though his hunch wasn't entirely misguided. It seemed highly likely that Mannering was blackmailing his former wife, even if he didn't kill her. But he had a strong suspicion that Gary wouldn't be pleased to learn Mannering was no longer a suspect, particularly after telling him they expected to have the case wrapped up by the weekend. Now his credibility was on the line, to say nothing of the £2,000 Gary promised him for exclusive briefings. He needed to reinstate himself rapidly as a reliable source and for that he needed to get the lowdown on this new suspect, Paul Priestley. The problem was that he was out of the loop. He had seen the photocopies of the letters, but that was this morning and Straker had given him only the barest summary when they spoke again this afternoon.

As he joined the slip road to the Services he reached for his mobile and tapped in Becky's number.

'Hi, Becks. It's Kevyn.'

'Hi. Are you still in Manchester?

'No, I'm on my way back.'

'How's it gone with Mannering?

'Not as well as it seems to have gone with you. Sounds like you made a bit of a breakthrough last night.'

'Yes. We struck it lucky, I guess.'

'And all down to you and DC Taverner.

'It's Taverner who deserves the credit, not me. He'd found three of the letters before I got in on the act. '

'I could have done with your company last night, Becks. I went to a great restaurant, but it's not much fun eating on your own.'

'I know. Maybe another time...'

'So what are you up to right now.'

'Actually I was just about to go to bed.'

'Pity. I was thinking of calling on you on my way home, so you could bring me up to speed.'

She laughed. *'Thanks Kevyn, but I'm practically asleep already. Can't we talk in the morning?'*

'We can. But just give me the gist of what you've learned today. It will give me something to think about on the long drive down the motorway.'

As Becky described the events of the day, she sounded more animated and excited than he could remember. She was still talking as he locked his car and made his way across the Services car park and bought himself a double cheeseburger.

'Tell me what you know about Priestley himself, Becks. What about this wealthy background he talks about?'

As Becky continued to describe her day, Wakeman took careful notes. Gary said he would call by 7.00pm and he wanted to make sure he had chapter and verse.

'That's about everything Kevyn,' said Becky at last. *'I'm in first thing tomorrow. If I remember anything else I'll brief you then.'*

'Thanks, Becks. Sounds like you've had a great day. Doing anything tomorrow night?'

'I don't know... Nothing as far as I know.'

'Do you like Johnny Cash?'

'Johnny Cash? He's dead, isn't he?'

'Yes, he's dead, all right. But a friend of mine runs a pub outside Oxford and he's doing a tribute

129

evening. Thought you might come with me. We don't have to stay if it's crap.'

'Sounds good. What time?

'We can go straight from work. Call in somewhere on the way for something to eat.'

Ending the call Wakeman smiled to himself. So, the day wasn't completely wasted. He was about to fetch himself a coffee when his mobile vibrated.

'Wakeman?'

'Hello mate. It's Gary. Any progress?'

'Hii Gary. Yes, it's going well.'

'Have you found Mannering yet?'

'Yes. He's out of the frame Gary.'

There was a pause. *'What did you say?'*

'I mean, as far as the murder is concerned. No, he has an alibi. We may bring other charges in due course though.'

'Other charges? You mean, conspiracy to murder, something like that?

'No. We don't think he had anything to do with the murder. Actually we're working on a new lead.'

'Wait a minute, Kevyn. When I called you on Sunday you said the investigation was practically sewn up? Are you now telling me that Mannering's in the clear?'

'What I'm saying Gary is that we're following up a significant new lead.'

'Christ, Kevyn. I stuck my neck out based on what you told me on Sunday. You saw Monday's Herald? And this morning's follow up. Two double page spreads in two days. All that stuff about his laptop. You said it was practically sewn up.'

'Be fair, Gary.' Wakeman felt himself getting hot. 'I said we had good reason to suspect Mannering. It was down to you what you made of it.'

But Gary wasn't letting it go. *'So, what are you telling me? That he has a cast iron alibi for Friday night. It's my credibility we're talking about here. And yours. I told them my source was absolutely kosher.'*

'What I'm telling you, Gary is that we have significant new lead. If you'll just give me a chance...'

'You don't mean Mr Walrus?'

'Yes, Mr Walrus. We've turned up a lot of new information about him.'

'Okay. Tell me what you've got on Mr Walrus. What's his name for a start?.'

'There's a press release going out tonight.'

'Fine, everyone can read that. Give me what it doesn't say.'

'Steady on Gary. We haven't even located the man yet.'

'Okay, so tell me what you know and why you're so keen to talk to him. Where he lives, where he comes from, what you've got on him. A head start, Kevyn. That's all I need. The rest we can find out for ourselves. Are you sure you've got the right man this time?'

'As sure as I can be'

'Right, spill the beans. Don't worry, Kevyn. Nothing will be printed that we couldn't have sourced elsewhere.'

Chapter Five

Wednesday, 11th April 2012

He stares in dismay at the headline. The other newspapers have moved on, but not the Daily Herald. The story fills the entire front page and there is even a photograph to replace the Photofit picture. It must have been the one taken at Father's funeral because he is wearing a tie. And today they have named him – Paul Priestley, living in the Croydon area and known to be a long standing member of Susan Linton's fan club. They even give the make and model of his camper van and the registration number. Yesterday he thought it must have been someone he worked with who called the police, someone who remembered him but didn't know his second name. Now they know everything. They even have a photograph. Who, except David, could have given them that?

He looks at the line of people queuing at the checkout. None of them will recognise him without his moustache, but what about the people at the camp site? What if they have seen the registration number of the van and reported it? The police could be there even now, waiting for him to return. Should he end it now, once and for all, or go back and face them? He has to decide.

'I'm sorry, Steve, but you know we're out again tonight.'

Straker was about to leave. 'I know. I'll be there.'

Emily came forward and put her arms round him. 'Once this play is over you can resign your membership. And so will I.'

'There's no need for that. It's my own fault. I should never have let Anton talk me into it.'

She followed him out to the car. 'Good luck today. I'm really pleased about the breakthrough. You deserve it.'

He managed a smile. 'Don't bother about supper. I'll get a sandwich and go straight there.' Reversing out of the drive, he gave her a wave. She was still standing there as he turned the corner.

Something was going on between her and Masterson, he was sure of it. She came home yesterday full of the children's party and what a fantastic job Dan had done getting it together. And for weeks now he had sensed a growing intimacy between the two of them. The way she brightened and became more alert whenever he appeared. The way she teased him and laughed at his jokes. How much had she confided to Dan Masterson in their cosy little afternoon get-togethers, supposedly to rehearse their lines? Probably quite a lot, because Emily was a born communicator, always telling him how glad she was to have her girlfriends, because he was such a hopeless person to talk to. But she knew that when she married him. She knew he was no good at sharing his worries and concerns with anyone, even her. Deep down he was still just same as he was the day he first set eyes on her in his final term at university.

It was the evening of his father's funeral. A friend called round suggesting they go to the university's production of Twelfth Night. It was the last thing he wanted to do that night, but he felt it would be discourteous to refuse. To his surprise, he found himself quite enjoying the play and particularly the performance of the pretty student playing the part of Viola. So much so that he was unable to sleep that night for thinking about her. The next day he joined the drama society, though there were to be no more productions until the autumn, and attended the next three meetings resolving each time to go over and to introduce himself. But each time his nerve failed him and he returned home frustrated and miserable. Then, at the final meeting before the summer break, she walked purposefully across the room and introduced herself. To his shame, he was too tongue tied and nervous to engage her in a proper conversation and he returned to his flat that night cursing himself for failing even to get her telephone number.

Fortunately the story had a happy ending. Three years later they met again working on a fruit farm near Brisbane and he resolved not to lose her a second time. But how to win her? He wasn't witty, or good at telling jokes. He wasn't knowledgeable about the theatre, or cinema, or music, which he knew to be her interests. To his surprise, none of this seemed to matter. The last thing she wanted, she said, was another extravert like herself.

Arriving at his desk, Straker dragged the pile of newspapers towards him to check the response to yesterday's press release. Emily was right. He had got things way out of proportion since coming down from Shropshire. He had become too much focussed on his career and it was affecting their relationship. But the consultation had knocked him sideways. To learn after twelve years of marriage that he was incapable of fathering a child, and probably never had been, had sent him right back into his shell. He wished he could talk about it but he couldn't.

'Seen the papers Steve?'

He looked up to see a concerned looking Jerry Rawlings standing in the door jamb. 'Morning Jerry. No, I haven't been through them yet.'

The Chief came in and sat down. 'The Herald is still making it their lead story, though their readers must be getting a bit confused. Yesterday they were practically accusing George Mannering of the murder. Now they seem equally certain it was Paul Priestley. I must say, they seem to know a hell a lot about him already.' He pulled the paper from the pile and drew it towards him. 'Listen to this.

> **'Linton Murder. Police name Mr Walrus**.
> *The police have identified Paul Priestley as a person they urgently want to interview in connection with the murder of Susan Linton. Living in the Croydon area, sources close to the investigation suggest that he is a significant witness. Our own investigations reveal Paul Priestley to have been a long standing member of Susan Linton's fan club. He also is rumoured to have had a long history of mental illness...*

Rawlings thrust the paper at Straker. 'Member of her fan club? Long history of mental illness? Our press release gave none of that information, surely.'

136

Straker ran his eyes down the report. 'No, we kept it short and sweet, Jerry. Though we did release the registration number of his vehicle, so maybe they've leaned on someone at the Vehicle Licensing Office to get Priestley's address. Once they had that, they could easily have got over to Croydon and got the information from neighbours.'

Rawlings sighed. 'But describing Priestley as '*a significant witness.*' Would they risk going that far, unless they had it on good authority from someone in the team?'

Straker shrugged. 'I warned everyone at the outset that this was going to be a high profile investigation. All media enquiries were to be directed to the Press Office.'

Rawlings got to his feet. 'Well, not much to be done about it now, and the publicity might just work in our favour. Okay Steve, I'm here all morning. Give me a shout if there are any developments.'

ii.

Becky stared distractedly at the columns of figures in Susan Linton's investment portfolio. Maths had never been her strong subject and she knew virtually nothing about stocks and shares. She was also finding it difficult to concentrate, because she had one eye on the door, watching for Kevyn Wakeman. When he rang off last night, she was as excited as she had been in months. It was only as she was getting into bed that she remembered what it was that had been niggling her ever since his call. Mark had invited her to watch him play his gig on Wednesday night. She hadn't exactly said yes, but nor had she said no.

What she should have done, of course, was call Kevyn back and tell him she couldn't see him after all. But, to her shame, she didn't do that. Instead she telephoned Mark to say she couldn't make the gig because her mother was ill and she needed to go over and look after her. The deed done, she went to bed and was soon fast asleep. But at 1.00am, she woke up with a start. What if tomorrow morning, Kevyn came over to confirm arrangements? With Mark only a desk away, he would be bound to overhear their conversation and it wouldn't take him long to put two and two together.

What was she to do? Call Kevyn and ask him to be discreet about their night out, especially in front of Mark? Too risky. There was only one solution. To back out of the date with Kevyn as well. It was a pity, but she liked Mark and would hate to hurt his feelings. Reaching for her mobile she texted her message to Kevyn. Then, her conscience salved, she went back to sleep.

But now it was 8.30am. Kevyn still wasn't in and nor had she heard from him, Could she rely on him to have checked his messages?

'Hi Becky.' Mark arrived at his desk and switched on his computer.

'Hi.'

'How's it going?'

'Not too well. I may need some help on this.'

He came across and looked over her shoulder. 'I can take a look, if you like. The fan mail is sorted now and we haven't found anything else worth following up. I don't think Susan Linton sent begging letters to anyone apart from Priestley... Sorry about your mother. Is she bad?'

138

Becky felt herself blushing. 'She's okay. She's been a bit up and down since my dad died. It's depression as much as anything.'

'Well, I'm sure she'll be all the better for seeing you.'

'You'll must tell me the date of your next gig,' she said quickly.' I'd really like to come.'

He smiled. 'Good. I'll hold you to that. Not that I've got anything firm in my diary right now. It's gone a bit quiet on the music scene. At least, it has for me.'

'Becky slid the portfolio in front of Mark. 'Do you know much about stocks and shares?

'A bit.'

'I'm due to go and see Kate Bellingham this morning. Any chance you could come with me? I'm sure you understand this stuff better than me.'

'Don't see why not. What time are you going?'

'I don't know yet. The boss said he is due to talk to her this morning. He said he would arrange a time for me to go over.'

'Good morning, folks.'

They turned to see a cheerful looking Kevyn Wakeman coming towards them.

'So, the two of you made something of a breakthrough while I was away.'

'We were just lucky,' said Mark, getting up and retreating to his own desk. 'Someone had to find the letters sooner or later.'

'Any sightings of Mr Walrus yet? Or Paul Priestley, as we now know him to be?'

'Not that I've heard.' Becky hardly dared look at him. Had he seen her text message? She was starting to suspect he hadn't.

As Mark got up and walked over to the coffee dispenser, Wakeman picked up the investment portfolio and opened it at the first page. 'About

139

tonight, Becks. Shall we go straight from here or would you rather go home first and change?'

Becky felt hot. Kevyn had the kind of voice that carried. 'Oh...you didn't you get my text then?'

'Text? No. When did you leave it?'

'Last night.' Becky lowered her voice. 'My mother's ill. I have to go and see her.'

'Really?'

Mark was back at his desk.

'Yes. She phoned me...'

'When?'

'Last night. After you...' Her voice trailed away.

Closing the portfolio, Kevyn tossed it on to her desk. 'Not to worry. Another time.' Getting up he glanced towards Straker's office. 'Better go and see what the boss man's up to.'

Blushing, Becky turned her attention back to the portfolio. She was certain Mark heard everything.

'Let me know what time you're going to see Kate Bellingham. I should be able to join you.'

As she turned and looked at Mark, he smiled. 'In the meantime, I'll see what I can make of the portfolio.'

iii.

Straker put down the telephone. Maybe The Herald got their information from Priestley's landlord. A journalist had called him at around 8.00pm last night, wanting to know everything about his tenant. He told him very little, or so he said. He wasn't aware that Priestley had a history of mental illness, or that he was a fan of the murdered actress. He hadn't even heard of Susan Linton until he learned of her murder.

'Hi boss.' Wakeman strolled into Straker's office. 'How goes it with you this morning?'

Straker managed a smile. 'We're making progress. Have you finished your enquiries into George Mannering?'

Wakeman pulled back the chair and sat down. 'Yes. For the time being. I don't have enough to arrest him as yet.'

'Have you confirmed his alibi for Friday night?'

'No. Though I think he was probably telling the truth.'

'Meaning you no longer think he was involved in the murder.'

Wakeman looked a little sheepish. 'I suppose you could say that, yes.'

'Do you think he was blackmailing her?'

'He laughed when I put it to him. Said he was in enough trouble already without risking new charges? Besides, he knew she had no money, so what was the point of trying to blackmail her.'

'I see. So, all in all, you trip to Manchester hasn't been very productive.'

Wakeman drew the pile of newspapers towards him. 'All right, Steve. No need to rub it in. Even you have to admit Mannering was behaving suspiciously, disappearing like he did. He said he did it deliberately to give us the run around.'

'Okay, we'll leave it there, ' said Straker, deciding that there was nothing to be gained by humiliating Wakeman further.

Taking the Herald from the pile Wakeman opened it at a double page spread. 'I see we're still getting good coverage in the media. That's something to be pleased about, at least.'

141

'Rather too good,' said Straker. 'In fact, I'm getting a bit suspicious. Did you notice that the Herald is using the same nickname for Priestley as Becky Reedman came up with at Monday afternoon's briefing?'

'So they are. Probably a coincidence. With a moustache like that, not too many other nicknames come to mind. '

'Now, today, they've come up with a whole lot of information that wasn't in our news release. And they're even describing Priestley as a *significant witness*. That's really jumping the gun.'

'Well, he is, isn't he? Having read those letters you sent over, I would go so far as to say he's our prime suspect.'

'Maybe. But we didn't use the term *significant witness* in our news release. Nor did we mention where he lives or anything about his health or about him being a long standing member of Susan Linton's fan club. Yet it's all here in this morning's coverage.'

'I haven't seen last night's press release yet. What did it say?'

Straker handed him a copy. 'All we gave was Priestley's full name and photograph, plus the registration number and description of the camper van.'

Wakeman looked at Straker with incredulity. 'You mean, that's all you said? In spite of the threats in his letters and his history of mental illness? Steve, Priestley is a knife wielding maniac. The public needs to be warned.'

'But we don't know yet that he's the murderer,' said Straker patiently. 'In spite of what he said in his letters, he may turn out to be completely innocent.'

'Come on man, he's as guilty as hell. What more do you need? In that last letter he even gave her an

142

ultimatum. Give me back my money, or it will be the worse for you.'

Straker tried to remain calm. 'I know that, Kevyn. But we need evidence, forensic evidence. Or a confession, at the very least. There's no way the CPS is going to take on the case, based merely on what he says in his letters.'

With a sigh Wakeman got up and walked over to the window. 'Well, Steve, it's not how I would have handled it. I would have said a lot more in that press release. We have a duty to protect the public. You must see that.'

Straker looked hard at Wakeman. 'Have you talked to any journalists in the last couple of days?'

'Absolutely not. What reason would I have to talk to journalists? Anyway, I've been out of the loop since Monday, as you've just been reminding me.'

Straker picked up the newspaper again. 'The administration team have seen the letters, of course. So, I suppose any one of them could have leaked the information.'

'And if so, what harm has it done?'

Now it was Straker's turn to look incredulous. 'What harm? Just suppose for a moment that Priestley turns out to be innocent? His life won't be worth living after all this publicity.'

'But he isn't innocent. The man's mental. And he's dangerous. Are you telling me, after reading those letters, that you don't think he killed Susan Linton?'

Straker didn't answer.

'I tell you this, Steve. The media isn't going to help us unless we are prepared to toss them a few crumbs.' Crossing to the door, he turned to face him. 'Still, you're the boss. Far be it from me to tell you how to do your job.'

As Wakeman left, Straker turned back to his computer screen. There had been forty 'sightings' of Paul Priestley since the release of his full name and photograph, but he couldn't give much credence to any of them until the camper van was located, The report in the Herald still rankled, but maybe Wakeman was right. The publicity should help them secure an early arrest.

iv.

David Priestley slammed down the phone. Why couldn't these people take no for an answer? Four calls already, two from the same newspaper and he wasn't even dressed yet. He told them the first time that he had nothing to say, so why ring again? Drawing his dressing gown round him, Priestley sank dispiritedly into the sofa. He should be in chambers by now. Thank God it was a quiet week, because there was no way he could show his face while all this was going on. The trouble was, it might go on longer and get worse. Until yesterday he was still hopeful that his fears would prove groundless. But those letters were deeply worrying.

He went over to the drinks cabinet. It was only 10.00am but he needed something strong. Lifting the decanter he tilted it carefully until the stem was resting on the lip of the glass. But his hand was shaking so much that whisky slopped down the sides and gathered in untidy pools on the silver tray. What on earth had Paul got himself into? That he had sent the actress money was beyond doubt. He had checked Mother's bank account and found several

ATM cash withdrawals, all made within days of each other and as recently as last month. Mother would be mortified. Had he kept a closer eye, as she had charged him to do, this madness might have been prevented. Which was all very well, but Paul wasn't an easy person to keep tabs on. Mother kept telling him to involve him more in his own life and introduce him to his friends, but that just wasn't practicable. They would have run a mile and so would Paul. No, it was out of the question.

Refilling his glass, he crossed to the window. Okay, he had been remiss. If he had just checked Mother's bank account every week or so, none of this would have happened. Now he was going to have to pay for his negligence. Soon his name would be all over the media as the brother of Susan Linton's murderer. Because he was sure of it now. From the moment those two detectives rang his doorbell yesterday afternoon, he knew it could only be Paul.

Taking the empty glass out to the kitchen he placed it on the worktop. He should get dressed and go to work. There was nothing to be achieved by hiding himself away. If Paul was charged with murder, it was a situation he would have to deal with. There would be practical issues, like getting him a good lawyer, discussing what plea to enter and determining what mitigating circumstances might get him a shorter sentence. Insanity perhaps. That might be the best option.

The telephone rang again. He cursed as he reached for the handset. 'WHO IS THIS?'

'David?'

'Oh. Hello Mother. I thought it was the press again.'

'David, what is happening. I've just had someone from the newspapers telephoning me. And the vicar has had a call too. They are all asking about Paul.'

'Yes, I'm sorry. I know it shouldn't happen, but there's nothing we can do to stop it. I've had calls too.'

'I've rung Paul's mobile almost every hour since Saturday and all I get is his message service. Do you think he's taken fright after seeing that awful picture in the papers. And now they've named him and printed his photograph. So it is definitely Paul the police are looking for, isn't it.'

'I'm afraid so. But that doesn't mean he's guilty. As you say, he may have taken fright, just knowing the police are looking for him. I don't think we should fear the worst just yet.'

'Then why are the police so anxious to interview him? I've only seen The Scotsman, but the vicar tells me the Daily Herald is referring to Paul as though he is the main suspect.'

'Maybe. But it's all speculation at this stage.'

'Are you sure you're telling me everything you know, David? I hope you're not just trying to protect me.'

Priestley hesitated. Should he tell her about Susan Linton's letters, or about the visit by the two detectives? No, not yet. 'Really Mother, I'm as much in the dark as you are. As you say, Paul has probably taken fright at all the publicity. But he has to turn up before long. By the way, I think it would be a good idea if we put a stop on your bank account for a few days.'

'Why? Has he been withdrawing money? I never look at the statements.'

'He's been making cash withdrawals. Quite a number in fact. I know it sounds cruel, but if we put a stop on the account, he will have to come home eventually, or make himself known to the police.'

'But I don't want him not to have money, David. How will he eat if he has no money?'

146

'Really Mother, it would be for the best. The sooner we find him, the better for everyone, including Paul. Will you call the bank and put a stop on the account?'

'Well, if you think it's for the best. But what am I to say if I get more calls from the newspapers?'

'I suggest you unplug your phone. You can always plug it in again if you want to ring me. For now, I don't think you should talk to anybody.'

'But you must do something, David. The newspapers have no right to say Paul is the main suspect. Think how that must make him feel. He'll never live it down. People don't live down things like that. He'll have to carry the burden for the rest of his life.

'I know, Mother. It's highly irresponsible.'

'No, you don't know, David. You don't understand. I'm telling you to do something. I want you to telephone the newspapers and tell them that if they say one more thing about Paul that is in any way detrimental to him, you will see them in court. And you can telephone the police too and make sure they are not colluding with the newspapers. Because they do, you know. They do it all the time. Get on to them, David. I would do it myself, but you are a lawyer. You are supposed to have influence.'

v.

Straker tapped Kate Bellingham's number into his mobile. It was answered almost immediately.

'Kate Bellingham.'

'Good morning, Miss Bellingham. Steve Straker.'

147

'Inspector. Good morning. I was hoping it might be you.'

'Are you going to be at home this morning?'

'Yes. Why? Are you coming and see me?'

Straker hesitated. He had determined not to see Kate Bellingham again, at least not on his own. But the possibility that George Mannering was blackmailing his former wife, was something he hadn't asked her about. Might he go instead of Becky? Not really. She was perfectly capable of asking the relevant questions. 'I'm sorry, I'm not able to come myself today. But we do have a few questions. Would it be convenient for one of my team to call on you?'

'Oh...' She sounded disappointed.

'Detective Constable Becky Reedman. We want to find out a bit more about George Mannering's relationship with Miss Linton.'

'I'm not sure there's anything I haven't told you already, Inspector.'

'DC Reedman has also been looking at Miss Linton's investment portfolio and she would like to go over a few points with you. I doubt if it will take more than half an hour of your time.'

There was a pause. *'Do you know, Inspector, I didn't go out of the house once yesterday in case you called.'*

'You didn't?'

'I know it's silly, but every time the phone rang I was just hoping it would be you. And now you tell me I won't see you today either. Won't you try and come yourself, Inspector? I feel so safe talking to you.'

'Well... I would need...Let me see..... are you available all day?'

'I am available to you at any time, you know that...' She gave a small laugh. *'I'm sorry. I didn't put that*

very well, did I? What I mean to say is that if you can spare the time, I will make sure I'm here.'

Straker hesitated. 'Well...perhaps I could move one or two things around. Let me call you back?'

His hand trembled as he returned his mobile to his pocket. *Available to him at any time.* It sounded very much like a sexual invitation. Yes, he would go himself. He would tell Becky that he needed to see Kate Bellingham on another matter and could deal with anything she wished to discuss at the same time. Stepping out of his office he was about to call her when he saw an anxious looking Jerry Rawlings approaching, newspaper in hand.

'We need to talk Steve.'

'Of course.'

The Chief closed the door firmly behind him. 'I've just had that lawyer brother of Priestley on the phone. He's seen the piece in this morning's Daily Herald and he's on the warpath.'

'Well, I can't say I'm surprised.'

'He said he's already been on the phone to the editor, threatening proceedings if they print another word prejudicial to his brother's name and reputation.'

'Good. I'm glad to hear it.'

'But he's suspicious of us too, Steve. He says someone in our team must be feeding them information.'

'Does he have any evidence for saying that?'

'No, of course he hasn't. Naturally, I told him that we take all allegations of professional misconduct very seriously.'

'And he wasn't satisfied with that?'

'He wasn't. He's convinced someone here has been feeding them information.'

'I don't think that's likely, Jerry. I've Just spoken to Kevyn about the Herald's coverage and he thinks they're getting their information from neighbours. His landlord, for example. I talked to him earlier. He says a journalist rang him at around 8.00pm last night asking a lot of questions.'

Rawlings unfolded the Herald on Straker's desk. 'But listen to this, Steve. *Sources close to the investigation suggest that Priestley is a significant witness...* 'Sources close to the investigation'. They would never use that phrase unless their information had come directly from a member of the investigating team.'

Straker sighed. 'But, what would you like me to do, Jerry? There are up to twenty personnel now working on the case at any one time. Interviewing all of them would take the best part of a day and I'm not sure what it would achieve, apart from a general lowering of morale.'

Rawlings pondered this. 'Yes, a witch hunt is the last thing we need right now, but I need something to tell Priestley's brother.'

'I could have a word just with the people who were involved in photocopying and transcribing the letters. Plus Becky Reedman and Mark Taverner, of course. But then there's the Forensics team in Oxford who are examining the letters for fingerprints.'

'So, how many are we talking about?'

'About twelve in all, I would guess.'

'Well, make a start with the people here in Aylesbury and we'll deal with Oxford later. And get someone from Human Resources to sit in, so we're seen to be doing things by the book. Then I can call Priestley back and tell him we've launched a full internal enquiry.'

Becky watched in puzzlement as yet another member of the administration team was ushered into Straker's office. Something was definitely amiss, because Josie Prior from Human Resources was in there with them. Staff had been going in at ten minute intervals for most of the last hour. Why? She had asked around, but no one seemed willing to talk. Probably Kevyn would know, but he and Mark had gone off to Croydon and weren't expected back until late afternoon at the earliest. She was due to be seeing Kate Bellingham this morning but, so far, had heard nothing. With all this kerfuffle, maybe Straker had forgotten to set up the appointment.

'Becky.'

She looked up to see Straker signalling to her to join him. Picking up the portfolio she went to join him.

'Do sit down.' Straker, closed the door behind her and returned to his desk. Josie Prior gave her a friendly smile.

'I'm sorry about this, Becky,' said Straker, 'but I'm having to carry out an investigation. Have you seen today's newspaper reports?'

'I've seen a couple,' said Becky. 'I haven't read all of them.'

'Paul Priestley's brother has complained about today's coverage in the Daily Herald. He believes someone in the team has been leaking information to one of their journalists.'

Becky frowned. 'I haven't spoken to anyone.'

'No. I'm sure you haven't, but it seems someone has. Their coverage this morning contains rather more information than we gave out in last night's press release. For example, it mentions that Priestley lives in the Croydon area. I realise they could have got that information via the number plate of his camper van, but they also mention that he has mental health problems and was a long standing fan of Susan Linton. That information, only we know from his letters.'

'As I say, I haven't spoken to anyone.' Did Straker seriously think she would talk to journalists?

'Of course, they could have gleaned some of their information from neighbours. Although I spoke to Priestley's landlord this morning and he tells me that Priestley tends to keep very much to himself. On the other hand, several members of the investigating team have had sight of the letters. Not just yourself and DC Taverner. All the staff involved in the photocopying and preparation of transcripts.'

Becky could feel herself bristling. 'I don't think anyone in the team would leak information, sir.'

'No, and I agree with you. ' Straker unfolded the newspaper and placed it in front of her. 'But the paper does use the phrase '*Sources close to the investigation*' and that concerns me. Usually when newspapers use that phrase, it means a member of the investigating team. As I say, I'm sorry to be putting these questions to you, but be assured I am interviewing everyone who has had access to the letters. Are you sure you haven't let anything slip to someone outside the team? '

'Positive, sir.'

'Not even to journalists you've had dealings with in the past?'

'Absolutely not.'

'Friends, family members?'

'Nobody.'

Then, were you surprised at yesterday's headline in the Herald?'

So that was what it was all about. *Mr Walrus.* 'Yes, I was a bit taken aback. Although it's a pretty obvious nickname, when you think about it, for a man with a walrus moustache.'

' I suppose it is.' Straker smiled at her as he put the newspaper down. 'Thank you Becky, that's all for now. I have one or two more people to see, so may I ask you not to discuss the content of this interview with anyone. Can I rely on you for that?'

Becky nodded and stood up to go. Josie Prior rose too and moved towards the door to see her out. Then, realising that she still had Susan Linton's portfolio in her hand, she turned. 'My interview with Kate Bellingham, sir. Did you agree a time?'

Straker paused. 'Ah yes, of course. Actually, Becky, on second thoughts I need to see her myself today, once these interviews are over. Some new information has come to light that I need to discuss with her.'

'I could deal with that too sir, if...'

'No, I think, in the circumstances, it's better that I go. Make me some notes of the things you wanted to ask her about and I'll deal with them at the same time.' He looked at his watch. 'It will have to be this afternoon now. Shall we say, by 2.30pm?'

vii.

Back from Croydon, Wakeman paused in the car park for a cigarette before going up. He was worried. On the return journey Becky called with the news that Straker was going overboard about the coverage in

153

the Herald. Convinced that someone was leaking information, he was interviewing everyone who had had sight of Priestley's letters. So far he had seen six members of the admin team plus herself, and she was very upset about it. Being interrogated in front of someone from Human Resources was humiliating enough, but that wasn't the main reason. She had been due to call on Kate Bellingham today, but Straker ended the interview with the news that he had changed his mind and he would see her himself instead.

Crossing the road, Wakeman strolled slowly down towards the roundabout. So Straker was conducting an internal enquiry. Most likely Priestley's brother was kicking up a fuss to Rawlings and the Chief needed to cover his back. Well, so be it. In his experience internal enquiries never came to anything. All the same, it was an unwelcome development. Taking out his mobile he tapped in Gary's number.

'Hi, Gary speaking.'

'Gary, it's Kevyn.'

'Hi Kev. How's tricks? Got something for me?

'Listen mate, you've haven't played fair. You promised me that you would cover my tracks.'

'And so I did Kev. I passed on nothing that we couldn't have got from other sources. Like Priestley's medical history and about him being in her fan club. Other people we've talked to since have confirmed both. I told the Herald to print nothing that, given more time, we couldn't have got for ourselves.'

'But you let them use the phrases 'significant witness' and 'sources close to the investigation. What's a source close to the investigation, Gary, if it's not a police source?'

'Are you sure the paper used those exact phrases, Kevyn?'

'You know they bloody did, Gary! That's why I'm ringing you, for Christ's sake.'

'Then the editor must have changed my wording. Leave it with me Kev, I'll deal with it.'

Wakeman sighed 'It's too bloody late, and you know it. The damage is done.'

'Come off it, what damage? You said yourself you've got a pile of evidence against Priestley. I mean, it isn't as if he's going to sue us for libel, is he? And I am paying you a couple of grand, remember.'

'You can forget your money, Gary, I don't want it. You realise, don't you, that thanks to you, this whole thing could blow up in my face.'

'Okay, if that's how you want to play it. We'll pay you for what you've given us so far. Then we'll call it a day. How much do you want to settle?

'I don't want any of your money. And don't ring me again, do you hear? I don't want to hear from you again, ever. Is that understood?'

Ending the call Wakeman made his way back through the car park to the entrance, noting as he did so, that Straker's parking space was empty. So he had decided to go and see Kate Bellingham again. Why this time? Had the housekeeper come up with yet another piece of information too important to be communicated to anyone but the senior investigating officer. He very much doubted it.

Back at his desk he sat down, pondering his options. Should he come clean with Straker about talking to a journalist? It would get Becky off the hook, but could he trust Straker to keep it under his hat? No. Better to hunker down and wait for the storm to blown over? Which it would, once Priestley was apprehended and charged.

Arriving at Kate Bellingham's Elleswood cottage, Straker felt like a teenager on his first date. *'I am available to you at any time, Inspector.'* Her meaning could hardly have been clearer and now the ball was in his court. Pausing a few moments to steady his breathing, he pressed the doorbell and stood back.

'Inspector.' Kate Bellingham gave a gasp of delighted surprise as she opened the door. 'I was beginning to think you weren't coming.'

Straker squeezed past her, lowering his head as he entered her small lounge. 'I'm sorry. There were one or two matters that delayed me.'

She followed. 'I decided it was cold, so I made a fire.'

Seating himself at the far end of the sofa, he glanced up at her. In her grey cowl neck jumper and slim black pencil skirt, she could have walked straight out of a fashion magazine advertisement. His hand trembled as he put his briefcase down on the thick woollen rug.

'I'll just make some tea and then we can talk...Though, I suppose I couldn't tempt you to a glass of wine.'

He hesitated. He could do with a glass of wine right now. 'Thank you, no. Not while I'm on duty.'

She laughed. 'You are incorruptible, Inspector. I should have known.'

As she went out into the kitchen Straker opened his briefcase and took out the investment portfolio. She was flirting with him, no question, but maybe it was just to put him at his ease. Opening the portfolio he ran his eyes down the first page. Several items were highlighted, with Becky's notes alongside, but her tiny

156

handwriting was almost impenetrable. He wished now he had taken the time to go through them with her before setting off.

'I've made a lemon drizzle cake in your honour.' Kate Bellingham returned with a small tray and placed it on the coffee table. 'I hope at least I can tempt you with that.'

'Thank you. That's very kind.'

Instead of moving to the armchair opposite, she sat down next to him and proceeded to pour the tea and cut the cake.

'Do you really think Paul Priestley could be involved in Susan's murder, Inspector, after being so generous to her?'

'It's too early to say.' Straker took the plate she handed him. 'Though, we do have reason to believe that he is the person you saw outside Miss Linton's house.'

'Really? But how could you possibly know that? Or shouldn't I be asking such questions?'

Taking a bite of the cake, he wondered if he should tell her Yes, why not? Particularly as she had been so helpful. 'We've found several recent letters in the filing cabinet from a man signing himself as Paul. We were able to establish that it was the same Paul Priestley who sent Miss Linton a gift of a thousand pounds some months ago.'

'But why do you think he was the man I saw?'

'It became clear from what he said in his letters. It appears that Miss Linton was asking him for money.'

She looked at him in surprise.

'According to our information, her ex husband was blackmailing her. Since he was demanding the money in cash, Priestley decided it was safer to deliver it by hand.'

Kate Bellingham shook her head in dismay. 'Susan writing to Paul Priestley? I can hardly believe it. And as to blackmail, I can't say I cared much for George, but I can't believe that of him either. Have you questioned him?'

'We have and he denies it.'

Straker met her eye. The smile had gone. Her expression was serious and businesslike. Perhaps he was mistaken. Perhaps the phrase she used wasn't a sexual overture at all. Well, at least he hadn't made a fool of himself. Reaching into his pocket he took out his pen. 'Which brings me to the main reason for my visit, Miss Bellingham. Do you know of anything in Miss Linton's past that might have made her susceptible to blackmail?'

She smiled. 'I'm sure we've all done things in our lives, Inspector that we wouldn't wish made public. And being so much in the public eye, Susan had more to lose, of course.'

'So, there was something that could have damaged her if it came out. Is that what you are saying?'

She shrugged. 'George used to joke sometimes that he had photographs of Susan that would have damaged her clean cut image.'

'And did he, as far as you know?'

'Possibly. Once when we were drama students, Susan and I agreed to do a photo shoot for a seedy German magazine in return for cash. The photos were hardly pornographic by today's standards, but I know she worried about them ever coming to light.'

'And George Mannering may have come across them. Is that what you are saying?'

'He claimed to have come across them in one of his girly magazines. Although I think he was bluffing. He never produced the evidence to prove it.'

'So, it is possible that he was blackmailing her.'

158

Kate Bellingham took a tissue from her sleeve. 'To tell you the truth, I don't know what to think any more. This has all been such a shock. Susan was my friend for more than thirty years. Yet, she kept all this from me...'

'I'm sorry.'

'No... no. She took his hand and drew it into her lap. 'You have your job to do. Please go on.'

He leaned nearer, willing her not to let go. Perhaps he wasn't wrong after all.

She released it and pulled the tray towards her. 'Another piece of cake. I shall only throw it away if you don't eat it.'

'No more, thank you.'

Disappointed, Straker reached for the investment portfolio and opened it at the first page. 'Perhaps I could ask you about Miss Linton's investments. There have been a number of draw downs of capital in recent years. I was wondering if...'

'I know nothing about Susan's investments, Inspector. You will have to ask Michael.'

'But, presumably, the money went into Miss Linton's bank account. Might I take a look at her bank statements?'

'Of course, but they only go back a year. I don't keep them beyond a year.'

'I see. No matter.' Straker stood up. He should go. It was foolish of him to have come in the first place.

Rising with him Kate Bellingham caught hold of his hand a second time. 'Oh dear, Inspector. Now you're going to think your visit has been a complete waste of time.'

'Not at all...You've been most helpful.'

'Please don't leave.' She brushed a speck of dust off his lapel. 'I was hoping you would tell me about this play you're in.'

159

How easy it would be now to take her in his arms. 'Oh, I don't think so. I really don't think ...'

His words petered out as she began to trace small circles on his palm with the tip of her finger. 'I can't think your wife's very happy right now. I mean, do you ever manage a day off?'

'Oh, no. Emily's fine...'This was more than flirting, surely. 'To tell you the truth, she's been barely aware of me since rehearsals began.'

'That's right, you told me. She has a leading role. Is it what we used to call the romantic lead?'

Unable to answer, he could only nod.

'Are you jealous?'

He studied the delicate lines around her eyes and mouth, the two or three strands of grey in her hair. 'Actually, I think she may be having an affair.'

'Then she doesn't know how lucky she is.' Leaning towards him she kissed him lightly on the lips. 'If I were your wife, I wouldn't let you out of my sight.'

Suddenly his arms were around her as he drew her towards him and buried his face in her neck. He was breaking every rule in the book, but he didn't care. As he held her he felt her hand move down to his thigh, then slide inside his zip.

A vibration came from somewhere but he was barely aware it as she took hold of him, gripping him tightly. And again, this time accompanied by an insistent buzz. He cursed under his breath.'

'Ignore it'

'I cant...'

'You can. 'With her other hand she felt in his pocket and took out his mobile. 'There, see. I've switched it off...'

Wakeman called Straker's number a second time. Strange. Now, it didn't even ring, but went straight to voicemail. Had he switched to silent, or off entirely? And if so, why? Could it be that Detective Inspector Steven Straker was up to something that he shouldn't be? Something that amounted to serious misconduct in any circumstances, but even more so when it involved a key witness in a murder investigation. Whatever he was up to with that woman, it was totally unacceptable. Here he was with a major development to report and his senior investigating officer had put himself out of contact. There was only one thing for it. If he couldn't be contacted by phone, then it was his duty to seek him out and give him the information in person? And if his hunch was right, he might just get there time to turn the situation to his advantage.

Why otherwise would Straker decide to call on Kate Bellingham again today, instead of sending Becky? Unless he really did believe it was Becky who leaked to the Herald. But even if he did, there was no need to go himself. He could have sent someone else in her place.

Driving up the hill towards Kate Bellingham's cottage, he was pleased to see Straker's car still parked outside. So far, so good. Parking his own car a few yards further down, he walked up the road and the few steps to the front door. He peered through the sitting room window but there was no sign of Straker or Kate Bellingham. He looked through the smaller window to his left. They weren't in the kitchen either. So, where were they? There could only be two more rooms - the bath room, probably behind the kitchen and, to its right, Kate Bellingham's bedroom.

He walked along the narrow path at the side of the cottage; then, bending low, crept past the frosted bathroom window until he was below the bedroom. Now, he could hear voices; a woman's, then a man's. Rising on to his toes he peeped through the small gap in the curtains. Kate Bellingham was on the far side of the double bed, under a sheet but, from what he could see of her, naked. The nearside was empty. Now he heard a tap running. Damn. Straker must have gone to the bathroom. Returning to the front of the cottage he was briefly tempted to ring door bell and confront them there and then, but he decided against it.

Ten minutes later, back at the station, he stopped at Becky's desk. 'Hi Becks, what are you up to right now?'

She sat back wearily. 'Not much. I was supposed to be examining Susan Linton's investment portfolio, but since the boss has taken it away with him, I'm marking time until he gives me something else to do.'

Dragging a chair across he sat down beside her. 'You know we've found Priestley's camper van.'

'Yes. I just heard.'

'So, it's good news.'

She gave a non committal shrug

'So, what's this work you were doing on the portfolio?'

'I doubt if it was that important. Quite a lot of Susan Linton's shares have been sold over the last few years. I just wanted to see where the money went.'

'Why? Do you think something funny has been going on?'

'Possibly. Or George Mannering was extracting money from his ex-wife for longer than the letters indicate. Anyway, the boss decided to go in my place, so maybe he'll come back with something.'

'Did he say why he wanted to see her today?'

'Only that there were other matters he wanted to talk to her about. He suspects me, doesn't he? He thinks it was me who leaked to the Herald.'

'Come on Becky. He doesn't suspect you, or anyone else for that matter. It's my guess that Priestley's brother has been leaning on Rawlings. The interrogation is just a charade to make it look as if we're doing something.'

'Then why did he decide to go and see Bellingham in my place? It's as if I'm no longer trusted even to carry out a routine interview.'

Wakeman touched her arm. 'You're reading too much into this, Becky. Anyway he knows my view. No one here has been leaking information. Once we released Priestley's surname and the registration number of his vehicle, any journalist worth his salt could have his address within five minutes. And once they had that, they could get their information from any number of sources. Don't worry. I'll have a talk with him.' He looked at his watch. 'It's 5.30pm. Why don't you head off? There's nothing more any of us can do now until we find Priestley.'

'I can't do that. I went home early yesterday I can't leave early two days running.'

'I thought you said mother was ill.'

Becky reddened. 'She is, but I don't need to leave early. I said I would be there by seven to cook her a meal.'

Getting up, Wakeman squeezed her shoulder. 'Leave it with me, Becks. I'll get things sorted. And let me know when your mother's feeling better so I can take you out for that meal I promised.'

x.

As Straker arrived back, Wakeman followed him into his office.

'So, you finally got my message. I tried you several times.'

'Yes, sorry. My phone was on silent. I gather they've found the camper van.'

'Yes, at a campsite at Westleton in Suffolk, at around 2,00pm. The owner spotted the number plate. It's being brought over tonight. Forensics will start work immediately.'

'But no sightings of Priestley.'

'Not in that area' Wakeman glanced at the blue folder sitting on Straker's desk. 'Did Bellingham tell you where the money went?'

'Actually, we didn't talk much about the investments. She said we would have to talk to Bristow.'

'I see. So, what else did you go and see her about? I thought Becky was due to interview her, but then you decided that you needed to see her yourself.'

'That's right. I did.'

Wakeman waited. 'Well, fill me in Steve? I am supposed to be your number two.'

'All right, Kevyn. I don't need an interrogation right now. Actually I decided to follow up the claim that Miss Linton was being blackmailed by Mannering.'

'Really? I thought you had already dismissed that idea.'

'I had, but I thought it worth checking. I asked her whether there was anything in Susan Linton's past that might have made her vulnerable to blackmail.'

'And was there?'

164

'Possibly. In her youth she had some photographs taken that she wasn't proud of.'

'Pornographic?'

'More top shelf stuff, I gather.'

'Couldn't Becky have got that information from her just as easily?'

'She could, but I also wanted to update her on progress to date.'

'Update her? Why would you want to do that?'

Straker gave a weary sigh. 'Miss Bellingham gave us a very important lead on Monday, Kevyn. It seemed only reasonable to me that I should update her on our progress.' He paused. 'I see you don't agree.'

'No, not particularly Steve, I don't. As far as I'm concerned, Kate Bellingham is just another witness in a murder investigation. Maybe she's reliable, maybe she isn't. Yet you, the senior investigating officer, take it upon yourself to drive all the way to her house to fill her in on our progress. For all you know she and Bristow may have been robbing the lady blind. Have you thought of that? And you do know that Becky was very upset today at having her integrity called into question.'

Straker flinched. 'It couldn't be helped. Priestley's brother called Rawlings this morning raising hell about the Herald's coverage of the investigation and insisting I talk to everyone who had access to Priestley's letters. But I handled the interviews gently. I certainly gave Becky no reason to think I suspected her more than anyone else.'

'Though you did have someone from HR sitting in on all the interviews.'

'That was Rawlings idea, not mine.'

'So, first you interrogate Becky about the coverage in the Herald and then you cancel her interview with

Kate Bellingham. Did it occur to you that she might see a link?'

Straker looked angrily at Wakeman. 'What is this, Kevyn? Have you been talking to her?'

'I have, actually.'

'Well, if she's upset, I'll have a word with her. Now, can we get on?'

Making no move to leave, Wakeman leaned back in his chair and grinned . 'You've got the hots for that woman, haven't you, Steve?'

Straker blanched. 'What the hell is that supposed to mean?'

'Come on. You know as well as I do. I was watching the two of you on Saturday. The way you were looking at her and the way she was sucking up to you. I remember thinking at the time, that woman has an agenda. I mean, you're not a bad looking guy, but you're not exactly Brad Pitt.'

Straker reddened. 'All that happened on Saturday, was that I showed Miss Bellingham some courtesy, while you were treating her as if she was our prime suspect.'

'And since Saturday you've found reasons to make three further visits to her cottage in the space of five days. Has she invited you to shag her yet? Because if she hasn't, I suspect she soon will.'

Straker got up from his desk and walked towards the door. 'We'll end this conversation here and now, Kevyn. You may be my number two, but I can still ask for you to be taken off the team.'

Wakeman got up slowly. 'I'm only telling you for your own good, mate. She's leading you on. Cool it before you get yourself into deep water.'

'Thank you,' said Straker, opening the door. 'When I want any further advice, I'll let you know.'

xi.

'THANK YOU EVERYONE, BUT LET'S DO IT AGAIN.'

Anton strutted down the centre aisle and up the steps onto the stage.

'AND THIS TIME WITH A BIT MORE OOMPH PLEASE. MATTHEW, YOU NEED TO COME IN SOONER. YOU'RE SUPPOSED TO CATCH THE LOVERS AT IT, NOT WAIT UNTIL THEY'RE COMING UP FOR AIR.'

He turned to Emily and Dan Masterson. *'BUT WHAT HAS HAPPENED TO OUR TWO LOVEBIRDS TONIGHT? WHERE'S THE PASSION? WHERE'S THE CHEMISTRY? I WAS BEGINNING TO THINK THE TWO OF YOU MUST HAVE FALLEN OUT. COME ON DARLINGS, SHOW US YOU REALLY MEAN IT...'*

Getting up from his seat Straker strolled slowly up the aisle to the exit. Yes, come on darlings. A bit more oomph. Surely the passion hasn't cooled already? But then, I don't know how much screwing you've gone in for over the past three months. Twice a week... three times? Because sexual passion burns out, you know. Or so they say. Don't take my word for it. I'm still a novice in such matters.

Walking on between the parked cars to the railings Straker felt his eyes smarting with angry tears? How could he have been so fucking stupid? Five days ago he was given the career opportunity of a lifetime - officer in charge of the highest profile investigation the division had seen in years -a role that many of his colleagues would have given their eye teeth for. So, how does he respond to the trust that has been placed in him? Just when they are on threshold of a major breakthrough, he takes the afternoon off to go to bed with one of the key witnesses. Why? A year ago, such a transgression would have been

167

unthinkable. It would have been a betrayal of everything he stood for, both as a police officer and as a husband. And all for what? A few minutes of excited anticipation, followed by a lifetime of regret.

What made him do it? That was the question he had been asking himself ever since he left her cottage. Why did he even go there in the first place, knowing the likely outcome? Because an attractive woman had made a play for him? Yes, but that wasn't the main reason. Ashamed as he was to admit it, he went there to level the playing field, to get even. If Emily was prepared to cast aside her marriage vows, then so could he. But it had brought him no satisfaction, only guilt and humiliation. Whatever the future held, this was a day he was going to regret for the rest of his life

Returning to the rehearsal he was just in time to see Emily and Dan Masterson in their final embrace.

'MUCH BETTER DARLINGS.'

Anton skipped up the steps.

'YOU'VE OBVIOUSLY KISSED AND MADE UP. OKAY, ON TO SCENE 3 AND THE ARRIVAL OF THE POLICE. MR PLOD, ARE YOU WITH US?'

He peered into the auditorium

'AH, THERE YOU ARE, STEVE. UP HERE PLEASE...CHOP, CHOP. AND YOU CAN LEAVE YOUR BOOK BEHIND. YOU SHOULD BE WORD PERFECT BY NOW.'

Chapter Six

Thursday 12th April, 2012

i.

Becky gazed despondently at her monitor screen. She had come in early out of habit, but there was precious little for her to do. She had lost Straker's trust, she was convinced of it. Yesterday afternoon, when Kevyn offered to plead her case, she was full of optimism. But when he emerged from Straker's office, she could tell the meeting hadn't gone well. And instead of coming over to report on their conversation, he went straight back to his desk looking grim and determined. Five minutes later he gave her a perfunctory wave as he made his way to the exit. She stayed on another hour, willing her phone to ring with the message that the boss wanted to see her, but in vain. Shortly after 6.00pm, he too made his way to the exit without so much as a glance in her direction.

She drove home as miserable as she had been in months. According to Straker, someone in the team had leaked information to the Herald and he was determined to get to the bottom of it. Kevyn took a different view. As he pointed out, it wasn't as if there was anything in Wednesday's coverage that couldn't have been obtained from friends or neighbours. But she was inclined to agree with Straker. Newspapers didn't use phrases like 'sources close to the investigation' and 'significant development' without at

169

least a nod and a wink from someone central to the investigating team.

But why was she so much under suspicion? Surely not because of that stupid nickname she came up with at Monday's review meeting. Though even she was taken aback to find *Mr Walrus* blazoned across five columns of the Herald's front page the following morning. No. Most likely it was because, as at Tuesday evening, she was the only officer other than Straker himself who was fully up to speed with the day's developments. But questioning her was one thing; effectively cancelling her duties for the rest of the day was quite another. He might just as well have hung a notice round her neck saying she was the culprit.

Of course, it wasn't strictly true that she was the only police officer up to speed with developments on Tuesday evening? It had crossed her mind more than once that Kevyn Wakeman was also in the picture, because she briefed him herself when he rang on his way back from Manchester. But would Kevyn have talked to the media? Surely not. He was a senior police officer as well as number two in the investigating team. No, Kevyn had too much to lose.

Hearing footsteps, Becky felt herself grow hot. As if it wasn't enough that she was about to be thrown off the investigation, any moment now she was going to have to face Mark. When she accepted Kevyn's invitation, she had momentarily forgotten the invitation to go with him to his gig last night. Why did she have to come up with that stupid lie about her mother being ill. She could easily have called Kevyn back to say she had just remembered she had a prior engagement. That way, she could have gone with Mark to his gig and still seen Kevyn another night. Mark wouldn't risk being stood up a second time.

170

Which was a pity, because she was beginning to think that watching Mark play his gig might have been more enjoyable than having dinner with Kevyn Wakeman.

'Hi, Becky.'

Mark arrived at his desk, jauntily swinging his briefcase. If he still felt sore, he was disguising it well. Dragging his chair across he sat down next to her.

'How's your mother?'

She blushed. 'A lot better, thanks. And last night's gig. Did it go well?'

'Didn't happen. I got the call yesterday afternoon on my way back from Croydon. Not enough tickets sold.'

'But that's a bit unfair, isn't it. Cancelling you at such short notice.'

'It happens. At least I didn't waste your evening.' He unfolded the newspaper he was carrying and laid it in front of her. 'Seen today's Herald? They're really going overboard on Priestley. He's the son of a laird. Did you know that? And they're continuing to make the link with Susan Linton by saying he was a longstanding member of her fan club. That wasn't in any press release.'

Becky turned to face him. 'Well, they didn't get it from me. Just in case you're wondering.'

He looked at her, eyebrows raised. 'Why would I think it was you?'

'Because that's what Straker thinks. In fact he's convinced of it. He hauled me in yesterday and interrogated me in front of Josie Prior from HR.'

'Just you?'

'No. He also interviewed several people from admin. But I was the only police officer.'

'So, why do you think he suspects you in particular?'

171

'It was obvious from the way he questioned me. You remember my 'Mr Walrus' remark at Monday's review meeting. He asked if I was surprised that the Herald used the same nickname in Tuesday's paper.'

'What did you say?'

'I said, I was a bit surprised. But he didn't stop there.....'

Mark listened as Becky described her humiliation at being asked to name all the journalists with whom she had ever had contact, together with anyone she might have talked to about the case on Monday and Tuesday night, even including members of her own family. Tears came to her eyes as she described her shock at the way Straker called her back just as she was about to leave and told her he had changed his mind about her going to interview Kate Bellingham. He had decided to see her himself, he said, so she should prepare notes of any matters she wished him to raise on her behalf.'

For several seconds Mark looked thoughtful. Then he gave her a sympathetic smile. 'I don't think he suspects you, Becky.'

'Of course he suspects me. The Herald wouldn't have risked going to print merely on the say so of a member of the admin team.'

But you weren't the only police officer who knew about Tuesday's developments.'

'Yes, I was. Unless you include Straker himself and the Chief.'

'What about Kevyn Wakeman?

'He was in Manchester all day Tuesday.'

'Yes, but you talked to him on Tuesday night, didn't you?'

Becky blushed. 'I did, actually. He phoned me on his way back, just as I was going to bed.'

'So you briefed him on the day's developments.'

'I suppose so, yes.'

'Which means that by Tuesday night he knew everything you knew.'

Becky shook her head. 'Kevyn wouldn't put his career at risk by giving such sensitive information to the Herald.'

Mark gave her a wry smile. 'When was the last time you heard of a serving police officer being fired, or even disciplined for leaking information to the media?' He stood up. 'I'll take a look at that portfolio now, if you like.'

'I don't have it any more. Straker took it with him when he went to see Kate Bellingham.'

'Okay, when he returns it.'

She looked up at him. 'Mark.... I'm sorry about last night...'

He raised a hand. 'Don't be. It was only a gig in a lousy pub. Anyway it was cancelled, so we couldn't have gone anyway.'

'The truth is that when Kevyn asked me out I'd completely forgotten about your gig.'

'Don't fret. It's not important. Anyway, you only said you might come. You didn't exactly commit.'

'But I would have liked to have come, really. I'm sorry.'

He smiled. 'May I infer from that, that next time I ask you out, you might say yes?'

She nodded.

'In that case...how about tonight?'

David Priestley sighed in exasperation. First it was the Herald. Now the Telegraph and the Express were jumping on the bandwagon. *Did Paul have a criminal record? Was it true he had a history of mental illness? Did the family know he was obsessed with Susan Linton?* It was all too much. This morning the Herald was even telling the world that Priestley came from a wealthy background and had a barrister for a brother. He doubted anyone in Chambers read the Herald, but it wouldn't be long before word got round. '*London barrister 's brother convicted of Linton murder.*' What impact would a headline like that have on his career, to say nothing of his social life?

Crossing to the sideboard Priestley poured himself a large whisky. This was getting to be a bit of a habit, but he needed something to calm his nerves. Fortunately things were quiet work wise and he had called in on Monday to say he was taking a few days break. But he was due in court next Wednesday, so he would have to go in on Tuesday at the latest. On reflection, it was probably a bad move telling that Indian fellow he was Paul's brother. And arriving in the Bentley wasn't too smart. On the other hand, he had to make a powerful impression or he might never have gained access to the flat and found those letters. At least they would support a defence plea for mitigation on grounds of extreme provocation.

Priestley sat down and closed his eyes as he pondered the best way forward. A plea of insanity would be best, but only if it could be sustained. Better to have a brother pronounced insane rather than branded a murderer. Yes, far better. Handled carefully, it could win him sympathy. And confined to

174

a secure institution, Paul would be well looked after and living at the Government's expense instead of being a burden on the estate. Mother might even be persuaded to change her will and leave everything to him.

Refilling his glass he went over to the window. But could such a plea be made to stick? That was the problem. Although Paul was emotionally unstable, it might be difficult to persuade a jury that he didn't know right from wrong. He looked down at the street. Commuters hurrying to work. Shoppers making their way to Harvey Nichols and Harrods. How he envied them, all of them. Because, nothing could ever be the same for him now. Wherever he went, there would be whispers. *You know who that is, don't you. David Priestley. It was his brother who murdered Susan Linton.* He would be the subject of gossip and innuendo for the rest of his life.

The telephone rang and Priestley let out another long sigh as he waited for it to go to voicemail.

'David, are you there? I've tried your office and they tell me you are on vacation....'

Priestley grabbed the phone. 'Hello Mother. I'm sorry. I thought it was another journalist.'

'Oh dear. Have they been bothering you as well? I've had two calls already this morning and so have some people in the village. Mrs Jenkins, your old headmistress, She's eighty seven. They've no right to be bothering an old person like that.'

'And they've no right to bother you either, Mother. It's intolerable. You should disconnect your phone..'

'But I can't do that, can I. I'm desperate for news. Have you still heard nothing from Paul?

Priestley hesitated. He hadn't told her about Tuesday's police visit. Perhaps it was time to say

175

something. 'You know they've found Paul's van, don't you.'

'Yes, I saw it in the paper. But they haven't found Paul yet, have they? Do you think he's gone into hiding, David? But why would he hide? He didn't commit this awful crime. I know he didn't.'

'No, I'm sure he didn't.'

'Are you? Really? Come on David, I know that tone of voice. You think Paul is guilty, don't you?'

'Of course I don't think he's guilty. But, you might as well know. I went round to his flat on Tuesday morning, as soon as I saw that dreadful caricature in the newspaper. I spoke to his landlord and he said that he hadn't seen Paul or his camper van since Friday morning...'

'Well, it was the Easter weekend. We've talked about that. He often goes off in his camper van at weekends.'

'Yes Mother, but there was something else...' Priestley paused. How should he say this? 'I asked his landlord if I could take a look in Paul's flat. I thought maybe I would find a diary, or something that might give me a clue as to his whereabouts.'

'And did you?'

'No. But I found letters. Handwritten letters to Paul from Susan Linton herself.'

'You mean, personal letters? What did they say?'

'I'm afraid you won't like what I'm going to tell you. It appears that Paul had been sending Susan Linton money and I infer from their content that he was refusing to send her any more. They were cruel letters, Mother. Some of them very threatening.'

'But that's monstrous, David. You must give them to the police immediately.'

'I know. I've already done so,' he lied.

'And what did the police say?'

'Not much. They were more interested in asking me about Paul.'

She was silent for a moment. *'Oh dear David. Do you really think they suspect Paul of murder. Why would they? What evidence do they have?'*

'All I know, is that as long as Paul remains in hiding, the more the press are going to try and dig up dirt about him. If I were you, Mother. I would disconnect your telephone. You can always re-connect it if you want to ring me. I'll be here. I can't go back to work until he is found.....'

There was a buzz on the intercom.

'...I'm sorry, I have to go. There's someone at the door. Probably another journalist....'

'This is a nightmare David....' She began to sob. *'... an absolute nightmare. I'll call you again tonight'*

Replacing the handset Priestley walked through to the kitchen and pressed the answer button. 'YES! WHO IS THIS?'

'David?...'

'Yes.'

'It's Paul. Will you let me in?

iii.

Wakeman sat impatiently at his desk, watching Straker's door. It had been firmly closed for ten minutes now, ever since he was paged to take an urgent call. Evidently there had been a development, so why couldn't he share it immediately, instead of shutting him out like this. Getting up, he walked over to the coffee machine. He couldn't help smiling

177

though. Until yesterday he had tended to regard Straker as someone who lived by the rules, both at work and at play. Now he knew he was no better than the next man and possibly a good deal worse. For a police officer to screw around was one thing, but shagging a key witness in a murder trial - that was a different matter altogether. It amounted to nothing short of gross misconduct, a sackable offence. Okay, he hadn't seen him actually on the job, but he had seen enough. The question was how to turn it to his advantage.

He returned to his desk, his eye still on Straker's door. One thing was for sure. Straker and Rawlings were treating this business with the Herald much more seriously than it deserved. What was an internal enquiry supposed to achieve, apart from a general lowering of morale? He glanced across the room. Coffee breaks had begun and the room was almost empty, but Becky was still at her desk. At least she looked a bit brighter than she had done when he came in this morning. Getting up, he strolled over.

'Hi Becky. You look busy.'

She paused her fingers on the keyboard but didn't look up. 'I'm collating some background information on Michael Bristow and Kate Bellingham.'

'For the boss?'

'No, just for something to do. While I'm waiting to be re-instated.'

Wakeman studied Becky. 'You mean, the boss didn't call you in last night?'

'No, he didn't.'

'He should have done, I'll have another word with him now. So, what have you found on Bellingham and Bristow? Anything interesting?'

'Nothing that can be sustantiated.' She glanced up briefly, before turning her attention back to the screen.

178

'How's your mother?'

'Better, thank you.'

'Good' He sat down next to her. 'So, what have you found out. Don't tell me the two of them are having an affair.'

Minimising the document on the screen, she turned towards him. 'You obviously haven't read the report of my interviews with the friends at the Friday re-union.'

'I'm afraid I only skimmed them. Why? Did they contain something I need to know?'

'Two of the people I interviewed spoke of rumours that they were in a relationship long before Bristow's wife died, but I haven't been able to verify it, of course.'

'And you think I might be still going on?'

'I don't know, but it's possible.'

Wakeman grinned. 'Well, fancy that. Kate Bellingham sleeping with Michael Bristow. Who would have thought it?'

Becky shrugged. 'Even if she is, it's hardly a big deal. He's a widower and she's single.'

'Ah, but you haven't met Michael Bristow yet, have you?'

'No. And I doubt if I will, judging by the way I was treated yesterday. Anyway, I doubt if any of this is relevant to the investigation.'

'Maybe. Maybe not.' Wakeman paused. 'So your mother's feeling better, is she?'

'Yes, much better, thank you.'

'Good. Then perhaps we can arrange that evening together. What about tonight?'

She looked away. 'I'm sorry, I've already made plans for tonight.'

He studied her. She seemed cooler towards him than she did yesterday. Maybe she would warm up once Straker had talked to her. Or had she guessed it was him all along? Maybe he should come clean. But he could hardly do that without first having to admit everything to Straker. And that he was not about to do. He stood up. 'Okay Becks. Not to worry. I'll check my diary and get back to you.'

iv.

Ending his call to Jerry Rawlings, Straker breathed a long sigh of relief. The news couldn't have come through at a better time. Shortly after 9.00am this morning, Paul Priestley had turned up at his brother's flat, very much in need of a wash and some rest. David Priestley said he would be bringing him over to Aylesbury by lunchtime at the latest. Such was Rawlings excitement at the news that the internal enquiry wasn't even mentioned.

Getting up from his desk he went out into the main office and beckoned to Wakeman to join him. Becky was at her desk too. That reminded him. He needed to talk to her and put her mind at rest.

'We've had some good news, Kevyn,' he said as Wakeman closed the door behind him. 'Paul Priestley has turned up at his brother's flat this morning. It seems he slept rough overnight, so he's put him to bed for a couple of hours and then he's going to drive him over here.'

Wakeman smiled. 'So that's why you've been shutting me out. I thought something must be going on. What were you doing, talking to the Chief?'

'Among other things, yes.'

'Has Paul Priestley said anything to his brother?'

180

'Only that he wasn't anywhere near Elleswood House over the weekend.'

'Well, he would say that, wouldn't he. Okay, so who's going to lead the interview, you or me?'

Straker paused. 'You do it, Kevyn. See if you can get a confession out of him by 4.00pm. That's when I said I'd give the Chief a progress report.'

'Excellent.' He paused. 'By the way, did you know that Kate Bellingham is sleeping with Michael Bristow?'

Straker stared at him. 'Who told you that?'

'Becky.'

'When?

'Just now. It's been going on for years, or so the rumour goes. Even before Bristow' wife died. Not that it's not absolutely for definite, but two of the people at last Friday's reunion mentioned it when she interviewed them. It's in her report. I must say I missed it myself when I read it.'

Kate Bellingham sleeping with Michael Bristow? No, it was impossible. Wakeman was just goading him to see his reaction. 'Well, even if she is in a relationship with Bristow, or anyone else for that matter, I don't see it as particularly relevant to the investigation.'

Wakeman grinned. 'No. I just thought you'd be interested, that's all. So, there you go, Steve. Seems I was wrong about her being a dyke. Unless she's ambidextrous of course.'

Straker stood up abruptly. 'Okay Kevyn, thank you. I'll let you know when I get word that the Priestley brothers have arrived. In the meantime, maybe you could touch base with Jack Meredith and his team in Croydon. See if they've found any more letters from Susan Linton.'

181

Shutting the door behind him, Straker returned to his desk and sat with his head in his hands. Kate Bellingham sleeping with Michael Bristow? No. It was just a malicious rumour. Why would she choose a scruffy, unkempt, toad of a man like Michael Bristow when she could have any man she chose? The man smelled. His entire office smelled. No, he didn't believe it. It was all just tittle tattle. Even so, he felt a cold shiver as he walked over to the door and signalled for Becky to join him.

'I just wanted to talk to you about yesterday, Becky,' he said, as she came into the office and sat down. 'I gather you were upset about me going in your place to see Kate Bellingham.'

Becky nodded, but said nothing.

'I'm sorry. I'm afraid I didn't handle things well. Let me assure you the decision had absolutely nothing to do with the possible leak to the Herald. The truth is that when I spoke to Miss Bellingham yesterday morning she mentioned something to suggest that George Mannering was blackmailing his ex wife. I know our focus is on Priestley now, but I thought it best to check out exactly what she had to say. As it turned out, Miss Linton was susceptible to blackmail. By which I mean there were things in her past that could have been damaging to her reputation, had they become known but, well, Mannering appears to have a sound alibi for the night of the murder....' Straker paused. He had said enough. He didn't need to explain himself any further. 'And as for the Herald's coverage, I'm afraid I had to talk to everyone up to speed with developments on Tuesday night. You understand that, don't you? We have to be so careful about what we say to the media. It can get us into a lot of trouble.'

Becky nodded again. 'I understand.'

182

'As to the queries you wanted to raise about the investments, I'm afraid I didn't make much progress. Miss Bellingham said she doesn't keep bank statements beyond a year, so we'll need to talk to the bank.'

'I've already done that, sir.'

'You have? And does anything come to light.'

'I've listed all the credits over the past five years. If you've finished with the portfolio I can make a comparison.'

Straker hesitated. 'I gather, by the way, that you think she might be in a relationship with Michael Bristow.'

'Yes, though it's only a rumour. I don't see that it's any concern of ours. Unless, we find that Bristow has been misappropriating funds, or something of that kind. In which case, maybe they were doing it together. I'll need to study the bank statements before I can form a view about that.'

'Yes, of course. In the meantime, there's been another development, Becky. David Priestley is bringing his brother in at around lunchtime.'

Becky's eyes widened. 'In that case, maybe I should put this line of enquiry on hold.'

'No...no. Not at all. What you're working on is important. If Bristow, or the two of them together have been stealing from Susan Linton, it needs to be followed up. Though probably as part of a separate enquiry. Do you need any help?'

Becky hesitated. 'Maybe Mark Taverner could work with me on it.'

'No problem. I'll arrange it now.'

David Priestley stood at the door of the spare room listening to the rhythm of his brother's snoring. Should he wake him? He had been there for two hours now but, judging from the state of him when he arrived, he might go on sleeping all day. So far he had managed to get very little out of him, beyond a flat denial that he had anything to do with Susan Linton's murder. He was nowhere near Susan Linton's house on Friday, he said. He drove straight to Suffolk on Friday afternoon and stayed over the five days at camp sites near the nature reserve at Minsmere. But it was evident from his exhausted, bedraggled state that last night he slept rough and he was badly in need of a bath and a change of clothes. So, first of all, he had sent him off to the bathroom, telling him to leave his clothes outside the door.

He looked at his watch.10.15am. His clothes were washed and in the tumble drier. Could he afford to leave him any longer? No, this business had gone on too long already. Knocking gently, he called out. 'Paul, time to wake up.' He put his head round the door and withdrew it quickly. Paul was lying on top of the bedclothes, snoring. He was wearing one of his brother's old dressing gowns, but most of it was crumpled beneath him, exposing his, fat, white body.

'What time is it?'

Hearing Paul's plaintive voice he put his head round the door a second time. He was still lying on his back but, thankfully, had gathered the dressing gown over his belly and private parts. 'It's 10.30am Paul. I'm going to make you some soup and then you're to get dressed and we'll drive together to the police station in Aylesbury.'

Paul sat up with a start. 'No! I don't want to go to the police!'

'But we have to.' David Priestley spoke the words patiently, as one might speak to a small child. 'There's nothing to be afraid of. Don't worry, I'll be there with you.'

'I said I don't want to go to the police! They won't believe me, David... they won't believe me...' He began to sob.

'Of course they'll believe you. All they want to do is question you so they can eliminate you from their enquiries. They can't hold you if there's no evidence.'

'They can. They think I'm mad, don't they. Everyone does. I've seen it in the papers. Everyone thinks I did it.....' Rolling on to his side he buried his face in the pillow.

David Priestley came over and sat on the edge of the bed. 'No one has said you're mad or that you're a murderer. But we have no choice, Paul, because I've already told the police that you're here. I said I would drive you to Aylesbury police station this morning. That's where the investigation is based...... Come on now. It won't be so bad. If you weren't at Susan Linton's house, there will be no evidence against you, will there?'

'But there will, that's the point.' Paul swung his legs over the side of the bed. 'You don't know everything. I wrote her letters, you see... lots of letters.'

Priestley looked sternly at his brother. 'Yes, I know about the letters. And so do the police. But we won't talk about those right now. I'll get your clothes and then I'll make you some soup.'

Ten minutes later Paul came into the kitchen. He still looked bedraggled in his creased shirt and trousers, but at least he no longer smelled.

'I see you've shaved off your moustache.'

185

'Yes, well...' Paul picked up the spoon and began to slurp his way through the soup. He was never a tidy eater.

'You know, don't you, that they've found your camper van. They found it yesterday afternoon.'

Paul continued spooning the soup into his mouth. 'I knew they would eventually. That's why I abandoned it and came to London.'

'And they've also talked to your landlord and searched your flat.'

'They won't find anything.'

'No, they won't,' said Priestley. 'But I did. I found some letters, Paul, some very unpleasant letters, from Susan Linton. They were sitting on your desk.'

Paul look at him warily. 'How did you get into my flat?'

'Your landlord let me in when I came looking for you.'

'When was that?'

'On Sunday morning. We were desperate to find you. Mother has been going out of her mind worrying about you. Why were you writing to Susan Linton, Paul?'

Tears came to Paul's eyes. 'I was trying to help her. She said she needed money because she was being blackmailed.'

'And you believed her, did you?'

'Yes. Why wouldn't I believe her? She said her ex husband was blackmailing her. You know, George Mannering, who went to prison.'

'I see. So you sent her money.'

'Yes... but then she kept asking for more....' Tears began to run down his cheeks. 'She was horrible to me. When I said I couldn't send her any more money she started threatening me. I said if George Mannering was blackmailing her, she should go to the

186

police. But she wouldn't listen. She just wanted me to keep sending her money... But I didn't kill her, David...It wasn't me...'

Priestley took a handkerchief from his pocket and handed it to him.

'She was threatening me. Saying she would write to Mother if I didn't pay up. Said she would go to the police and tell them I was harrassing her.'

David Priestley leaned forward and met his brother's gaze. 'Paul. Are you quite sure that you didn't visit Susan Linton last Friday evening?'

'No. I told you. I never went near her house.'

'All right. If you say so, then I believe you. I'm only asking you the questions the police will ask you.'

Paul reached across the table and gripped his hand tightly. 'I'm frightened. Don't let them put me in prison, David. They'll kill me. Please don't let them put me in prison.'

vi.

At 1.12pm came the news that the Priestley brothers had arrived at Aylesbury Police Headquarters. Wakeman went the observation room to monitor their arrival. Straker was about to follow when he learned that David Priestley had requested an urgent meeting in private.

'I have something for you, Inspector.' Priestley sat down and opened his briefcase. 'I'm sorry, I should have passed these to you before now.' Taking out a large brown envelope he handed it to Straker. 'I found these letters on Tuesday when I visited Paul's flat.'

Straker looked crossly at Priestley. 'You realise, don't you that withholding evidence can lead to a charge of perverting the course of justice.'

'Yes, I know that. But my brother is very vulnerable, Inspector. Reluctantly I have come now to the conclusion that he is guilty of this awful crime. But I hope you will agree when you've read these letters, that he was provoked beyond endurance.'

Straker opened the envelope and peered inside. It contained several handwritten letters. 'Has your brother admitted to you that he murdered Miss Linton?'

'He hasn't. In fact he denies being anywhere near the actress's house that night.'

'But you don't believe him.'

'No. Not after reading those awful letters. They are vicious and threatening. I just hope they will be taken into account when determining sentence.'

'Well, that is a matter for the judge, Mr Priestley. My job is simply to find Miss Linton's killer and produce enough evidence for him to be brought before the courts.'

'Then all I ask, Inspector, is that you read those letters before you question him. Paul is not a strong man, but nor is he a bad man. Certainly he bears no resemblance to the grotesque caricature we've all seen in certain parts of the media.'

'Does your brother know that you have handed these letters to me?'

'He doesn't. And naturally, I would prefer for it to stay that way. But, of course, I leave that to your discretion.' David Priestley rose. 'Thank you for seeing me, Inspector.'

As Priestley left, Straker took some tweezers from the drawer and carefully removed the eight letters from the envelope. Neatly handwritten on Basildon

Bond paper they seemed to belong to a simpler, more innocent age, before the arrival of the internet. He browsed through them one by one.

9th January 2012
...sorry not to have written to you for a while but I have been very worried, so much so that it has made me quite ill... You see, Paul, I did something very stupid once when I was young... George is demanding £5,000 and he wants it straight away...Unless I pay him the £5000 in cash he will release everything to the press and my reputation will be ruined..appeal to you on my knees

23rd January 2012
... can't thank you enough.... sure he will be satisfied with £2,000... cash is best because he wants it that way... Can you deliver it to me Paul? There is a post box at my gate.... put the money in a sealed envelope I can get it when I am by myself ... Tell me what day you will come and what time.... this must be our secret Paul... can't bear for anyone to know...

7th February 2012
...You have to help me again...George is demanding another £1,000.... promise I will never ask you again...

20th February 2012
... don't know what to do... he wants another £1000 or he will go to the

189

media...Please help me this last time Paul....please, I am counting on you.

From this point on the relationship deteriorates rapidly as Susan Linton's letters become more demanding and more threatening.

27th February 2012
...stop this silly talk of going to kill people. All I was asking for was £1000, which I will pay back with interest if you insist.... Think again Paul or I will start to wonder if you are really the kind and loving person I took you for...

5th March 2012
...Why have you not replied to my letter... Maybe you are not my friend after all. I must have the money, Paul and I must have it by Wednesday the 7th March...Don't let me down.

13th March 2012
...bring it this Friday the 16th, Paul at 8.00pm. If you don't I am warning you I will telephone your mother and tell her about you and how you have been stealing from her...

20th March 2012
...So you have decided to refuse me...now I know the kind of person you are... I realise now you are not right in the head with your talk of finishing people off and all your sick fantasies about me...No, I will not return your money...I warn you Paul... I will

definitely call your mother and tell her you are stealing from her and can't wait for her to die...don't even think of coming to see me because I won't let you in. I will ring the police immediately...you can be sure they will put you away for a very long time...

Had he learned anything that he hadn't gleaned already from Priestley's side of the correspondence? Not really. Either Susan Linton was a woman driven to the point of desperation by her former husband, or she was a scheming, lying bitch, deliberately exploiting the generosity of a loyal but simple minded admirer. But did it matter either way as far as the investigation was concerned? To a judge, perhaps, but not to him. His job, simply, was to find Susan Linton's murderer.

Returning the letters to the envelope, he called admin to arrange for photocopies to be distributed to all members of the investigating team before sending the originals for fingerprints analysis.

vii.

Joining Wakeman in the observation room Straker watched Paul and David Priestley sitting at the table in earnest conversation. Without his moustache, Paul Priestley bore little resemblance to the E-fit image and even to the photograph supplied by his brother.

'Okay, Kevyn. Let's make a start. Softly, softly, as the saying goes.'

As they entered the interview room the brothers

ended their conversation abruptly. David Priestley gave Straker a polite nod. Paul Priestley offered no greeting.

'Good afternoon gentlemen,' said Straker. 'We appreciate that Mr Priestley is here of his own volition. We will, however, be conducting the interview under caution.'

Wakeman switched on the video recorder. 'Interview with Paul Priestley conducted by Detective Inspector Steve Straker and Detective Sergeant Kevyn Wakeman, in the presence of his brother, David Priestley.....'

As Wakeman delivered the caution, Straker studied the two men. They were as unlike one another as two brothers could be. Were they close, he wondered? Was there any real fondness between them?

'Mr Priestley,' began Wakeman. 'Did you murder Susan Linton?'

His tone was aggressive and Paul Priestley looked momentarily taken aback. Already there were small beads of sweat on his brow.

'No.. I didn't murder her.'

'Then, can you tell us where you were last Friday evening?'

'I was in Suffolk, in my camper van?' Unlike his brother, Paul Priestley spoke with a mildly Scottish lilt.

'And where was this exactly?'

'At a campsite near Minsmere.'

'Minsmere is a bird sanctuary,' said David Priestley. 'It's in Suffolk about ten miles south of Southwold.'

'Do you have the address?'

'No, but I often stay there. The owner knows me.'

'So, he can verify that you stayed there last Friday night, can he?'

Priestley stared at him blankly.

'You have a receipt, for example, showing the date of your arrival.'

'No. The owner doesn't do receipts.'

'But he will confirm that you stayed at his site that night, will he?'

'I didn't arrive until after seven. I called on him next morning to book in.'

'I see.' said Wakeman icily. 'So he can't confirm that you were there last Friday evening.'

Priestley stared glumly back at Wakeman but said nothing

'Did you go for a meal locally, Mr Priestley?' said Straker, deciding to introduce a more conciliatory tone. 'Or a drink perhaps?

'No. I stayed in my van all evening.'

'So, you have no way of proving where you were on the night of the murder,' continued Wakeman. 'Is that right?'

Paul Priestley shrugged, but didn't answer

Wakeman leaned forward. 'Then let me put it to you, Mr Priestley that last Friday evening you weren't at a campsite in Suffolk at all. You were at Elleswood House, the home of Susan Linton.'

Priestley looked suddenly startled. 'No... that not true. I was nowhere near Susan's house' His voice trailed away and Straker could see that his knee was shaking under the table..

Wakeman stared accusingly at Priestley for several seconds. 'So, you stayed at the Westleton campsite until yesterday. Is that what you're saying?'

'No, I moved on a couple of times.'

'Why did you do that?'

'The first two were too noisy, with lots of kids. I like it quiet.'

'I see. But then, on Wednesday you decided to abandon your camper van and sleep rough, before coming to your brother's flat in London this morning. What made you do that?'

'Because I knew that once you gave out the registration number of the camper van, it was only a matter of time before someone would recognise me.'

'I see. Then, you were aware that the police were looking for you.'

'Yes. It was in all the newspapers.'

'But, since you say you were nowhere near Susan Linton's house last Friday evening, why didn't you just pop into the nearest police station and make yourself known. Wouldn't that have saved everyone a lot of time and trouble?'

Priestley didn't answer. There were tears in his eyes as he stared down at the table.

David Priestley put out his hand and rested it on his brother's arm. 'It's all right Paul. Just tell the inspector everything you told me.'

'Why didn't you make yourself known to the police, Mr Priestley?' repeated Wakeman.

'Because... I didn't think anyone would believe me.'

'Really. Why not?'

'Because... of what it said about me in the newspapers. And because...'

'Yes, because of what?'

Priestley didn't answer.

Wakeman opened the folder containing the transcripts of his letters and began to leaf through them. 'Was it because of these letters by any chance? The letters you were writing to Miss Linton right up to a couple of weeks before her death?'

Again Priestley didn't answer, but stared down at the table.

'We know from the letters that you delivered most of them by hand, which means that you came to

194

Susan Linton's house on several occasions in recent weeks?'

Priestley looked apprehensively at his brother, but said nothing.

'Why were you writing to Susan Linton, Mr Priestley?'

David Priestley touched his brother's arm. 'It's all right, Paul. Just tell the inspector what you told me.'

Priestley looked up. 'I saw her on television, talking about her accident and how she didn't have enough money, even for food. So I sent her a cheque for £1,000.'

'That was a bit generous, wasn't it?'

'Well...I felt sorry for her... It was after that, that we started writing to each other.'

'You mean personal letters?'

'Yes. She said she was lonely. She said she liked getting letters from me.'

'And then you started to visit her at her house.'

Priestley shook his head vehemently. 'No, I never actually met her. I came to her house, but only to deliver letters to her mailbox. I never went in. I never met her in person.'

'If you weren't going to meet her, why didn't you just post the letters and save yourself the long drive?

'Because she didn't want her housekeeper to know,' said Priestley, his voice now barely more than a whisper. 'The housekeeper dealt with the post, you see. And also because...'

Wakeman leaned closer. 'Speak up please. We didn't catch that.'

'Because I was bringing her money.'

'More money?'

'Yes, she wanted it in cash and it wasn't safe to send it through the post. She was being blackmailed, you see. By her ex-husband. He was demanding

195

£5,000, for some old photographs, she said. It was only a loan. She said she would pay me back.'

'So you agreed to lend her £5,000.'

'No, I didn't have that amount. I wrote saying that maybe I could send her £2,000.

'And she accepted that, did she?'

At first, she did.'

'And you delivered the money to her mailbox.'

'Yes.'

'And was she happy with that?'

'No.' Priestley was beginning to get increasingly agitated. 'But, I didn't have any more money to give. I was having to borrow it from my mother's bank account. Eventually I said I couldn't give her any more money. I told her that if she was being blackmailed by her ex husband she shouldn't give in to it. She should go to the police.'

'And what did she say?'

For a moment Paul Priestley was silent. Then his face crumpled as he let out a choking sob and tears ran down his both his cheeks.

'Was that when you and she began to fall out?' said Wakeman, taking one of the transcripts from the folder.

Burying his head in his hands Priestley continued to sob.'

'She started to get nasty with you, didn't she, Mr Priestley. Insulting you, making threats to contact your mother'

But Priestley was no longer listening as he sobbed in long choking gasps.

'So you decided to get nasty too, didn't you? Let me remind you of what you said in your letter dated the 17th March this year, just three weeks before Susan Linton was murdered. *'Dear Susan, How can you be so cruel after all I have done for you and the money I have sent you. I have been a fool all these years to love you. You have been using me Susan that is what I think. Well you will not get your £1000 whatever you do and I don't care what this man does to you because you deserve it"* Wakeman paused and looked up at Priestley before continuing. *And I give you a big warning Susan not to try and talk to my mother. Anyway she won't listen to you. But if you do I am warning you keep away from my family or it will be the worse for you. And if I am not good enough for you then my money isn't good enough for you either and I want it back. I will give you a week to get it and then I will come....'*

'Yes, but I didn't mean it!' cried Priestley, almost hysterical now. 'It was Mannering who put her up to it, treating me like she did. I only wanted my money and letters back.'

'But you gave her an ultimatum, didn't you. Return my money and letters within a week or it will be the worse for you. That's what you said. What exactly did you have in mind when you wrote that?.'

Priestley buried his face in his hands. 'I only wanted to frighten her. I never meant her any harm.'

'Really? Are you sure about that? Did you keep those letters from Susan Linton?'

'Yes.'

'All of them?'

'Yes. Because now she was blackmailing me, I thought I would take them to the police.'

'Then why didn't you?' said Wakeman. 'Wouldn't it have been a lot better if you had done exactly that?'

Priestley was shaking now as tears ran down his cheeks. ' I didn't kill Susan...why would I kill her... I loved her.....'

There was a knock on the door and Mary Chandos came in with an envelope. The room went quiet as

197

Straker and then Wakeman examined the contents of the envelope, It was the news they had been hoping for. As she left the room Wakeman resumed the interview.

'Did you know that Susan Linton wore a catheter, Mr Priestley?'

The two brothers looked at Wakeman in bewilderment.

'No, of course you didn't. Why should it have occurred to you?'

Now David Priestley turned to Straker. 'This appears to be a strange new line of questioning, Inspector. Is it relevant?

'Highly relevant as it happens,' said Straker, passing the document to Wakeman. 'We have just received the report following the forensic examination of your camper van, Mr Priestley. Tests confirm that traces of urine found in the driver's foot well match urine spillage into the carpet around Susan Linton's body. This was due to her catheter tube coming away from the bag, presumably as she struggled with her attacker.'

David Priestley stared at his brother in shock.

'Paul Priestley,' said Straker. 'I am arresting you on suspicion of the murder of Susan Linton.'

Chapter Seven

Friday,13th April 2012

i.

At 7.45am Straker crept out of the house, leaving Emily still fast asleep. He wasn't needed for last night's rehearsal, so he had an entire evening to brood on the events of the previous forty eight hours. He wished now he had responded when Emily tentatively touched his shoulder as she slid into bed beside him. It would have been so easy to turn over and take her in his arms. Instead he just lay there, consumed by guilt.

Arriving at his desk, he dropped the pile of newspapers on his desk and took off his coat. In a couple of hours it would all be over. With DNA evidence putting Priestley incontrovertibly at the scene of the crime, he had decided to delay further questioning until this morning, calculating that a night in custody would give him time to reflect on the hopelessness of his situation. He had also granted his brother full access to persuade him of the benefits of a guilty plea, rather than contesting the charge in front of a jury.

Straker lifted the Daily Herald from the pile. Last night's press release consisted of a single sentence confirming Priestley's arrest on suspicion of murder. But was enough, to bring the story back to the front page under a banner headline - *LINTON MURDER – MR WALRUS ARRESTED.* Inside was yet another with double page spread of interviews with acquaintances and former work colleagues, most of them continuing to characterise Priestley as a loner, a misfit or a weirdo.

Rawlings put his head round the door. 'Morning Steve. Ready for the big day?'

Straker looked up cheerfully. 'I think so, Jerry. I'm not expecting any hitches.'

'And how has the Herald responded to our latest press release?'

'Much as we have come to expect.' Straker handed him the newspaper.

Rawlings shook his head as he scanned the front page before turning to the inside spread. 'You know, I'm amazed their legal boys let them get away with this.' Folding the newspaper he placed it back on the pile. 'I assume you got nowhere with your interviews.'

'I'm afraid not. And I don't see I can question everyone a second time'

'No, of course you can't. Anyway, it's the Herald's lookout, not ours and I doubt if David Priestley will cause any further trouble once his brother's been charged. Let's hope we get a quick confession this morning. We could all do with a weekend off.' He turned to go. 'Well, I'll leave you to it. You've done a great job, as I knew you would. How's Kevyn Wakeman been performing, by the way? Have you found him competent?'

Straker hesitated. 'He's a bit headstrong at times, but yes, I think he's sound.'

Rawlings pondered this for a few moments. 'You know, Steve, if I were you, I'd let him lead again this morning. I know he can be a bit aggressive, but that might be just what we need to get the case wrapped up quickly. Anyway, I'll let you get on. I'm here all day if you need me.'

As Rawlings departed, Straker took the two folders of letters from the drawer. It grated that Jerry rated Wakeman so highly, but he was probably right about letting him lead today's interview. He was conscious that no one needed a free weekend more than he did. His suspicions about Dan Masterson for example. It was all speculation. He had no proof, none at all. He needed to get control of himself, or he might really have something to worry about.

'Morning Steve.' Wakeman strolled in and sat down. 'All set?'

'I think so. Anyway, it's over to you to finish the job. I'll just sit in as before.' He picked the Herald off the top of the pile and passed it across to him. 'Our friends have been busy again.' He watched as Wakeman ran his eyes down the page. 'We need a confession, Kevyn. Do you think you can deliver it?'

'Don't worry, boss. He'll crack.'

The phone rang to say that David Priestley had arrived and once again was requesting a word in private prior to the interview. As he was shown in, he looked relaxed and confident.

'Good morning gentlemen. I thought it best to have a word before you interview my brother today.' He paused. 'You will appreciate that Paul was a frightened man when I brought him here yesterday. Which is hardly surprising given the newspaper coverage of the past couple of days. I don't know if you had time to see this morning's Herald.'

'We have,' said Straker, 'and we are as concerned as you must be.'

'They seem to have had it in for Paul ever since you released that E-fit image. It's clear that they have already decided that he's guilty.'

201

'Yes, I'm sorry about that,' said Straker, 'but I'm afraid we have no control over what is published in newspapers. All I can tell you is that we have been absolutely scrupulous about the information we've released to the media.'

David Priestley looked sharply at Straker. 'Are you absolutely sure that no one in your team has been talking to journalists?'

'As sure as I can be.'

David Priestley shrugged. 'Very well. Then I'll have to take your word for it. But let me come to the main reason I wanted to speak to you this morning. I talked to Paul last night and he has now admitted to me that he wasn't telling the truth when you interviewed him yesterday. He has assured me that what he will be telling you today is the absolute truth and I trust he will keep his word. I've warned him that he is under caution and that it's in his best interests to hide nothing from you, nothing at all.'

'Thank you,' said Straker. He looked at his watch. 'We said we would begin at 9.30am, but I'm happy to make it earlier if you are both ready.'

ii.

At 9.17am, Straker and Wakeman entered the interview room.

'Good morning, gentlemen,' said Wakeman, sitting down opposite Paul Priestley. 'I trust you had a comfortable night, Mr Priestley.'

Paul Priestley didn't answer.

'If you're ready, we'll begin.'

As Wakeman switched on the DVD recorder and proceeded to deliver the caution, both brothers looked surprisingly relaxed.

'Mr Priestley,' Wakeman's tone was sharp and businesslike. 'Where you were last Friday evening?'

For a few seconds Paul Priestley stared at him as if he hadn't understood the question. Then he answered, almost in a whisper. 'I went to Susan Linton's house.'

'I see. So you weren't at the camp site in Suffolk, as you told us yesterday.'

'I was, but I arrived there later.'

'What time did you go to Susan Linton's house?'

'At about 7.30pm. Susan told me not to come any earlier.'

'You mean, Susan Linton invited you to visit her last Friday?'

'Yes. She telephoned me.'

'When was this?'

'It was on the Monday, or Tuesday of last week. I don't remember exactly.'

'On your mobile, or on your landline?'

'On my landline. She said to come on Friday, but not before 7.30pm. Her housekeeper would definitely be gone by then.'

'Did she say why she wanted you to visit her?'

Priestley looked at his brother, as if seeking reassurance.

'Take your time Paul,' said David Priestley. 'They just want the truth.'

'She said she wanted to apologise for the way she had treated me.' Paul Priestley's voice was firmer now. 'She said she also wanted to pay back the money I lent her. She said I could have all my letters back too, if I wanted.'

Wakeman studied him with scepticism. 'I see. Quite a turnaround then from what you told us yesterday. Did she say why you were to come last Friday rather than any other day?'

'Yes. She said her housekeeper was going to be in London on Friday evening, so she would definitely be on her own. She told me to ring the door bell twice so she would know it was me, and then to come straight in. I would find her in her sitting room at the top of the stairs.'

'And you agreed to that, did you?'

'No...not straight away.' Priestley paused. 'I told her I didn't want to see her. I said just to leave the money and the letters in the hall where I could find them and I wouldn't trouble her again.'

'And what did she say to that?'

'At first she kept insisting that she wanted to apologise in person. But in the end, she agreed.'

Now Straker intervened. 'Why didn't you want to see her, Mr Priestley?'

Priestley's eyes became tearful. 'Because of all the nasty things she said in her letters. I just wanted my money back. And my letters.'

'Go on.'

'Anyway, eventually she agreed. She said she would leave the money in an envelope on the hall table, together with my letters. Then, if I still didn't want to see her, I could just take everything and go. But she hoped I wouldn't do that. She hoped I would come and see her before I left.'

Wakeman leaned forward. 'Why have you completely changed your story since yesterday, Mr Priestley?' .

Priestley turned back to face Wakeman. 'Because... I was afraid. I was afraid you wouldn't believe me.'

204

His brother put a hand on his arm. 'It's all right, Paul. Just explain everything as you explained it to me last night.'

Yes, Mr Priestley. Tell us exactly what happened when you arrived at Susan Linton's house last Friday evening.'

With his brother's hand still resting on his arm, Paul Priestley described how he, arrived at the house a few minutes early so he parked in the road opposite the drive. Then, at 7.30pm, he walked across the road to the house, rang the bell twice as instructed and went in. Here he turned to his brother, as if awaiting permission to continue.

'And was the envelope on the hall table, as promised?' said Wakeman

Priestley shook his head. 'No. There was just a note from Susan saying she had the money and the letters, but I was to come up and see her in her sitting room at the top of the stairs.'

'So, you went upstairs?'

'Yes, but she wasn't in the sitting room. I looked in all the bedrooms, but she wasn't there either. So I came down again to the hall. Then I realised she must be in the lounge because I could hear the television. I hadn't noticed it when I first came in. So I tapped on the door and opened it and...' Priestley stopped in mid sentence and stared at Wakeman, eyes glistening.

'And what?'

He began to shake his head. 'The room...it was all messed up...things all over the floor... papers, books, drawers pulled out. It was like there had been a burglary.'

'And Susan Linton. Was she there?'

He nodded. 'Yes, she was there...though I didn't see her at first. The television was on and her wheel chair was next to it, but it was empty....' Tears began to run down Priestley's cheeks. 'Then I saw her. I could only see her foot at first because the sofa was in the way. So I went in a bit further. She was lying on her back... covered in blood. I bent down to see if she was alive, but I could tell she wasn't.... it was horrible...'

'What did you do?'

Priestley stared at Wakeman. 'I just turned and ran out of the house and back to my van. I tried to start the engine. But I was shaking so much I couldn't even put the key in the ignition.... Then I thought... what have I done? It would look like it was me that killed her, because I must have left fingerprints everywhere. So I went back to the house and wiped all the doors and the handles. Everywhere I'd been. Then I went back to my van and drove off.'

'Where to?'

'I thought at first of going home. But then I decided I couldn't just go home, not after what I'd seen. I decided to drive out to Minsmere.'

'Why Minsmere?'

'Because that was where I was planning to spend the Easter weekend. I mean, before Susan rang me.'

'I see,' said Wakeman with a sneer of contempt. 'You had just found Susan Linton lying in a pool of blood, so you decided to drive to Minsmere. Is that right? You didn't think to call the police. Or your brother.'

Priestley responded with a small shake of the head.

Wakeman gave a sigh of impatience. 'And what you are telling us today is the absolute truth, is it Mr Priestley?'

Priestley nodded.

'Unlike yesterday, when it was all lies.' He leaned forward. 'Why do you expect us to believe you today,

Mr Priestley, when you now admit that what you told us yesterday was a pack of lies?'

Priestley didn't answer.

'Isn't the real truth that you drove to Elleswood House last Friday evening determined to get back your money and your letters. ' Wakeman opened the folder and took out the transcript of Susan Linton's final letter to Priestley. 'Here is what she said to you on the 13th March, barely four weeks before she was found murdered.

So you have decided to refuse me. All right, if that is your decision. I thought you were someone I could trust but now I know the kind of person you are. You need help Paul because I realise now you are not right in the head with your talk of finishing people off and all your sick fantasies about me. .

And now you dare to threaten me.   No, I will not return your money. I wouldn't even if I had it because it wasn't yours to give, was it. I warn you Paul, if I ever hear from you again I will definitely call your mother and tell her you are stealing from her and can't wait for her to die. And don't even think of coming to see me because I won't let you in. I will ring the police immediately and give them all your letters Then you can be sure they will put you away for a very long time.

No, but I didn't kill her,' cried Priestley, by now very agitated. 'Yes, it's true that I was angry with her...but I would never have harmed her.'

'So you want us to believe that she was already dead when you got to the house.'

'Yes, it's true... that's how I found her,' sobbed Priestley.

You're telling us that someone got there before you and murdered her. Is that what you're saying? That on the very evening that you decided to call on Susan

Linton to retrieve your money and letters, by sheer coincidence, someone else broke in just ahead of you and stabbed her to death'

'Yes. She was already dead!'

'And who might this unlikely assassin have been, do you think?'

'I don't know... Burglars, maybe. I told you...the place was done over.'

'Come on, Mr Priestley, you don't really expect us to believe this, do you? And I'm pretty sure a jury isn't going to believe it either. Isn't it the truth that the only person who broke into Elleswood House last Friday night, was you? And isn't it the truth that you didn't come to the front door and ring the bell, as you just told us, because you knew perfectly well that once she saw you through the spy hole, there was no way she was going to let you in. I put it to you that you arrived at Elleswood House last Friday evening with every intention of confronting Susan Linton. And the only way to do that was to take her by surprise. Which is why you crept round the house and broke in by the back door.'

'That's not true!' cried Priestley.' I didn't even know there was a door at the back.'

'And once inside, you went in search of Susan Linton, didn't you? Eventually finding her in the lounge watching television. But when you asked for your money and your letters, she continued to refuse you. Isn't that the truth? And that's when you started to lose your cool. She laughed at you and insulted you, just as she did in her letters. Until eventually she drove you to such a frenzy of rage that you stabbed her to death...

'No...no! That isn't what happened...'

'And then, realising what you had done, you came suddenly to your senses. You had to cover your tracks, make it look like a random break in. So, you went round getting rid of your fingerprints and then you ransacked the place. And once you had done that, you drove all the way to Suffolk. First, to establish your alibi and then to lie low until the story blew over. It must have come as a big surprise to see that description of you in the newspapers, then your name, plus a photograph...'

I didn't kill Susan,' wailed Priestley. ' Why would I kill her? I loved her...I loved her...'.

Now David Priestley intervened. 'Enough, Gentlemen, please! Paul has given you a clear and honest account of what happened last Friday evening. If you have evidence to contradict what he has told you, all well and good. But I suspect you haven't, or you wouldn't be attempting to undermine him.'

All right,' said Straker, switching off the recorder. 'We'll take a break. Resume in thirty minutes.

iii.

'I think there's a very good chance that by tonight it will all be over.' said Becky, handing Mark the car keys and walking round to the passenger side.

'You think so?' said Mark climbing into the car and fastening his seat belt

'Kevyn may not be everyone's cup of tea, but he has a Rottweiler reputation as an interviewer. I wouldn't like to have to face him.'

Mark didn't respond as he concentrated on manoeuvring out into the heavy traffic. She gave him a glance. What was going on in that head of his? Something, that was for sure. Well, at least he had

209

got some recognition at last, and so had she. This morning Straker had the grace to call her into his office and apologise for his clumsy handling of Wednesday's interview. She had done a great job over the past week, he told her, and she could be confident that she would get the recognition she deserved. He then called in Mark and congratulated him too on his excellent contribution.

'So you think Wakeman will get a confession out of Priestley this morning, do you?' said Mark as the traffic began to thin.

'He's probably got it already. In which case we are wasting our day seeing Bristow and Susan Linton's solicitor.'

Again Mark didn't respond.

'But you're not so sure. Is that it?'

'Not entirely, no. In the meantime, I'll be interested in what Michael Bristow has to tell us.'

'Come on, Mark. If Bristow was quietly fleecing Susan Linton of her money, it's hardly relevant to what we're dealing with right now.'

'It might be. Until we get that confession from Priestley I just think we should keep an open mind.'

Becky sat back with a sigh and for several minutes they drove on in silence.

'Didn't two of those who attended last Friday's reunion say there were rumours about Bristow and Kate Bellingham being in a relationship?'

'Yes, but does it matter? Look Mark, I know this is frustrating but we have to stay focussed.'

'It's just that I've been studying the investment portfolio and I think something fishy has been going on. Something that could involve the housekeeper as well.'

'Something relevant to Susan Linton's murder?'

He smiled. 'Who knows? First we thought George Mannering was our man. Then it was Paul Priestley...'

'And still is Paul Priestley. Thanks mainly to you.'

'Yes, but he hasn't been charged yet, has he. All I ask is that you let me put the questions I want to put to Bristow and we'll take it from there.'

'Fine, over to you. I'll just listen in.'

Don't you want me to brief you first?'

Becky laughed. 'Not really. I'd rather you told me about this band you play in.'

iv.

Sitting across the desk from Michael Bristow, Becky tried to imagine what qualities he possessed to persuade the actress to employ him in the first place. Judging by the way he greeted them at the door, charm wasn't one of them.

'I have to say I was surprised to get your call,' said Bristow, clasping his hands to reveal chewed down fingernails. 'If it's to ask about Miss Linton's investments you you really should be talking to Horizon. They manage the portfolio now.'

'We know that, sir.' said Mark. 'But we understand that you managed her investments from around the time of her accident until January of this year?'

'That is so.'

'Even though you were her theatrical agent and not her accountant.'

'Susan never employed an accountant. She didn't see the need for one. She had some investments that she'd inherited from her family so, initially, surplus income went into one or another of those. After her accident, of course, her circumstances changed dramatically and it was necessary to draw down income to supplement the meagre amount she was getting from the state.'

'And you felt competent to deal with her investments, did you, sir?'

Bristow gave Mark a suspicious look. 'It wasn't that complicated to begin with. But, as you know, the markets have been somewhat turbulent in recent times. All I can say is that I did my best.'

Mark opened the portfolio. 'At the time of Miss Linton's accident her investments were valued at £1.4 million. At the last valuation, which was in October last year, they stood at £547,000. That's a 61% decline in just five years?'

'There are several reasons for that. First of all, you may not know that Miss Linton settled £200,000 on George Mannering at the time of her divorce.'

'Yes I do know that. But even without that £200,000, we are still talking about a 55% decline.'

'And, as I'm sure you are aware that there was a massive fall in the stock market in 2008 from which it has still not fully recovered.'

'We are aware of that too, 'said Mark patiently.

'Another point you may not have considered is that, following her accident, Miss Linton had only a meagre disability allowance from the state. Yet she insisted on continuing to live in that vast house which was extremely costly to maintain and run. Sometimes I had to sell shares at unfavourable times to meet her needs.'

'So it appears. You sold shares to a total value of £141,295 over five years to the end of 2011. Although I notice that the proceeds from those sales didn't find their way all that quickly into Miss Linton's bank account. In fact, until January of this year, there was a shortfall of almost £48,000.'

'That is possible. As you observed yourself, I was a theatrical agent, not an accountant. I think Horizon will confirm that the books were in order when they took them over.'

Are you a gambler by any chance, Mr Bristow?'

'I have a flutter, from time to time.'

'Using cash presumably, given your current credit rating.'

Bristow glared angrily at Mark but said nothing

'Did you meet up with Miss Linton regularly to discuss her investments?

Bristow shook his head. 'No. Susan had no head for figures. She simply wasn't interested. Most of my dealings were with Miss Bellingham who looked after her day to day finances.'

Mark studied the portfolio. 'I see that in 2008 a holiday apartment in Marbella was purchased for £97.000. Miss Linton approved of the purchase, did she?'

'Of course,' said Bristow brusquely. At the time, it looked like a good investment. Besides she was able to walk short distances back in 2008 and her condition seemed to be improving.'

'So you thought she might manage to visit the flat herself and get a little Spanish sun.'

'We hoped so, yes.'

'Even though it was a second floor flat, with no lift.'

'As I say, at that time Susan was making good progress. But the notion that she might be able to make use of it herself from time to time was only secondary. I saw it as an investment opportunity with a potential for good returns.'

'In fact, you and Miss Bellingham have made use of the flat yourselves on two occasions. Is that right?'

Bristow reddened. 'What gives you that idea?'

'I spoke to the community office today and they told me that you had spent two weeks at the flat, the first in 2010 and the second last summer with a lady they assumed to be your wife. Their description appeared to match Miss Bellingham's

'Yes. It was necessary for me to visit Marbella couple of times, strictly on business. There were matters to discuss with the community office and the rental agents.'

'But you chose to take Miss Bellingham with you?'

'As a friend, yes. Kate didn't get much opportunity for holidays. It was on a strictly arm's length basis, I assure you.

'You mean, it made sense to stay at the flat rather than paying for a hotel.'

'Exactly.'

'May I take it then that you and Miss Bellingham are, shall we say, intimate friends?'

'I wouldn't use that word to describe our relationship. But close friends, certainly. I've known Sarah as long as I've known Susan.'

'Close enough to share a one bedroom flat?'

Bristow paused before answering. 'I really don't see where this line of questioning is leading. Actually it has turned out to be one of Susan's more successful investments with an annual return of close to 4%.'

'So I see,' said Mark. 'Although that may not continue for very long. The lady I spoke to this morning told me that community charges are now two years in arrears and that local taxes amounting to some1,500 euros are still outstanding on the account.'

'That's because I'm in dispute with both of them.' Bristow turned to Becky. 'I must say I find your colleague's line of questioning very intrusive. What of

214

it if I took Miss Bellingham with me? We are both unattached.'

Becky turned to Mark. 'Are we nearly done?'

Mark closed the portfolio. ' Yes. Thank you Mr Bristow. That will be all for now. You have been most helpful.'

v.

Declining Straker's invitation to join him for lunch, Kevyn Wakeman walked to the roundabout and on towards the park. All morning Paul Priestley had stuck to his story and for the first time he was beginning to have doubts. Not that they had the wrong man - he was in no doubt on that score - but whether they had enough evidence to charge him. The problem was that this new story Priestley had come up with effectively neutralised the forensic evidence against him. Which meant that without a confession, or compelling new evidence, the CPS would be unlikely to proceed.

It was Straker's fault. The time to break Priestley was yesterday when he was at his most vulnerable, not this morning when he was fresh and better prepared. But no, Straker thought differently. No need to bully the man, he insisted. Give him a night in custody to reflect on the hopelessness of his situation and by morning, he'll be putty in our hands. Which might have been so, had he not also had the bright idea of enlisting David Priestley's help. Spend time with him, he urged. Make him understand that a full confession is in his best interest.

215

Did Straker seriously believe that David Priestley would do anything of the sort? He was a lawyer, for God's sake. Even if he believed his brother was as guilty as hell, wouldn't his first instinct be to look for ways to undermine the evidence? Which he did, brilliantly. The story he was now coming up with stretched credibility to the limit, but that didn't matter. All Priestley had to do was come up with an explanation that would sow seeds of doubt in the minds of the jury.

Yes, David Priestley had used his time well. Yesterday his brother was a pathetic, snivelling wreck. Today he was different man completely. Far from cracking, he appeared to gain in confidence as the morning progressed. And now they were back to square one. Or worse. Because, for as long as Paul Priestley stuck to his story, no amount of forensic evidence would persuade the CPS to put him before a jury.

Arriving at the far end of the park Wakeman turned and began to make his way slowly back. Was it possible that Paul Priestley was telling the truth after all? No. Absolutely not. Because if he didn't murder Susan Linton, who did? Not George Mannering, he was fairly sure of that. But what about Kate Bellingham? As sole beneficiary in Susan Linton's will, she stood to gain a good deal from the actress's death. though not for maybe another thirty or forty years. Not that she could have committed the murder herself, unless everyone attending Friday night's London reunion alibi was in on the conspiracy. But she could have employed an accomplice. Someone like Michael Bristow perhaps.

As he walked back past the High School towards the police station, for the first time Wakeman felt vulnerable. Until this moment it hadn't occurred to him

216

that his briefings to the Herald could blow up in his face. Now it seemed they might. Guilty or not, if Paul Priestley walked free, he sensed that his brother wouldn't be satisfied with filing a suit for damages against the newspaper. He had already accused the police of collusion. Might he go a step further and register a complaint with the Independent Police Complaints Commission? And if he did, what was the risk? Gary wouldn't give him away. Journalists could generally be relied upon not to reveal their sources. But someone in the investigating team might name him, particularly under the pressure of an independent enquiry. Taking out his mobile he scrolled down his contacts.

' *Becky Reedman?'*

'Becks, it's Kevyn. How are things?

'They are good thanks, Kevyn.'

'Where are you right now?'

'On the A40 with DC Taverner. We've just been to see Michael Bristow at his office in Wembley?'

Damn. He was hoping she would be on her own. 'And where are you this afternoon?'

'At 2.30pm we're due to see Susan Linton's solicitor in Hammersmith. How's it gone with Priestley?'

'Not good. He's proving a tougher nut than we were expecting. He now admits to being at the house, but denies murder. He insists Linton was already dead when he got there.'

'Well, he would say that, wouldn't he?'

Wakeman sighed. 'I don't know, Becks. I gave him a hard time all morning, but I haven't been able to shake him from his story. He says Susan Linton asked him to come to the house last Friday so she could pay him back his money. But when he arrived

217

he found her lying dead in the lounge covered in blood.'

'Are you still questioning him?'

'I'll have one more go this afternoon, but I'm not holding my breath. Meanwhile his brother is demanding that he be released unconditionally. It's a mess Becky. By tonight we could be back to square one.'

'I'm sorry.'

'Well, you win some, you lose some. How did you get on with Bristow?'

'Fine. DC Taverner questioned him. He seems a pretty dodgy character altogether. And the way he's been managing the portfolio looks little short of criminal.'

'You mean he's been embezzling funds?'

'I wouldn't go quite that far until we've looked into it a bit more. But we did find out one thing of interest. It appears that the rumours about his relationship with Kate Bellingham are true.'

'Wakeman grinned. 'Really? How did you find that out?

'It's a bit complicated. I'll tell you when I see you.'

'You do that. Okay. Thanks, Becks. I'd better let you get on.'

I'm not sure we can get back for the review meeting, Kevyn. You know what Friday afternoon traffic is like."

'Not to worry, Becks. We'll talk in the morning.'

Still smiling at Becky's last piece of news Wakeman walked up the stairs to the incident room and back to his desk. Everything depended now on his final session with Priestley. Would he break? He wasn't optimistic. Maybe it was time to come clean about the leaks to the Herald. Yes, maybe now was the time to have a little talk with Detective Inspector Straker and get him onside.

vi.

Becky stared thoughtfully at the road ahead. For the first time since she had known him, Kevyn, sounded uncertain, even worried. If Priestley stuck to his story, the CPS wouldn't risk going to trial, which meant that all their hard work of the past week would have come to nothing.

'Do I gather that Priestley hasn't confessed?' said Mark, sensing the drop in Becky's mood.

'No, he hasn't. And it sounds like he's not going to. He admits coming to the house, but not to killing her. According to his new story, Susan Linton telephoned him to apologise for the way she had treated him and offering to return the money he had given her. But when he arrived, he says he found her lying dead in the sitting room.'

'I see. So that explains the traces of blood and urine found in the foot well of his van. Very clever.'

Wakeman was right. Unless Priestley cracked this afternoon, they were back to square one. Tonight or tomorrow at the latest, Straker would face the humiliation of having to announce that Paul Priestley had been released without charge. Moreover, given the media storm that would follow, they could hardly risk disclosing that they were not looking for anyone else in connection with the crime, even though that was the true position. Gradually the team would be run down and disbanded and the Linton investigation would join that long list of unsolved cases, to be dissected, analysed and written about for years to come.

Still, the day had had its compensations. She had very much enjoyed Mark's company. If he was a geek, she decided she was partial to geeks, especially if they were as amusing and interesting as Mark.

'If they can't charge Priestley, they'll have to release him,' said Mark, 'The Herald won't be pleased. It could cost them a fortune in damages.'

'We could find ourselves facing questions too,' said Becky glumly. 'There could be an independent police enquiry .'

'I thought the boss gave you reassurances about that this morning. He said you were in the clear.'

'I know, but next time it will be out of his hands. I'm bound to face another grilling.'

Mark turned towards her. 'In which case, you will have to tell them everything, even if it means betraying a colleague.'

Becky didn't answer but she knew Mark was right. She would have to reveal that she gave Kevyn a full briefing on the day's events last Tuesday. And why shouldn't she? If Kevyn had talked to the Herald, then he hadn't he been straight with her. Maybe he thought that with Priestley's arrest, the affair would blow over. Well, it hadn't and, in the meantime, he had let her carry the can.

vii.

At 2.30pm Becky and Mark arrived at the Hammersmith offices of Harwood and James. Announcing their arrival, they had barely sat down when a genial looking man in late middle age appeared from one of the offices. 'Good afternoon. Geoffrey Harwood. Sorry to keep you waiting. Please come this way.'

Becky and Mark followed Harwood into his office.

'I expect you could do with some refreshment.' Without waiting for an answer, he picked up the phone. 'Coffee and biscuits for three, if you please, Mary.' Returning the phone to its cradle, he took a folder from his in tray. 'Yes, a terrible business. Quite terrible. I'm only sorry that I didn't learn of it sooner. You see, we were on a walking holiday in northern Spain where mobile phones don't operate too well. And, as for English newspapers, well, they just weren't available...'

'When did you learn that Miss Linton had been murdered?' said Becky.

'Not until yesterday at the airport. I was browsing the front pages on the newspaper stands and there it was. Someone had been arrested for Susan Linton's murder I couldn't make out at first what had happened. But when it sunk in, I called the office at once. I wasn't due back until next Monday but I said I would be happy to come in today, if an appointment could be arranged.'

'For which we are most grateful, sir. Did you know Miss Linton well?

Harwood shook his head. 'Not really. She was my late partner's client. In fact, I only met her for the first time a few weeks ago. Like most people, I guess, I remembered her as she was in her prime, so it came as quite a shock seeing her in that wheelchair, so thin and wasted.'

Becky, opened her briefcase and took out her notebook. 'We appreciate that you have a duty of confidentiality, Mr Harwood, but we would be most grateful if you could be as open with us as possible. We'll try not to put you on the spot. Perhaps we can start by asking you a few questions about Miss Linton's estate.'

'Yes, of course.'

'You say you met her recently,' said Becky. 'Was that here or at her house?'

'At her house. I visited her there twice, in fact.' Harwood opening the file in front of him. 'I had a call from her on Friday the 6th January, asking if I could possibly pay her a visit at home as she had something important to discuss. Now, I'm not normally in the habit of calling on my clients at home but, in her case, I made an exception. She asked if I could manage an evening appointment, as she needed to see me on her own. As you may know there is a Miss Bellingham who looked after her during the day.'

'And what was the date of your visit?'

Harwood referred again to his notes. 'Monday the 9th January. Then again, a week later on the 16th January.'

'And would we be right in thinking that your two visits had something to do with Miss Linton's will?'

Harwood gave a long sigh. 'I'm afraid the duty of confidentiality doesn't end with a client's death. But, in view of the circumstances, I think I can divulge her reason for wanting to see me. Yes, she wanted to change her will.'

'Did she say why?' said Becky, suddenly alert.

Harwood hesitated a few moments before answering. 'She didn't go into detail. But I got the strong impression that she no longer trusted Miss Bellingham or, for that matter, her former agent Mr Bristow. She said that she called the two of them to a meeting on the 2nd January this year when she put her concerns to them both. It was a few days after that meeting that she rang, asking me to visit her.'

Becky paused. She knew she had to tread carefully. 'We understand that Miss Linton' previous will named Kate Bellingham as sole beneficiary. Are you able to tell us if that remains the case?'

Harwood sighed. 'Now you are taking me into difficult territory. Unfortunately I am unable to tell you that, which must seem absurd to you since I have the new will right here in front of me. But, if you can furnish me with a warrant, I can send it over to you immediately.'

'Then, we'll do that,' said Becky, deciding there was no point in trying to push him further. 'Thank you for your time Mr Harwood. You have been most helpful. We will get back to you just as soon as...'

'One moment,' said Harwood, rising from his chair. 'Perhaps I could go and check through the archives to see if there is anything else relating to Miss Linton that might be relevant to your investigation. My late partner tended to be rather untidy with his filing, you understand. Just give me a couple of minutes...'

As he left the room, Becky and Mark looked first at the file where Harwood had left it and then at one another.

'Are you going to look?' said Mark. 'Or shall I ?'

They reached for it simultaneously, but Mark's arm was longer. In less than a minute they had found the information they were looking for. By Harwood's return, they were sitting back in their places.

'No, nothing at all, I'm afraid' said Harwood. 'But be assured. As soon as you are able to furnish me with a warrant, I will get the will over to you without delay.'

Once out of the building, Becky and Mark broke almost into a run, in their haste to get to the car.

'How long will it take us to get back?' said Becky, fastening her seatbelt.

'At this time of day, ninety minutes at least. I doubt if we'll be back by 4.00pm.'

She took out her mobile. 'When they've heard what we have to tell them, I think they might be prepared to wait.'

viii.

'Could they have done it?'

It was Becky who broke the silence that had lasted all the way round the North Circular as far as the A40.

'Well, they certainly had a motive,' said Mark, braking once again in the long line of crawling traffic. 'Or she did. After that row, it must have crossed Bellingham's mind that Linton might decide to cut her out of her will.'

'And Bristow's too, I would imagine,' said Mark. 'since we have now have good reason to believe that Bellingham and Bristow are in a relationship. Even in its present state Elleswood House must be worth a couple of million. That's a lot to lose.'

'So, you think they conspired together to murder Linton before she got round to changing her will.' said Becky. 'Is that your new hypothesis?'

'Well it makes sense, doesn't it. Bellingham sets up her alibi by organising a London reunion of friends for the night of the murder, leaving her boyfriend to do the dirty work.'

'Only one problem, ' said Becky. 'Where does Priestley fit into this new scenario? Or was it sheer coincidence that he happened to turn up at the house on the very evening they decided to despatch Linton?'

Mark frowned. 'I agree. It can't have been a coincidence, can it? There has to be an explanation.'

They were making good time now as they drove along the A40 as fast as the speed limit would allow. But their thoughts were racing even faster as each grappled with the problem of how to fit Priestley into their new scenario. Passing the M25 turn off, it was Mark who spoke first. 'I think I've got it. Let me try this on you.'

'I'm listening.'

'I think Priestley was framed.'

'You mean, by Bellingham and Bristow?'

'Yes. Think about it, Becky. Priestley was a loner. He had a history of mental illness and, best of all, they had letters showing him to be in an increasingly acrimonious correspondence with Susan Linton right up to within a few days of her death.'

'Yes, but Kate Bellingham wasn't to know that, was she?' said Becky. 'unless she somehow managed to gain access to Susan Linton's fan mail.'

Mark smiled. 'We only have Bellingham's word that Linton kept her fan mail to herself. For all we know she was intercepting Priestley's letters from day one. I could even go one step further. How do we even know that Linton wrote the letters to Priestley? Maybe they were written by Kate Bellingham.'

'You mean, posing as Susan Linton?'

'Why not?.'

By now they were at the Beaconsfield turn off. In half an hour they would be back in Aylesbury.

225

'Slow down Mark. Let's go through it all again. Before we get to the meeting, let's make sure your hypothesis stands up....'

ix.

Rawlings gave Becky and Mark a broad smile as they took their places at the conference table. 'Your call couldn't have come at a better time, Becky. We were just about to issue a press release to the effect that Paul Priestley had been released on police bail. It was nice being able to add that we were pursuing an important new lead.' He tapped on the table. 'Right, fill us in on your meeting with Harwood.'

As Becky delivered her report she sensed that only Rawlings and Jack Meredith were fully engaged. Straker looked tense and distracted. Wakeman, chewing gum as usual, looked as if he would rather be elsewhere.

'Thank you,' said Rawlings, as she completed her account. 'So, Stoke Mandeville Hospital gets everything and Kate Bellingham gets nothing. Is that your understanding?'

Becky nodded. 'We only had time to skim the document briefly, but I don't think there are any other beneficiaries apart from the hospital.'

Rawlings peered round the table. 'So there we have it, ladies and gentlemen. Thanks to Susan Linton's solicitor we have a new line of enquiry to pursue. Whatever the meeting on the 2nd January was about, it must have been pretty acrimonious for Susan Linton to decide to change her will and Kate Bellingham must have been worried to say the least.'

He turned to Straker. 'But enough to want her dead? What do you think, Steve?'

Straker looked uncomfortable. 'I suppose it's possible. Susan Linton didn't have much ready money but the house itself must be worth quite lot.'

'I go along with that,' said Jack Meredith. 'Though we know Bellingham couldn't have murdered Linton herself. She was at a reunion party in London last Friday night, wasn't she?'

'But her boyfriend wasn't in London,' said Mark confidently.

'Boyfriend?' said Straker, scathingly.' What boyfriend?'

'He means Michael Bristow,' said Wakeman, suddenly taking an interest. 'That's right isn't it Becky. You've been doing some digging.'

'Yes, we believe they are in a relationship sir, said Becky. 'In fact, Bristow more or less admitted it this morning.'

'I see,' said Straker sarcastically. He more or less admitted it, did he?'

'I can explain,' said Mark.

They listened as he told them about Susan Linton's apartment in Marbella and of his conversation with the Community Office.

'All right,' said Rawlings. 'Let's accept for the moment that Linton and Bristow are in a relationship. Also that the two of them conspired to murder Susan Linton before she had time to change her will. It still leaves the problem of how Priestley fits into the jigsaw. It seems a remarkable co-incidence that he should just happen to turn up at Elleswood House on the very day that they decided to despatch Linton.'

Becky looked apprehensively at Mark. 'Actually, sir... we have a theory about that too.'

All eyes fixed on Mark Taverner

227

'Well, let's hear it, Taverner,' said Rawlings. 'Don't keep us all in the dark.'

Mark took his notebook from his briefcase and placed it in front of him. 'This is going to sound far-fetched sir, so I hope you'll bear with me.'

For the next ten minutes the meeting listened in silence as Mark delivered the hypothesis that he and Becky had worked on all the way back from Hammersmith.

'That's our theory, sir,' said Mark, addressing Rawlings directly as he concluded his exposition. 'We don't have all the answers as yet, of course.'

'No, of course not. But thank you, Taverner, and you two, Becky. Rawlings turned to Straker. 'A plausible hypothesis, Steve. Wouldn't you agree?'

Straker shook his head. 'You're forgetting one thing. The correspondence between Linton and Priestley goes back months. Long before Kate Bellingham had any reason to believe her inheritance was at risk.'

'And you're forgetting something else, Mark' said Jack Meredith. 'Fingerprints. Priestley's letters bear the actress's fingerprints, not Bellingham's. As do her letters to Priestley.'

'Do they?' said Mark. 'I knew the earlier letters bore Susan Linton's fingerprints, as well as Priestley's. I haven't heard anything yet about the later ones.'

Meredith took out his mobile. 'Give me a moment. I'll check.'

Rawlings turned to Straker. 'Does Bristow have an alibi for last Friday evening?'

'He said he went to the cinema.' said Straker. 'To the early evening showing. He showed us his admission ticket to prove it.'

'It doesn't mean he stayed to watch the film.'

They waited while Jack Meredith ended his phone call and returned to the table.

'Mark, I owe you an apology. Only those letters exchanged between the 27th July and the 1st September last year bear Susan Linton's fingerprints. After that date the only prints we could find on any of the letters are Priestley's.'

'Not Susan Linton's? ' said Rawlings.

'No, and not Kate Bellingham's either.'

Wakeman looked scornfully at Mark. 'So, what do you make of that, Taverner?'

Mark didn't answer.

Becky turned towards Straker 'To answer your query, sir, we think that initially Susan Linton and Kate Bellingham probably worked together - Susan Linton composing the letters to Priestley and Bellingham doing the actual writing.'

'To what end?' said Straker, looking puzzled.

'To persuade him to send money. We're not suggesting that Bellingham had it in her mind to kill Linton back then. Last year their main concern was lack of money. Priestley had already sent £1,000 following the feature on Breakfast Television. We think they were simply trying to tap him for more.'

'But then, in September, we think Miss Linton backed off,' said Mark.

'Backed off? Why?' said Straker

'Well, they weren't having much success, were they?' said Becky. 'Between April and September last year they had written Priestley four letters, without receiving a penny in return? Maybe by then they had come to the conclusion that they were flogging a dead horse.'

'But Kate Bellingham decided to keep on writing. Is that what you're saying?'

Becky nodded. 'Yes, sir. but not immediately. After the letter dated the 5th September there was a break in the correspondence of four months. Then, in early January this year it resumed. Priestley received another letter, once again begging for money. Only this time on the grounds that she was being blackmailed by her former husband.'

Rawlings nodded. 'Early January. About the same time as the big fall out with Susan Linton.'

'Exactly.' said Becky. 'And this letter was followed more letters in quick succession always demanding money and each letter more insistent and threatening than the previous one.'

'You mean that, by this time, it wasn't really the money they were after. They wanted to provoke Priestley, drive him into a frenzy.'

'That's out theory, sir, yes'

'No, I don't buy this at all, 'said Wakeman. 'What if Priestley failed to turn up that night and had an alibi to prove it?'

Becky looked confidently back at Wakeman. 'Then it would look like a random break in. The glass in the back door was smashed, remember. Although, when you think about it, they did their best to make sure Priestley did turn up that night. He says he received two phone calls in the week before the murder telling him to come to the house on Friday the 6th April, no earlier than 7.30pm. Very precise instructions, wouldn't you say?'

Wakeman snorted dismissively. 'Well, we can soon check whether your theory holds water. We can get a handwriting expert to compare the handwriting in the will with the letters found in Priestley's flat.'

'We can,' said Meredith. 'Though I suspect the CPS will want more than the evidence of a handwriting expert.'

'True.' said Rawlings. 'We'll need some hard evidence as well. Or a confession. Otherwise, we could end up the same situation as we are with Priestley.' He sighed. 'But thank you, Taverner. And you too Becky. You've given us a great deal to think about.'

X.

As Becky left his office, Straker leaned forward with his head in his hands. Kate Bellingham a murderer. Two days ago he would have poured scorn on such a notion. Not any more. After all, two days ago he wouldn't have believed that someone as sophisticated and elegant as Kate Bellingham would be prepared to share a bed with a grubby little worm like Michael Bristow. Did she really conspire to murder Susan Linton? Far-fetched as it seemed, he couldn't ignore the fact that this new hypothesis dovetailed perfectly with Priestley's own account.

He would keep it low key to begin with. Becky and Mark Taverner would call on Kate Bellingham first thing tomorrow. No issue of a caution. Just an informal interview to tell her about the change of will and observe her reaction. But, sooner or later, he knew he would have to confront her and challenge her about the authenticity of the letters. And should she fail to come up with convincing answers, it would be his job to place her under arrest and remand her in custody on suspicion of conspiracy to murder.

'The Priestley brothers have left the building, Steve.'

231

Straker looked up to see Kevyn Wakeman standing at the door.

'I don't care for the position it puts us in. Do you?'

'Us? said Straker. 'I don't understand.'

Closing the door Wakeman came in and sat down. 'For a start, we could be facing an independent police enquiry. David Priestley has already said he won't be content with just suing the Herald. He's convinced someone in the team was feeding them information.'

'Yes, he did make that pretty clear.'

'Well, just to put your mind at rest, Steve. It wasn't Becky who talked to the Herald. It was me.'

Straker stared at his deputy. 'You? Are you saying it was you who leaked all that stuff about Priestley?'

'Not all of it, no. In fact, not even most of it. But I did talk briefly to a journalist on Tuesday evening. Someone I thought I could trust.'

'What did you tell him, for God's sake?

'Only that we regarded Priestley as a significant witness. Which he was, and still is as far as I'm concerned. As for the rest, they must have got it from other sources.'

'Wait a minute, Kevyn. You are now admitting that you told the Herald as far back as Tuesday, that Priestley was a significant witness, Why on earth did you do that? It's tantamount to saying that we'd identified the killer and weren't looking for anyone else.'

'Well, we're not looking for anyone else as far as I'm concerned. You don't go along with all that stuff that Becky and Taverner came up with just now, do you?'

Straker sighed. 'I don't know. I didn't at first. But the more I think about it, the more plausible it seems. And it fits Priestley's story exactly, doesn't it..'

'Come on, Steve, it's too clever by half. Besides, it's not in your interest for their theory to gain traction, is it?.'

'Not in my interest? I don't understand.'

'Think about it, Steve. Kate Bellingham isn't going to appreciate being accused of conspiracy to murder, is she?' Wakeman grinned. 'Especially by someone she's come to regard as an intimate friend.'

'I don't know what you're talking about.' Straker felt his face starting to burn.

'Yes, you do. You must know that if you lean too hard on Kate Bellingham, she could make life pretty uncomfortable for you all round.'

'I'm not sure what you're implying, Kevyn, but whatever it is, you had better come out with it straight.'

'Wakeman, looked steadily at Straker. 'Okay. You remember, two days ago, when I tried to contact you about finding Priestley's camper van.'

'Go on.'

'Well, since you weren't answering your mobile, I decided drive out and give you the news in person.'

Straker looked at Wakeman with suspicion. 'You mean you actually drove out to Kate Bellingham's cottage. If you weren't able to contact me on my mobile, why didn't you call me on Miss Bellingham's landline?'

'Yes, now you mention it, I suppose I could have done that. But it didn't occur to me at the time. All I could think about was that there had been a major development and our senior investigating officer, for some reason had decided to put himself out of contact. So, I drove out to Kate Bellingham's cottage and, sure enough, there was your car still parked outside. I didn't come to the door immediately. I decided to have one more go at ringing your mobile,

233

but again, no luck. So, I came to the front door and was just about to ring the bell when I observed through the window that you weren't in the lounge. Strange, I thought. maybe they're in the kitchen. Maybe I should go round to the back door. But no, you weren't in the kitchen either. It was then that I noticed the bedroom curtains were drawn. Not completely. There was a small gap ...'

'Okay, Kevyn,' said Straker, quietly. 'You can spare me the rest. So, you came to spy on me. If this is blackmail, at least come to your point.'

Wakeman gave him a look of innocent surprise. 'Steve, you and I are mates. We look out for one another. All I was going to say was that I think it would be best if I handled any interviews with Bellingham tomorrow, and you stayed well clear.'

'But I've already asked Becky to do the initial interview. I can't cancel her a second time.'

'Becky Reedman?'

'Yes, at Miss Bellingham's cottage. I thought it best to take things gently. See how she reacts to the news that she'd been cut out of the will. Then take things from there.'

'And who do you plan to send with her?

'DC Taverner. They seem to work well together.'

Wakeman shook his head.' You're taking a big risk, Steve. That's all I can say.'

'Then what do you suggest?'

'Let me go in Taverner's place. Becky can still do the interview, if you prefer it that way, but I can step in if Bellingham starts cutting up rough.'

'How do you mean?

Wakeman grinned. 'The usual method. Begin by putting the frighteners on her. Warn her that the police don't take kindly to having wild and unsubstantiated allegations thrown at them and she would do well to button her lip.'

Straker looked warily at Wakeman. 'Why are you offering to do this for me, Kevyn?

'I've told you. We're a team. Besides, I might need your help one day. I mean, if Paul Priestley walks free and David Priestley decides to have a go at us. Not that I'm expecting it, but you never know, do you?'

xi.

Switching off his computer Straker picked up his briefcase. Emily would be at rehearsal again tonight, so he would have the house to himself. Which was what he needed, because his head was still reeling. He checked his watch. 5.10pm. If he drove straight home now she would still be there. Better stop off for a pint so he wouldn't have to face her. By the time she got back, he could be in bed, pretending to be asleep.

Twenty minutes into his journey he pulled into a lay-by and switched off the engine. Too early. The pub didn't open for another half hour. Tilting the seat, he lay back and closed his eyes. It was the consultation. Everything stemmed from that bloody consultation - his loss of confidence, his mood swings, his withdrawal into himself. Because Donaldson didn't mince his words. *You have an exceptionally low sperm count, Mr Straker.* How was he supposed to react to such news? It was all very well Emily saying it didn't matter and that they would find a way through. There wasn't a way through. At least, not a way that he could accept.

235

Then, along came Kate Bellingham. Sure, she was good looking and well turned out for her age, but not especially so. Certainly not at that first interview when her mascara was smudged with tears. So, what was it about this forty eight year old woman that he found so irresistible? She had seduced him, deliberately, he could see that now. Lured him to her cottage, not once but twice. Then flattered him, got him to talk about himself and the problems in his marriage. Finally, took him to her bedroom and her bed. Wakeman was right. He was no Brad Pitt. There had to be a reason.

He was about to set off again when he saw a grey BMW approaching that looked familiar. It was Dan Masterson's car, with Masterson at the wheel. And sitting beside him was a female passenger who also looked familiar. Within twenty seconds he had swung the car round and was speeding back the way he had come until he had the BMW in his sights. Then, keeping a safe distance, he followed it through Princes Risborough and on towards Kimble. Unless he was very much mistaken, that was Emily in the car.

The BMW signalled to turn right. Straker followed on the narrow, winding road to Cadsden. Masterson continued on past the pub to the top of the hill and turned left into the National Trust car park. Driving thirty yards past the entrance, Straker pulled on to the grass verge and walked back in time to see Masterson and Emily, hand in hand, take the path into the woods at the far end of the car park. Quickening his pace he followed, but soon they were lost from sight as the path wove its way through the trees and down the hill. After about two hundred yards he came to a fork. There was no point in continuing as they could have gone either way. But nor could he give up and return to his car. Walking over to a large tree about thirty yards to the left of the fork he positioned himself behind the trunk and crouched down. With the rehearsal due to start at 7.00pm, he knew he wouldn't have to wait long

After about fifteen minutes he heard their voices before they came into view. They seemed to be in animated conversation, with Emily doing most of the talking. Then he saw them, still hand in hand, walking back to the car. He waited until they were well past before coming round from behind the tree and following. As they reached the edge of the car park, they stopped and Masterson put his arm round her. Then the two of them crossed the car park to his car. Here they stopped again. This time Masterson took Emily into his arms and held her. They didn't kiss, but it was a long embrace. A minute later they were gone.

Returning to his car Straker drove back down the hill to the main road and on to Saunderton where he turned in at the Rose and Crown. For the next two hours he sat there, brooding on what he had just witnessed. By 8.30pm, with the tables filling, he decided to drive home and confront Emily with what he had seen. But, by the time he pulled into the drive he knew he couldn't face her. He would go to bed and when she returned he would pretend to be asleep.

At just after 11.00pm he heard her key in the door. He listened as she walked into the kitchen, then came out again and began turning off the downstairs lights. Now she was coming up the stairs. The bedroom light was off and she didn't come in, but went straight to the bathroom. Ten minutes later she crept into the bedroom, slipped on her nightdress in the dark and climbed into bed, sliding her foot briefly down his calf as she snuggled under the duvet. He didn't respond.

Fifteen minutes later her rhythmic breathing told him she was asleep.

Two nights ago she had assured him that, much as she liked Dan Masterson, she wasn't attracted to him. Two nights ago she had assured him that she had never once been unfaithful to him and nor would she be, ever. Two nights ago he believed her. So, what was she doing in the woods today with Dan Masterson? What was it that she was confiding to him that he felt the need to take her in his arms and hold her for so long? After what he'd witnessed today, could he ever be confident again that she was telling him the truth?

Chapter Eight

Saturday,14th April 2012

i.

Becky sensed a renewed buzz of excitement around the incident room as she prepared for her10.00am appointment with Kate Bellingham. Overnight, photocopies of Susan Linton's letters to Paul Priestley had been emailed to a former colleague of Jack Meredith, retired forensic graphologist, Derek Glenton. Early this morning Susan Linton's new will had been biked over from Harwood and James's offices in Hammersmith and a photocopy of the page containing her signature, address and date was also emailed to Glenton. His verdict, received thirty minutes later, was unequivocal. The person who wrote and signed the letters found in Paul Priestley's flat was definitely not the person who had signed, addressed and dated Susan Linton's will on Monday the 16th January, 2012.

'Ready to go Becks?'

It was Kevyn Wakeman standing over her.

'Almost. I'm just waiting for Mark.' She flinched as she felt his hands rest lightly on her shoulders. 'Actually I haven't seen him yet this morning. I sent him a message, but he hasn't answered.'

'Probably because he's on the move. Change of plan, Becks. We've sent Taverner over to Wembley to keep Michael Bristow company while we search his property.'

'Then who's coming with me to interview Kate Bellingham?'

'It's your lucky day. You've got me.'

She rose angrily. 'But, why the change of plan? It's only a preliminary interview. It's not as if we're interviewing the woman under caution.'

'No, but we soon might be. Come on. We don't want to keep the lady waiting '

Still angry, Becky followed Wakeman down to the car park.

'But why you?' she said as they reached her car. 'Has the boss decided I'm not experienced enough to handle things without a more senior officer to hold my hand?'

'It's not like that, Becks. But you haven't met the lady yet, have you? I tell you, she's a slippery customer. Don't fret though. It's your show. I won't interfere.'

With a sigh of resignation, Becky unlocked the car and climbed in.

Tell you what,' he said, climbing in beside her. 'Get her to admit to writing the letters and we'll go out to tonight to celebrate.'

Becky didn't answer, concentrating instead on fastening her seat belt.

'On second thoughts, we'll go out anyway.'

She turned to reverse out of her parking space. 'Thanks Kevyn, but I'm already booked for tonight.'

'Tomorrow then.'

'Sorry, I can't. The thing is, I'm seeing somebody.'

Silenced by this, they were approaching Wendover when he spoke again. 'Not Mark Taverner, I hope.'

Becky gave a non committal shrug.

He touched her lightly on the knee. 'Come on Becks, you can do better than that. He's not in your league. You've only got to look at the man.'

240

Again Becky didn't answer.

'Anyway, it was Straker's decision to send Taverner to Wembley this morning, not mine. '

Becky paused at the pedestrian crossing on Wendover high street, 'You don't think much of this hypothesis of ours, do you Kevyn?'

'No, not a lot. I think Bellingham may have written the letters on Linton's behalf. But I don't go for your theory that they framed Priestley for the murder.'

Arriving at the cottage, Becky drew in to the side of the road and switched off the engine. Now she turned to face him.' It was you who leaked all that stuff to the Herald, wasn't it?'

He looked at her warily. 'Me? What makes you think that?'

'It was obvious. When I saw the report in the Herald on Wednesday morning I couldn't believe what I was reading. It was all there. Everything I told you over the phone...'

Wakeman smiled. 'Steady, Becks. You're getting carried away.'

'Everything I said, chapter and verse, even down to the nickname I coined for Priestley. *Mr Walrus.* You even gave them that, didn't you. And then, to cap it all, you let me take the blame. That's the bit I can't get my head round. One minute you're asking me out, the next you're letting me take the blame for something I didn't do.'

He put up a hand. 'Hold it, Becky. You're not being fair. Yes, it's true that I gave an off the record briefing to a journalist on Tuesday night, but I certainly didn't give him 'chapter and verse,' as you put it. Most of what you read, they must have picked up elsewhere.'

'Did you tell Straker that?'

'Of course.'

'When.'

241

'Yesterday.'

'Yesterday? You mean you waited while half the team were hauled in and given the third degree, before admitting it was you all the time.'

Wakeman sighed wearily. 'It wasn't like that, Becks.'

'What's that supposed to mean?'

'Yes, it's true I spoke to a journalist on Tuesday night. But only briefly. All I told him was that Priestley was a significant witness.'

'On Tuesday? Before we had even interviewed the man? '

'The truth is, Becks, I was being hassled. What happened was that this journalist rang just after I'd talked to you and asked if there was anything we could add to what we'd said in the news release. I said I hadn't seen the press release, but no, there wasn't. So then he started to have a go. He wanted to know about Straker and whether he was really up to the job. Not just him. All of us, the whole team. We'd been at this investigation for four days, he said, and as far as he could tell we still had nothing to show for it. Who was Paul Priestley? Was he a suspect or wasn't he? More to the point, was he dangerous? Okay, I went so far as to say he was a significant witness and we were keen to trace him. But that's all. I had to give him something, Becks. I had to let him know we were making progress.'

'Then, why didn't you tell Straker all this on Wednesday morning, before he started interviewing everyone?'

'You're right. I should have done. I realise that now. But when I saw Wednesday's paper, containing so much more detail than I'd given, I assumed someone else must have been talking. Not you, but maybe someone in the admin team. All I said was that

242

Priestley was a significant witness. As for the rest, it didn't come from me.'

'Not even *Mr Walrus*?'

Wakeman hesitated. 'I may have used that nickname. But that's hardly significant, surely.'

'Except that you waited until yesterday before mentioning any of this to Straker.'

'Not true. I talked to Straker on Wednesday night, just as I promised. I told him you were upset and he should apologise. Which he did, didn't he?'

For a few moments Becky, was silent. Then she looked at her watch 'We're late, Kevyn. We'd better go in.'

ii.

Kate Bellingham opened the door before they had time to press the bell. She looked at them sourly. 'I thought our appointment was for 10.00am.'

'It was. Sorry to have kept you waiting,' said Wakeman as they followed her into her sitting room. 'We'll make this as short as we can.' He smiled. 'Detective Sergeant Kevyn Wakeman. We met a week ago, remember. And this is my colleague, Detective Constable Becky Reedman.'

Kate Bellingham looked crossly at Wakeman, then at Becky. 'I thought I would be seeing Inspector Straker this morning.'

'I'm afraid he is on other business,' said Wakeman, moving towards the fireplace.

'I see.' She sat down and gestured for them to do likewise. 'Perhaps you could start by telling me what this is all about. I've already told Inspector Straker everything I know.'

'We just want to go over a few details, Miss Bellingham.' said Becky, determined not to let Wakeman take over before they had even begun. 'I'm sure it won't take long.' Opening her briefcase, she took out her notebook. 'Do you mind telling us again how the mail was dealt with when you were looking after Miss Linton?'

Kate Bellingham gave a weary sigh. 'I dealt with it. I brought it in from the mail box when I arrived in the morning and I posted any letters that needed posting on my way home in the evening.'

'But you've said previously that you only dealt with items such as bills etc. You didn't help Miss Linton with her fan mail.'

'No. At least, not since her accident. Susan was very protective of her fan mail.'

'So, she answered fan mail herself, but gave the letters to you to post.'

'No. To my knowledge she never answered any letters she received. Certainly she never gave me any to post.'

'What about the letter from Paul Priestley in March 2011? The one accompanying the cheque for £1,000. Did she deal with that herself?'

Kate Bellingham paused for a moment as if sensing a trap. 'No, I helped her with that letter. Susan had to show it to me because she needed me to bank the cheque.'

'And did she write back acknowledging the gift, or did you?'

'As I remember it, we wrote the letter together. She dictated, I typed. I have a laptop that I use for business correspondence.'

'But she signed the letter.'

244

'She must have done. I don't actually remember. In the old days we had a stamp for her signature, but that disappeared long ago.'

Opening her folder Becky took out photocopies of the letters found in Priestley's flat. 'You are aware, I believe, that since receiving that cheque for £1,000, Miss Linton was in frequent correspondence with Mr Priestley.'

Kate Bellingham nodded. 'Yes, the news came as quite a shock. According to Inspector Straker the two of them were exchanging letters every few days. Yet, I was completely unaware.'

'I suppose she could have retrieved letters from the mailbox before your arrival.'

'She could and occasionally she did. In fact in first year after her accident, when she was still having regular physiotherapy, she could even walk as far as the post box at the crossroads, using her walking frame. '

Wakeman leaned forward. 'Miss Bellingham. Did Inspector Straker tell you anything about the nature of the correspondence between Miss Linton and Mr Priestley?'

'A little. He didn't go into detail.'

Wakeman turned to Becky. 'Then you might like to give Miss Bellingham a flavour, Becky. It would be interesting to have her comments.'

Irritated at Wakeman's intervention, Becky picked out half a dozen of Susan Linton's more recent letters to Paul Priestley and began to read extracts from them. Kate Bellingham listened in silence, registering no reaction. It was only when she came to the last three letters with their cruel jibes and barely veiled threats that her eyes started to fill with tears.

'All I can say,' she said, dabbing her eyes with a handkerchief, 'is that this isn't at all the Susan I knew for thirty years. The only explanation I can give you is that she was deeply depressed when she wrote them. As I told Inspector Straker, Susan had become increasingly withdrawn and secretive over the past year. And hostile. Not just towards me, but also towards Michael Bristow, even though he had been her agent and friend for almost as long as she had known me.'

'So we gather, Miss Bellingham' said Wakeman. 'Hostile to the point of accusing you both of stealing from her.'

Kate Bellingham looked startled.

'She called the two of you to a meeting on the 2nd January this year. Isn't that so? 'Wakeman took one of the letters from Becky and held it out to her. 'Let me ask you something, Miss Bellingham. 'Do you recognise this as Susan Linton's handwriting?'

Kate Bellingham barely looked at the letter. 'I would say so, yes.'

'Are you quite sure?'

'As sure as I can be. Why do you ask?'

'You see. We were as puzzled as you that that she was able to get to the post box without assistance.'

'I don't see...'

'It occurred to us that maybe you wrote the letters for Miss Linton. Just as you typed the letter thanking Mr Priestley for the cheque.'

'I'm sorry. I don't understand what you're saying.'

'You see, we do have one sample of Miss Linton's handwriting that we know to be authentic.' Wakeman took the folder Becky was holding and withdrew a single sheet. 'This is a photocopy of the last page of Susan Linton's will, containing her signature, her address and the date, all handwritten by her. Not a large sample, but sufficient for a comparison, wouldn't you say? Here, take a look.'

Kate Bellingham's hands were noticeably trembling now as she took a pair of glasses from her bag and put them on to study the photocopy.

'Not the quite same, is it, Miss Bellingham? In fact, not the same at all.'

Kate Bellingham looked pale. 'You have to remember that Susan made this will a long time ago. Shortly after her accident, in fact. So I'm not surprised if the handwriting is somewhat different.'

'Ah, but this isn't from her old will,' said Wakeman. 'It's from her new will, the one she made on the 16th January this year. A few days in fact, after that rather unpleasant meeting you had with her when she accused you and Mr Bristow of stealing from her.'

'Her new will?' She stared back at him in astonishment. 'Are you telling me Susan made a new will?'

'That's exactly what I am telling you.' Wakeman now took a full copy of the new will from the folder and handed it to her. 'We had it biked over from her solicitor this morning. Yes, following that meeting on the 2nd January, Miss Linton decided to leave her entire estate to Stoke Mandeville Hospital.'

Kate Bellingham stared at Wakeman in bewilderment. 'But that's not possible...'.

'I'm afraid it is.' said Wakeman. 'Check for yourself.'

Grabbing the document she began flicking backwards and forwards through the pages.

'Page two, paragraphs three and four,' said Wakeman. 'I've marked the relevant sections.'

Turning to the page Kate Bellingham examined the document for several seconds before letting out a long howl of despair. 'After all I'd done for her!.....all those years of caring for her.... how could she be so cruel...' She turned away, her body heaving with her sobs.

'Did you write those letters to Paul Priestley, Miss Bellingham?' said Wakeman sharply.

She stared at him through her tears .

'Because we think you did. We think you wrote every one of them, pretending to be Susan Linton. Didn't you?'

Angrily, Kate Bellingham rose to her feet. 'I don't have to listen to this. You come to my house on the pretext of wanting to clear up some minor details, and then you make this absurd accusation.' She stared angrily at Becky, then again at Wakeman. 'Leave my house now, both of you. I refuse to be insulted like this. Leave my house at once!'

'So you refuse to answer my question...'.

'LEAVE MY HOUSE NOW!... or I'm warning you, I shall file a complaint. In fact I will file a complaint. I demand to speak to Inspector Straker who, unlike you, is a gentleman.'

Five minutes later Becky and Kevyn Wakeman were back in the car, driving towards Aylesbury.

'Well, thank you for that,' said Becky . 'Although I thought I was supposed to be leading the interview.'

'And so you did, Becks. I just thought we needed to move things along a bit' He grinned. 'You don't look happy.'

'I'm not.'

'I see. I suppose you would have preferred to have DC Taverner sitting alongside you.'

'At least we'd still be there instead of being thrown out on our ears.'

'Yes, but just wasting her time and ours. Okay we've done it Straker's way. Now I think even he will agree that it's time to bring her in.'

248

Straker was in conversation with Jack Meredith when Becky and Wakeman arrived at his office. Becky looked tense and angry.

'Well? How did it go?'

'Badly,' said Becky. 'She blew us out.'

'But we got her rattled, didn't we, Becks?' said Wakeman. 'Time to bring her in, I think.'

'You told her about the new will?'

'We did. We also confronted her with the discrepancy in the handwriting.'

'What did she say?'

'News of the new will took her completely by surprise,' said Becky. 'In fact she broke down when we told her. As for the letters she didn't admit to writing them, but nor did she deny it. That was when she blew us out.'

'She'll have to admit it sooner or later,' said Wakeman. 'We've got the opinion of an expert witness. I think we should arrest her now, Steve and question her under caution'

'On what grounds?'

Wakeman shrugged. 'Obtaining money by deception. Demanding money with menaces. Either will do.'

'I'm afraid that forensic graphology is a very uncertain science,' said Meredith. 'Some judges even refuse to accept it in evidence.'

'I know that,' replied Wakeman. 'But this isn't to get her in front of a judge. At least, not yet.'

Straker looked uneasy. 'I suppose we should bring her in. But you'll continue to question her, will you Kevyn?'

'I thought you gave that job to me,' said Becky petulantly.

'Yes, I'm sure Becky can take care of Miss Bellingham,' said Wakeman. 'I'll just sit in again.' He gave Straker a sly smile. 'Unless, of course, you would care to take over.'

'No. You started, so you may as well finish the job. Okay, bring her in.'

As Becky and Wakeman left, Straker felt beads of sweat forming on his brow. It wasn't so much what Kate Bellingham might say under the strain of an interrogation,. Accusations of sexual harassment against the police were common, and rarely followed up. He was more worried about what Wakeman might say when, over a few beers, he chose to describe his indispensible role in bringing the perpetrators to justice.

His phone rang.

'Straker.'

'I thought you were my friend.'

He recognised her voice at once. 'Where are you?'

'At home. Where should I be? Why did you let that animal loose on me, Steve? Haven't I done all I can to help you with your investigation?'

Straker closed his eyes. 'Yes. of course, you've been most cooperative. But DS Wakeman is an experienced police officer. I hope he didn't behave disrespectfully towards you.'

'He's just accused me of writing all those letters to Priestley. He has no grounds for making such an allegation.'

Straker hesitated. 'I'm sorry, but unless you are accusing him of misconduct, I'm afraid it would be improper for me to interfere.'

For a moment she was silent. *'I see. So you and I are not my friend any more. Is that what you are telling me?'*

'All I can say is that DI Wakeman had good reason to question you about the letters. Before coming to see you we sought the opinion of a forensic handwriting expert.'

'So he told me. Steve, if anyone is going to interview me, I want it to be you. Tell me one thing. Am I about to be arrested?'

'I'm sorry, but I can't answer a question like that.'

'Then should I be talking to a lawyer?'

'I think it would be wise to be prepared, yes.'

'If I'm going to be arrested, Steve, I want you there. Do I make myself clear?'

'Perfectly. I'm sorry, but I'm afraid my hands are tied.'

'Very well. But I'm counting on you, Steve. Remember that. I'm counting on you as my friend. Don't make me your enemy.'

iv.

Becky watched at the observation panel as Kate Bellingham and her solicitor were shown into the interview suite. She had changed out of the blouse and jeans she was wearing earlier and was now immaculately turned out in a neat, navy blue suit. She looked remarkably calm and relaxed for someone who had just been arrested.

Her mobile rang. It was Mark

'Hi, Becky. Sorry not to have responded to your messages, but I was on the road. Wakeman told you about the change of plan, did he?'

'He did. How's it going with Bristow?'

'Not as well as I was hoping.'

'Why? Was he uncooperative?'

'Not at all. He was most accommodating, almost as if he was expecting us. He baulked a bit at having to hand over his car keys as well as the keys to his office and house. But, on the whole, he seemed surprisingly unfazed. I drove him to Wembley Police Station while Meredith and his team began their search.'

'What reason did you give him for the search warrant?'

'I said we were looking into Susan Linton's financial affairs and we'd found some discrepancies in the portfolio that we were following up. I didn't let on that the search had anything to do with the murder investigation.'

'And he didn't object to handing over the keys to his car?'

'He did a bit. But Jack Meredith is a persuasive guy. He said he could have them back within the hour. Then I stayed with him at Wembley Police Station and we chatted until it was time to take him home.'

'Did you say anything about Susan Linton's new will?

'I did. I told him that Susan Linton had made a new will leaving her entire estate to Stoke Mandeville Hospital.'

'And how did he react?'

'Hardly at all. Just a shrug of the shoulders, as though it meant nothing to him. I took it as a bad sign.'

'Not necessarily. Kevyn Wakeman and I were with Kate Bellingham until about 10.30am. She could have telephoned him after we left to warn him we were on the trail.'

'So, how did Kate Bellingham react to the news?'

'Genuine shock. In fact she was almost hysterical.'

'But you haven't arrested her?

'We have now. We've just brought her in on suspicion of obtaining money by deception. I'm about to interview her again.'

'Sorry I'm not there. Who's doing it with you?'

'Kevyn Wakeman, worst luck. He keeps wanting to taking over. Sorry, I have to go, Mark. That's him coming to join me now. Maybe you should brief him before we have another go at Bellingham.'

Handing the phone to Wakeman, she waited while he took the call. She could tell from his expression that he didn't think much of their hypothesis, but there was nothing to be done about it. Obviously Straker had decided that Wakeman should sit in on the interviews, so she would just have to make the best of it.

'Okay, Becks,' said Wakeman, ending the call. 'Let's see how the lady reacts to being interviewed under caution.'

v.

As they entered the interview suite Kate Bellingham barely looked at them but her solicitor rose immediately to greet them.

'Good morning. David McBride. I'm acting for Miss Bellingham.'

253

'Have you had sufficient time to brief your solicitor, Miss Bellingham?' said Wakeman as they sat down.

'We're fine,' said McBride. 'Miss Bellingham has explained everything. I think we should be able to clear things up quite quickly.'

Becky switched on the video recorder. 'Interview with Kate Bellingham at 11.45am on Saturday the 14th April, 2012 in the presence of Miss Bellingham's solicitor, David McBride. Miss Bellingham, you have been arrested on suspicion of obtaining money by deception. I am now going to caution you. You do not have to say anything. But it may harm your defence if you do not mention when questioned something which you later rely on in court. Anything you do say may be given in evidence.'

Taking from her folder copies of the handwritten letters to Priestley she placed them on the table in front of her. 'We asked you earlier, Miss Bellingham whether you recognised the handwriting of these letter's as Susan Linton's. You said then that you did. Is that still the case?'

Kate Bellingham looked straight at Becky. 'I want to clarify what I said earlier. Susan didn't write those letters to Paul Priestley. I wrote them. It was stupid of me to deny it earlier.'

'You mean, you wrote all of them?' said Becky, taken aback by this unexpected admission.

'Yes. All of them. The truth is that, after receiving that gift of £1,000 from Mr Priestley, Susan came up with this idea of developing the correspondence. Her motive wasn't very honourable, I'm sorry to say. It was in the hope of persuading him to send more money.'

'So, you wrote the letters on Miss Linton's behalf.'

'Exactly. You see, following her accident, Susan found writing quite tiring. So she asked me to write

254

the letters for her. At first, I said I wanted nothing to do with her little scheme, but eventually I gave in.'

'Did she leave you to write the letters independently, or was she involved too?'

'Oh, yes. Susan was totally involved. She dictated the letters. I acted merely as scribe. I'm very ashamed now of what I did but, as I say, Susan was my closest friend. I couldn't refuse her.'

Becky looked down at her notes. Where did she go from here? This wasn't at all the answer she had been expecting.

'Was it true that George Mannering was blackmailing his ex-wife?' said Wakeman. 'Or did she make that up to try and extract money from him.'

'She made that up, I'm afraid. You see, by September of last year she was starting to get frustrated that the correspondence wasn't producing the results she had been hoping for. By this time, Mr Priestley had told us quite a bit about himself. For example, that he didn't have much money of his own, though his mother was wealthy and supported him a good deal.' Taking a handkerchief from her sleeve Kate Bellingham dabbed her eyes delicately. 'I tried to talk her out of it, telling her that what she was doing was immoral at the very least. But she was adamant.'

'So, she decided to put the pressure on,' continued Wakeman. 'Is that what you are saying?'

Kate Bellingham nodded.

'And this was around January of this year.'

'I don't remember exactly when it was.'

'And it was about this time that you asked for the letters to be delivered by hand?'

She shook her head. 'No, that was Paul's idea. He told us that since he was having to get the money from cash machines, he preferred to deliver it by hand, for fear of it getting lost in the post.'

'Why didn't you ask him deliver it to the door?' said Becky, 'so Miss Linton could thank him personally.'

Kate Bellingham hesitated before answering. 'Susan never wanted people to see her in her crippled state. Particularly former fans.'

'Really?' said Wakeman. 'Even though, a few months earlier, she made an appearance on Breakfast Television?'

'Yes, well, Susan was a very complex person. Besides, Mr Priestley never expressed a wish to meet Susan personally.'

'So, what did you do with the money that Priestley delivered?' said Becky. '£3,000 in total. Did you bank it?'

She shook her head. 'No. She didn't want me to bank it.'

'Why not?'

'I suppose she didn't want anyone to know about the begging letters. Particularly Mr Bristow. He would review the bank statements from time to time and he would have noticed a large amount like that.'

'I see.' continued Becky. 'So, where is that money now?'

'I don't actually know. I suppose we must have spent it quite a lot of it. If there is any over, I assume it is somewhere in the house, because Susan held on to it. She didn't ask me to look after it for her.'

'We've done a thorough search of the house,' said Becky, 'and we found no bundles of cash.'

Kate Bellingham gave a dismissive shrug. 'Then I can't help you I'm afraid.'

Wakeman leaned forward aggressively. 'Earlier this week, Miss Bellingham, you told us that you saw a man in a camper van delivering packages to Miss Linton's mailbox. Are you now saying you knew who he was all the time?'

256

For the first time Kate Bellingham began to look nervous. 'Yes, we knew it was Paul Priestley, of course. I'm sorry. I suppose when I was asked earlier, I was just trying to protect myself.'

Wakeman studied Kate Bellingham for a few moments. 'Since you were involved in writing the letters, Miss Bellingham, I assume that you also had sight of Priestley's replies?'

She hesitated, as if sensing a trap. 'Of course. We read his letters together.'

Opening the folder he took out the fingerprints report. 'Because there is something very odd about Mr Priestley's letters. The first four, the ones dated between the 30th July and the 1st September last year, all bear Miss Linton's fingerprints.'

'Really. I don't find that odd.'

'No, and nor do we. What we find odd is that we found none of Susan Linton's fingerprints on any of the later letters. I'm talking now about the letters written between the 9th January and Mr Priestley's final letter to Miss Linton, which is dated the 17th March this year. Can you suggest an explanation for that?

Kate Bellingham was silent for several seconds. 'Yes, I can explain that. By this time, even Susan was starting to feel ashamed of what we were doing. When I brought the mail in from the mail box each morning, she asked me to open anything from Priestley and just read it out to her. I suppose she didn't want to get her hands dirty, so to speak.'

'So she didn't handle the letters. She asked you to read them to her instead.'

'Yes.'

Wakeman smiled. 'In which case, we would expect to find your fingerprints rather than hers on those later letters from Priestley. Yet, oddly, we didn't. In fact, we

257

didn't find your fingerprints on any of letters, Miss Bellingham. Can you explain that?'

Kate Bellingham turned towards Becky and smiled. 'Some things are only odd to a man, I think. Yes I can explain why you didn't find my fingerprints on the letters. I always wore disposable household gloves in the mornings while I was dealing with Susan and getting her ready for the day.'

Wakeman looked sceptical. 'Even when dealing with Miss Linton's mail?'

'Yes, until I had finished all the chores. The gloves are quite thin. You tend to forget you are wearing them.'

'So, you also wore disposable gloves to write the letters to Paul Priestley?' said Becky.

'Is this line of questioning really relevant?' said McBride, suddenly interjecting, 'We do seem to be dancing on the head of a pin.'

'It's very relevant' said Becky sharply. 'Because I'm going to suggest a more plausible reason why none of Priestley's later letters bear Miss Linton's fingerprints.'

'And what is that?' said McBride.

'Because she never saw them. Because from January of this year she was totally unaware that you were continuing the correspondence in her name.'

'I don't understand,' said Kate Bellingham haughtily.

'Then let me put it more plainly,' said Becky. 'It's our contention that after the first few letters, Miss Linton decided to call it a day. She realised that in spite of all the hints about being short of money, Priestley was not going to play ball. But you decided that you would continue writing to Priestley without her knowledge. You thought you would try other ways of getting money out of him. Like inventing the story that George Mannering was blackmailing you and demanding £5,000....'

Tears began to welled in Kate Bellingham's eyes. 'I totally refute that accusation....'

'But you only got £3,000 out of him, didn't you? Where is that money now Miss Bellingham? In your own bank account? Or have you spent it?'

Now she began to cry. 'Everything I have told you today is the absolute truth! I loved Susan. She was my closest friend. I still love her, in spite of everything....'

'All right, we'll take a short break there ,' said Becky, switching off the video recorder. 'Resume in half an hour.'

vi.

David Priestley stood at the window. Where was he? Had he got lost? There were two vacant parking spaces down there at the moment. If he didn't arrive soon they might both be gone. They had picked up Paul's camper van from Oxford at around 3.00pm and returned in convoy via the M4. But at Hammersmith they were separated by the lights and there seemed no point in waiting for him. Crossing to the drinks cabinet he poured himself a large whisky. What a week! His own brother branded a murderer. It still hadn't fully sunk in. These last seven days he had barely been out, apart from taking Paul to Aylesbury and back, and no one had rung him. Which was a little surprising when he thought about it. He rang Chambers on Monday pleading a heavy cold but no one had called since to ask how he was. Thankfully his own name hadn't appeared in the papers so far, but someone might have made the connection. He had occasionally mentioned in passing that he had a dysfunctional brother, but there was no way he could prepare for this. Soon it would be all round the Inns of Court. *Brother of top London lawyer charged with Linton murder.* What would that headline do to his career? And it wouldn't be a one day wonder either. The story would run for weeks.

Come on Paul. Don't tell me you've decided to drive straight home to Croydon without a word of thanks and without even letting me know. If you have, don't expect any more help from me. He took a cigarette from the box on the table and lit it. Just one to calm the nerves. He had done pretty well since January. The same with the drinking. Not a drop before 6.00pm and then just a single glass of wine. But now he was back to his old habits. He daren't think how many empty bottles he'd thrown out this week. But he couldn't go on like this. He would have to go back to work on Monday, whatever happened.

With a sigh Priestley turned away from the window and returned to the drinks cabinet to replenish his empty glass. Well, so be it. If Paul had decided to reject his help, there was a limit to how much he could do for him. Stretching out on the sofa he put the glass to his lips and savoured the aroma as he tilted it slowly and felt the warm reassuring sting as the whisky washed over his tongue. Yes, let him find his own way if that was how he wanted to play it. He would get him a good lawyer, but that would be the end of it. Six months down the line he would be in a secure mental institution and then he would have his life back. It might even be better that way. At least he wouldn't have to look out for him any more.

The door buzzer jolted him out of his reverie. Stiffly he rose from the sofa muttering a curse as he went over to the window. Paul's scruffy old camper van was parked between a shiny Mercedes and the Bentley owned by the American couple directly below. Walking slowly to the hall he picked up intercom phone.

'It's me. Sorry. I got lost.'

'Okay, come up. I'll meet you outside the lift.'

A minute later, sweating profusely, Paul stepped out on to the landing. I think I must have entered the post code wrongly into the sat nav. I was at Hyde Park Corner before I realised.'

'Not to worry. Come in and get yourself a drink while I go down and put a parking permit on the van.'

As the lift descended Priestley resolved to check himself. Mother was right, he had to help him. Whatever his private thoughts about what happened in that house a week ago, he had to convince himself that his brother was innocent. Paul was slumped in the armchair when he returned, his legs splayed out in front of him, his head half submerged in the soft upholstery.

'So, what will you have Paul? A whisky?'

'I don't want a drink,' he answered sullenly.'Have you got any food?'

'Not much, I'm afraid. I haven't been out.' He picked up a bowl of peanuts and handed it to him. 'Here, have these for now and we'll go out to a restaurant.'

'No, I don't want to go out. People will see me.'

'No one's going to recognise you, Paul. Not without your moustache.' He hesitated. 'You look better without it, by the way.'

Paul took a large handful of peanuts and stuffed them into his mouth.

261

David Priestley sat down opposite his brother. 'Glad to get your camper van back? I had to pull a few strings to persuade them to release it so soon. It's a good sign Paul. It shows they don't have enough to charge you.'

'Then why didn't they release me?'

'They did release you.'

'Only on bail.'

'But without conditions. They didn't even insist on you staying here last night. Well, they did at first, but I talked them out of it.'

'Why did you have to talk them out of it? I've told them the truth, haven't I? They know now I didn't do it.'

'Of course they do. And they'll lift the bail soon. It's only a matter of time. The truth is they've messed up. If they had released you unconditionally yesterday they'd have lost too much face. And the police don't like to lose face, believe me.'

Now Paul became agitated. 'But what about me, David! What's going to happen to me now. I'll never get another job after what the papers said about me. Everyone thinks I killed her.' He put his hands to his face.' You still think I killed her, don't you? I can tell. You think I was lying yesterday. You think I'm a murderer!'

'Of course I don't!' Priestley had to check himself before continuing. 'I know you didn't kill her, Paul, but the important thing now is to convince a jury of that.'

'You think they're going to arrest me again, don't you?' He was sobbing now.

David Priestley took a handkerchief from his pocket and came over to him. 'Here, use this. It's going to be all right. I'm sure of it.'

For several seconds Paul was silent as he wiped the tears from his eyes. Then he screwed the handkerchief into a ball, put it in his pocket and got up out of his chair. 'I'm going home.'

Priestley made a move to intercept him, then let him pass. 'I thought we were going for a meal.' He followed his brother to the door. 'Call me when you get home. So I know you're okay. Will you do that Paul?'

He half turned. 'You don't have to come to the lift. I can see myself out.'

vii.

At 4.15pm Becky and Wakeman returned to the interview suite for one final session. Becky was convinced that Kate Bellingham was lying when she claimed to have written the letters only to Susan Linton's dictation. Similarly her assertion that she wore disposable gloves when writing to Priestley and reading out his letters. The problem was that she had stuck assiduously to her story all day and neither explanation could be disproved.

'Shall I continue, or do you want to take over?' Having spent several hours going over the same ground, she was beginning to wonder whether there was any point in continuing.

'No, Becks,' said Wakeman. 'It's your show. Though I have to say, I think you're on to a loser.'

As they entered McBride rose to address them. 'I trust this interrogation won't continue very much longer. We have been at it now for most of the day, in spite of the fact that my client has given you a perfectly reasonable explanation in regard to the letters, as well as the lack of fingerprints'

263

'We have no wish to detain Miss Bellingham any longer than necessary,' said Becky, 'but we do have a few final questions.'

McBride sat down with a sigh of resignation.

'According to Paul Priestley, in addition to receiving several letters from someone he assumed to be Susan Linton, he also received two telephone calls. The first was on the 26th March this year. A person whom he took to be Susan Linton, apologised for everything that had gone before and asked him to pay her a visit at Elleswood House so that his money and letters could be returned to him.'

Kate Bellingham stared blankly at Becky.

'Mr Priestley said that he received the second call two days later, the purpose of which was to agree Friday the 6th April as the date he was to come to the house to collect his money and letters. According to Priestley he then received a series of very precise instructions. He was to enter by the front door, which would be unlocked, and come into the hall. There he would find an envelope containing his £3,000, plus all the letters he had sent to her.' Becky paused. 'Did you make those telephone calls, Miss Bellingham, effectively luring Priestley to the house?

For several seconds Kate Bellingham didn't answer. 'Yes, I have to confess that I made those calls. Although I object to your suggestion that they were to lure Paul Priestley to the house.'

'Then what was their purpose?'

Kate Bellingham sat up firmly. 'As I've said many times today, I am deeply ashamed of the part I played in that correspondence with Mr Priestley. What Susan did to that poor man was utterly despicable and I felt badly about it. But that final letter she made me write was the last straw. Not only was it vicious and cruel - to my mind it was criminal of Susan to make those

264

dreadful threats about going to the police and contacting his mother. I decided enough was enough. The time had come to confront Susan. And so I did. I told her that what she had been doing was beyond the pale and that I wanted no further part. More than that, I gave her an ultimatum. I said that unless she returned the £3,000 to Mr Priestley, together with a fulsome apology I would go to the police myself and report her.'

'And what did she say?'

'She was angry with me, of course, but she had no choice. She agreed to my demand.'

'Why couldn't she just send Priestley a cheque with a letter of apology?' said Wakeman .

'You may well ask. But you didn't know the Susan I knew. I assure you that the Susan Linton of stage and screen was very different from the real Susan. She said if she was going to apologise, she would do it her way. She told me to telephone him and tell him to come to the house. She would see him in person to make her apologies, she said. Then and only then would she return his money and letters.'

'If you were so fed up with her,' said Becky, 'why didn't tell her to make the phone call herself?'

Kate Bellingham gave a dismissive laugh. 'To tell you the truth I was sorely tempted. But in the end I decided I didn't want to push things any further. I was just grateful that I had persuaded her to do the honourable thing and return his money and letters.'

'I see,' said Becky. 'So, you made the phone calls to Priestley and then you arranged to be away that night meeting friends in London. Was there a reason for choosing that evening in particular for your reunion?'

'Absolutely, there was. Having persuaded Susan to see Priestley, I resolved to be as far away from

Elleswood House as I could. I didn't want her telephoning me as soon as Priestley arrived, asking me to come down to the house and help her deal with him.'

'So you stayed overnight in London and returned to Elleswood House the following morning to find Miss Linton murdered. Do you have any theories as to the murderer?'

'I can only assume there was an altercation of some kind and that Priestley murdered her in a fit of rage.'

'But this was meant to be a meeting of reconciliation, surely.'

'I know. But Susan was a highly volatile person and from what we gathered from his letters, so was Mr Priestley. Beyond that, your guess is as good as mine.'

Becky turned to Wakeman to indicate that she had no further questions.

'I think we should end it there,' said Wakeman.

'Good, ' said McBride. 'May I conclude that my client is now free to go?'

'Not quite,' said Becky, switching off the recorder. 'You will have your answer shortly.'

Leaving Kate Bellingham with her solicitor, Becky and Wakeman made their way to Straker's office, where both Straker and Jerry Rawlings were waiting for them. They listened as Becky gave her account of the interviews, then asked Wakeman if he had anything to add. Wakeman shook his head.

'The question is whether we release her on police bail, or unconditionally,' said Rawlings. 'What do you think, Steve?'

'It's a difficult one,' said Straker. 'I agree with Becky that some of Miss Bellingham's answers were implausible. On the other hand, I find the main thread of her story believable. And so would a jury, I think, if it got that far.'

'Then we should release her unconditionally,' said Rawlings. 'The lesser charge of demanding money with menaces will hardly stand up with the main perpetrator dead.'

'I think we should release her on police bail,' said Becky. 'I mean, just until we've heard from Jack Meredith. By tomorrow we'll know if they've found anything to incriminate Bristow. '

Rawlings nodded. 'Yes, I think Becky makes a good point. Release her on police bail for tonight, with a promise that we hope to make it unconditional once we've had a chance to review all the evidence.'

viii.

Mark Taverner made his way to the conference room for the 5.00pm review meeting. At the head of the table sat the Chief, flanked by Straker and Wakeman on one side and Jack Meredith and Becky on the other. Their solemn expressions told him there had been no breakthrough.

'Well, ladies and gentlemen,' said Rawlings as he took his place next to Becky. 'I was hoping that by now we would be in a position to bring charges. But I have to say that I'm starting to have doubts about this new hypothesis. Miss Bellingham has admitted to writing the letters to Priestley and to making those two phone calls inviting Priestley to the house, so congratulations on that. But, given her claim that, in the first instance, she was acting on Susan Linton's instructions and, in the second, her motives were

267

entirely honourable, I doubt the CPS will decide to prosecute,' He turned to Straker. 'Miss Bellingham has been released, I take it.'

Straker nodded.

Rawlings moved his gaze round the table, 'So it seems that we are no further forward than we were this time a week ago.'

For several seconds his words hung in the air. Then Becky broke the silence. 'I can't agree that we are no further forward, sir.'

Rawlings gazed at her, eyebrows raised. 'You mean that after interviewing Kate Bellingham for the best part of a day, you are still convinced that she and Bristow framed an innocent man.'

Becky glanced at Mark. 'I do, sir, yes.'

'Then you haven't heard Jack Meredith's report, have you?'

Becky shook her head.

Rawlings turned to Jack Meredith.' Over to you Jack.'

'Yes. Sorry to be the bearer of bad news,' said Meredith, 'but my forensic team have spent much of the day going over Michael Bristow's house, office and car. We've vacuumed up dust particles in all three locations and it will be tomorrow before we have a detailed analysis. But I have to say that we are not optimistic of finding anything. The car in particular was in showroom condition, at least as far as the interior was concerned, and it is there, if anywhere that we were hoping to find DNA traces.'

'Don't you find that suspicious in itself,' said Becky. 'Having seen his office, I wouldn't have thought Bristow was the sort of person to care about the state of his car interior.'

Meredith smiled. 'I'm just a humble forensic scientist, Becky. All I'm saying is that I'm not optimistic

268

that we are going to come up with anything to support your theory.'

My money's still on Priestley,' said Wakeman. 'I'd like to bring him back in tomorrow and have another go at him.'

Rawlings looked directly at Becky. 'Run through your scenario again, will you Becky, just in case we've missed something.'

As Becky summarised their hypothesis for a second time, Mark studied the faces of those sitting round the table. Why were they so sceptical? Wakeman, in particular, seemed barely to be listening. Yet the notion that Susan Linton's death was the result of an angry altercation was no more plausible than their own theory. The autopsy report concluded that the murder weapon was a small sheath knife or kitchen knife. Would Priestley carry such a knife about his person, especially coming to what was supposed to be a meeting of reconciliation? Because, if not, at some point during his visit, he would have to have gone to the kitchen in search of one. And the evidence of the stabbings themselves. The conclusion from the autopsy was that death was caused not by any of the stab wounds to the chest or stomach, but by a single thrust under the left shoulder blade that pierced the heart.

'And we know that they had a motive,' said Becky concluding her account. 'They stood to lose everything if Susan Linton changed her will.'

Rawlings turned to Straker. 'You're still not convinced, are you, Steve? And neither are you Kevyn.'

Wakeman shook his head. 'I accept that the two of them may have been stealing from Linton. And that Bellingham may have continued trying to tap Priestley for money without Linton's knowledge. It's the idea that they framed Priestley for the murder that I don't buy.'

'So, you still think Priestley was the murderer,' said Becky, addressing Wakeman with barely disguised contempt.

'Absolutely, I do,' said Wakeman. 'I think the actress may have intended to give him his money back, just as Bellingham said. But then something changed her mind and he killed her in a fit of rage.'

'You mean, in a fit of rage, he retrieved a knife from somewhere, then crept up on her and stabbed her in the back? Because that's what the autopsy indicates.'

'No. There was a struggle, in the course of which he stabbed her six times. Five stabbings to her chest and stomach and once in her back. I don't have a problem with that.'

'And then he had the presence of mind to smash the glass in the back door, to make it look like a burglary?'

'No one has suggested that Priestley is stupid,' said Wakeman.

Rawlings picked up his briefcase. 'I think that's where we'll have to leave it for tonight. At least we have evidence putting Priestley at the scene of the crime, whereas we have nothing against Bristow. Or anyone else for that matter.' He rose from the table. 'Steve, my advice is to get Priestley back in tomorrow and let Kevyn have another go at him. The shock of being returned to custody might concentrate his mind.'

The meeting over, Mark and Becky walked down their cars. Although partly vindicated by Bellingham's admission about the letters and phone calls, Mark felt despondent.

Becky gripped his arm. 'Don't lose heart, Mark. We haven't had the final report from Forensics yet.'

270

He clicked the remote to unlock his car. 'Anyway, I'm off the case. So, at least I get tomorrow off.'

'Off the case. Who told you that?'

'Wakeman. On the phone this morning. He said I'd wasted enough police time with my half baked theories. He said in future I should keep them to myself and leave it to more experienced members of the team to decide what leads to pursue.'

Becky came round to face him. 'He's an idiot Mark. I don't know why I ever thought otherwise. But he's persistent. I'll give that to him. He even asked me out again yesterday.'

'Did you accept?'

'No. I told him my new boyfriend wouldn't like it'

'Your new boyfriend? You're a dark horse. Do I know him?'

She laughed. 'Why don't you come back to my flat for a meal and I'll tell you all about him.'

ix.

Driving home Straker knew he had to stay focussed. He had been given a job to do and whatever the stresses and strains in his private life, he had to bring Susan Linton's murderer to justice. As he opened the front door Emily was standing in the hall waiting to greet him. She was wearing the dark green dress she had bought for last year's university reunion and the gold necklace he had given her for her thirty fifth birthday. Her hair was different too, not tied back but hanging loose.

She came forward smiling and kissed him. 'Good. You weren't held up after all. I rang Mary and she said

271

you were just going into your review meeting. Have you charged anyone yet?'

'No.' He moved past her to take his briefcase into the study.

'I've booked a table at the bistro to make up for last Saturday. Why don't you go up and shower while I pour you a drink?'

Continuing into the lounge he walked over to the patio doors. Ominous grey clouds hung low overhead, darker than they had been in weeks. There was a sound like distant thunder, but it might have been an aeroplane.

'That's if you want to go out,' she said, coming into the room. 'I can order a take away if you...'

'I saw you and Dan Masterson yesterday,' he said, turning to face her.

'What?'

'You're having an affair with him, aren't you.'

She stepped back, almost tripping on the hearth surround. 'Steve, I thought we'd dealt with this. We're in a play. We're playing the part of lovers. We have to do what lovers do, hold one another, kiss...'

'I'm not talking about what you do on stage.'

'Then, what are you talking about?'

'Where were you yesterday afternoon?'

She hesitated. 'I don't remember. Here probably.'

'So, you didn't go out?'

'Well, yes. I did go out later. That's right. It was a nice afternoon, so I decided to go for a walk.' She reddened. 'Steve, why are you quizzing me like this? If you must know I drove up to the National Trust car park above Cadsden and went for a walk in the woods.'

'By yourself?'

She didn't answer.

'Did you go by yourself?'

272

'Oh, for God's sake Steve, I can't talk to you when you're like this.' Turning away from him she walked out into the hall and picked up the phone 'Okay, I'll cancel the table.'

He followed her. 'I know where you went, because I was there too.'

She looked at him in astonishment. 'What? You mean, you followed me?'

'Yes. I was there too, in the woods, above Cadsden.'

Carefully returning the phone to its cradle she stared at him. 'What on earth for?'

'I saw you as I was driving home. You were in Dan Masterson's car, coming the other way. You weren't expecting me back so early, were you? So, I decided to follow you, just to see where the two of you were going.'

'You mean you turned round and followed us? Steve, I can't believe what you're telling me.'

'I saw you leaving the car park and going off together into the woods. Laughing, talking, holding hands.'

'And you followed us all the way, did you?'

'No, I wasn't in time to see which route you took. So I waited by the fork in the path, until I saw you coming back. Why did you need to go to the woods? Wouldn't it have been more comfortable at his place, or ours? But then, I suppose it was more romantic doing it in the open air.'

'Steve. We went for a walk, that's all. Am I not allowed to go for a walk when I choose?'

'You never go for a walk with me.'

Now she was angry. 'That's because you never want to go for a walk. Because you're always at your bloody work, or glued to the television when you do come home. I can't believe I'm hearing this. What

273

exactly were you hoping to discover by following us Steve? Were you hoping to catch us having it off on a bed of leaves?'

Straker was beginning to wish he had thought things through more carefully before challenging her. But it was too late now. 'I saw what I saw, Em. The two of you walking hand in hand back to the car and then Masterson wrapping his arms round you. Don't tell me that was just rehearsing your lines.'

'He put his arms round me because I was upset!' She was almost shouting now 'Or perhaps you didn't notice that, even though you were watching us so closely.'

'Upset about what?'

Tears began to well in her eyes. 'Steve, I know Donaldson's verdict hit you hard, but the last few weeks haven't exactly been a picnic for me either.'

'Then shouldn't you be talking to me about that instead of going off for walks in the woods with Dan Masterson?'

'Talking to you?' Her eyes were blazing now. 'When could I ever talk to you? Certainly not these last few months. You've been too busy feeling sorry for yourself to listen to how I feel.'

Turning away from her, Straker walked over to the window. 'Did you talk to Masterson about not being able to have a child.'

'Yes, if you must know. It's no secret, is it.'

'And I suppose you told him why, did you?'

'I didn't actually. It's the fact that we can't have a child that matters to me, Steve. Whether the problem lies with you or me is hardly important compared to that?'

'Well, it's important to me.'

'Not more important surely.'

'You're not a man. You don't seem to realise....'

274

'What!' She looked at him in bewilderment. 'Is that what you're saying? That this blow to your self esteem means more to you than the fact that we can't have a family.'

'Not, when you put it like that. But the two things are interconnected Em. You can't have one without the other. Okay, you were disappointed, but this...'

'STOP!' she shouted, putting up both hands as to shield herself from him. 'I don't want to hear it! You know what, Steve? For twelve years I've been fooling myself. I realise that now. I've been fooling myself into believing you loved me.'

Stung by this he turned to face her. 'Of course I love you, but we're not talking about that...'

'No Steve, you don't! You don't love me. All these years I've chosen to believe you did, because the alternative was too unbearable to contemplate. But I can face it now. You don't actually love anyone, do you? The only person you care about is yourself.'

'That's not true...'

Yes it is. But it's my fault too. I suppose, from the beginning, I invested you with the qualities I was looking for, instead of accepting you for what you are.' She walked towards the door and out into the hall. 'I'm going outside. I need to clear my head. Don't follow me. When I come back I'll pack a suitcase and go.'

'Go where?'

'To Mum's. I'll come back during the week and get the rest of my things. In the meantime, you can make a list and we can decide how to share the spoils.'

With that she went out through the front door, slamming it behind her.

Straker stood motionless, too shocked to take in what had just happened. Emily was given to occasional shows of histrionics, but this was different.

Okay, he might have chosen his words more carefully, but was he really so out of order? He opened the front door and stepped out into the porch. As he did so, a jagged flash of lightning lit up the granite sky, followed almost immediately by a long crack of thunder so loud that the house shook. Had she gone to neighbours? They knew several to say hello to, but none well enough to call on, especially in the state she was in. He looked across the road at the footpath sign pointing across the field and up the hill to the wood. Surely she hadn't gone that way, not in that flimsy green dress.

Suddenly it was raining so hard that water was cascading over the gutters, splattering the flower beds and pummelling the road in a violent, misty spray. Without stopping to put on his raincoat he ran out of the house and across the road to the kissing gate. By the time he had gone thirty yards, his suit was soaked and his trousers caked in mud as his shoes slid and squelched in the mud. He stumbled on. He had to find her and get her safely back to the house.

As the path entered the wood, it wound its way over the top of the hill and down the other side. Surely she wouldn't just have stumbled on in this downpour. Except that there was nowhere to shelter because the trees were still bare of leaves. He looked round him. Maybe she hadn't come this way at all. Maybe she went down to the main road, or up the other way, through the housing estate.

Then he saw her, about thirty yards to his left, huddled against a large tree trunk, shivering. Her hair hung in dark streaks across her face, her green dress was soaked and dripping. As he picked his way through fallen branches to reach her, he saw that one of her shoes was missing and there were long bloody scratches on her calves.

276

'Emily!'

'GO AWAY! GET AWAY FROM ME!'

He came closer. 'I'm sorry. Em.... Please...I'm sorry!'

'No you're not!'

Taking off his soaking wet jacket he wrapped it round her shoulders and held her. At first she struggled to push him away, but he held on tightly until eventually she fell against his chest sobbing. He continued holding her, pulling her closer, smoothing the hair away from her eyes. 'Emily...I'm sorry... I'm sorry. Don't leave me, Em...Please don't leave me...'

Chapter Nine

Sunday, 15th April 2012

i.

Kevyn Wakeman studied his face in the bathroom mirror. The bags under his eyes were definitely getting more pronounced. And he could even detect the beginnings of a double chin. Was this how other people saw him? He switched off the mirror light. Better. But he would need to watch it. Too much alcohol wasn't good for his complexion. To say nothing of what it was doing to his sex life. Had Becky given him the elbow in favour of that geek, Taverner? What did she see in him, for God's sake, with his narrow frame and girly looks? What did Taverner have that he hadn't? Apart from a degree, probably, which was hardly a lot of use in this kind of work? This new theory of his, for example. Too clever by half. He knew it would come to nothing.

Still, at least now the focus was back where it should be. All the circumstantial evidence pointed to Priestley from the outset, and now they had forensic evidence to back it up. What more did the CPS want. It was totally unreasonable of them to insist on a confession as well. Still, if a confession was their stipulation, that was what he would get from Priestley, even if it took all day and all night to drag it out of him. The galling thing was that they would have had it three days ago, had Straker not been sitting next to him, ready to call a halt the moment the man started blubbing. By now he could have been charged and in custody and the whole team could be enjoying a well earned rest.

He looked at his watch. 8.25am. Two of the lads were driving over to Croydon this morning to bring Priestley back to Aylesbury. No hurry. Even on a Sunday it was unlikely they would get back before 10.00am. Walking through to the kitchen he filled the kettle. Yes, this morning he would nail Priestley once and for all. Though he had to admit there was the odd moment yesterday when he began to think he might be innocent after all. Which would not have been good. Even if his release didn't lead to a full independent enquiry, there were bound to be questions asked about how the media seemed to know so much. Could he rely on Straker to play dumb? Probably. But what about Becky? She had said nothing so far, he was pretty sure of that. But what if she were to be hauled in again, this time by Rawlings?

Pulling his front door closed, Wakeman set off for work. Well, so what? He would give Rawlings the same story he gave Becky and Straker. He might get a rap over the knuckles, but it was hardly a sackable offence. Still, why was he thinking like this? This morning he would extract a confession from Paul Priestley and he would be the hero of the hour.

As he approached the roundabout at the end of the dual carriageway his mobile rang. He pressed the hands free button. 'Kevyn Wakeman.'

'It's DC Jason Savage sir. Bad news, I'm afraid.'

'Tell me.'

'We arrived at Priestley's flat at 8.30am, but there was no answer when we rang the bell.'

'Go on.'

'His landlord saw us out of the window and said he should be there because his camper van was parked outside. Eventually he came down and let us in?'

Wakeman gave a groan. 'Don't tell me he's done a bunk,'

'No, he was there all right. We found him lying in the bath, with both his wrists slit ...'

ii.

Becky walked into the empty conference room and took her place at the table. She had received a text on her way in to say there was to be an unscheduled team meeting at 9.30am. A moment later Straker entered with Kevyn Wakeman and Jack Meredith, followed closely by the Chief. Judging by their purposeful expressions she sensed there had been a development. Rawlings sat down at the head of the table.

'Good morning.' His expression was grim. 'Before I hand over to Jack Meredith, I have to tell you that Paul Priestley has been taken to hospital following an apparent suicide attempt. He was found by two of our officers at 8.30am this morning lying naked in the bath with both wrists cut. He's lost a great deal of blood, but the hospital thinks he should pull through. I have to say that it was extremely fortuitous that our lads went there this morning, because in another hour he would certainly have been dead. The irony is that, if the information you are about to hear from Jack had come through yesterday, we would not this morning be making that arrest. So, as it happens, he's a very lucky man. Over to you Jack.'

Jack Meredith opened his file and took out a typed sheet. 'Yes ladies and gentlemen, I'm pleased this morning to report a significant development. Yesterday, as you know, our forensic team carried out an extensive examination of Michael Bristow car.' Meredith paused. 'An old car and very scruffy, yet the interior was in pristine condition. In fact, suspiciously so, as you remarked yesterday, Becky. Well, that set us thinking. So much so, that last night I and a member of my team returned to Bristow's house and that's where we got lucky. Normally, at Bristow's address, the recycle bins are emptied on a Friday. But because of the Easter Bank Holiday, Friday's collection was delayed until this coming Monday.

To cut a long story short, we took his recycle bin away for inspection and, sure enough, right at the bottom, we found a half full vacuum bag. By 9.00pm last night the bag was on its way over to our laboratories in Oxford where I've had a team working overnight to examine the contents.' Here Meredith paused and a bright smile lit up his face. ' I can now confirm, ladies and gentlemen, that in that vacuum bag we found DNA and other evidence linking Michael Bristow to the crime scene. Tiny fragments of glass that match the glass fragments found by the back door of Elleswood House. Microscopic fibres from the carpet in the foot well of his car containing traces of urine, just as we found in Paul Priestley's camper van. And, most significantly, rug fibres impregnated with Susan Linton's blood.'

As Rawlings leaned forward, he too was beaming. 'Thank you Jack. So, ladies and gentlemen, I believe we now have enough evidence to arrest Michael Bristow on suspicion of the murder of Susan Linton.' He turned to Straker. 'By the way, where is Taverner this morning?'

282

'I decided we wouldn't be needing him today,' said Wakeman.

'Well, he certainly deserves a day off, as we all do. Still, I would have preferred him to have been here, so I could congratulate him, along with you, Becky, on a magnificent piece of work. Is he back in tomorrow?'

'I'll make sure he is,' said Straker.

'Good. Then I'll come over and commend him personally,' said Rawlings. 'I can also tell you, ladies and gentlemen, that I've had a conversation just now with a senior crown prosecutor, setting out this morning's findings and they are confident of proceeding against Bristow. Which still leaves Kate Bellingham, of course. Do we bring her back in this morning for further questioning?'

'I would say so, yes,' said Straker, looking more relaxed than Becky had seen him in days. 'We can put them in adjacent rooms and interview them side by side. I doubt if we'll have to wait long before one incriminates the other.'

'Rawlings nodded. 'And who will do the interviews?'

'I will,' said Straker confidently. 'Together with DS Wakeman. We'll interview both of them.'

iii.

The interview with Michael Bristow lasted barely fifteen minutes. Confronted with the evidence from the vacuum cleaner bag, Susan Linton's former agent declined to answer any further questions. He was remanded in custody on suspicion of murder.

Making their way to Interview Room B, Straker and Wakeman paused a few moments to watch Kate

283

Bellingham through the observation panel. She looked tense and on edge as she sat talking to her solicitor. .

'Shall I lead this time?' Evidently still affected by the news of Priestley's attempted suicide, Wakeman sounded more subdued than usual.

'No, this is my call,' said Straker, his mouth dry with apprehension. He knew this was an interview he couldn't delegate.

'I would start briskly. Don't let her cosy up to you.'

'Yes, I know.'

'And if she starts getting cheeky, leave her to me.'

Straker gave his deputy a tight smile. 'Okay, let's go.'

As they entered the interview room Kate Bellingham rose immediately. 'Inspector, thank goodness. Please can you tell me what is going on?...'

'Sit down please, Miss Bellingham,' said Straker.' All will be revealed in due course.'

Taken aback by his businesslike tone she resumed her seat. 'Yesterday, Inspector, I was told that my unconditional release was more or less a formality. Now, this morning I am brought here a second time..'

'There have been some developments overnight,' said Straker, still avoiding her eye, 'Developments that lead us to the conclusion that you have not been entirely truthful in the evidence you have given us so far. So I am now going to caution you and remind you that this interview is being recorded.'

'Caution me? Again? But this is completely unacceptable, Inspector. Yesterday, I gave what I hope was a full and reasonable explanation for all my actions. I just hope that you know what you are doing, because ...'

284

'Miss Bellingham,' said Straker sharply. 'After I have cautioned you, it is in your own best interests to listen carefully to the questions I put to you and answer them truthfully, remembering that the answers you give may be referred to in court. '

Silenced by his harshness of tone Straker delivered the caution, then opened his notebook. 'Let me begin by asking you to describe your relationship with Michael Bristow.'

She looked at him, eyebrows raised. 'I would describe Michael as a long standing friend. Although I don't see what this has to do with anything.'

'Would you describe him as an intimate friend?'

She hesitated. 'If by intimate you mean someone in whom I would be happy to confide, then I would say yes.'

Straker lifted his eyes to meet hers. To think that four days ago, he went to bed with this woman. Today he didn't find her remotely attractive. 'And the two of you have been intimate friends for many years. You don't deny that.'

She looked mockingly at Straker for several seconds before answering. 'Come on, Inspector, what are you trying to get me to say? Yes, Michael Bristow and I are in a relationship and have been for many years. Does that satisfy you?'

McBride shifted uneasily. 'I must say, Inspector that your line of questioning does seem rather intrusive. Are you sure it is strictly relevant to your enquiry?'

Straker looked steadily at Kate Bellingham. 'Then you will be concerned to learn that, this morning, Michael Bristow has been remanded in custody on suspicion of the murder of Susan Linton. Furthermore, it is our belief that you conspired with Michael Bristow in that murder and together framed Paul Priestley for the crime.'

285

McBride seemed taken aback by this news, but Kate Bellingham remained calm. 'That is ridiculous, Inspector and you know it.'

'You have already admitted that it was you and not your employer who wrote all the letters to Priestley. You have also admitted that it was you and not your employer who telephoned Priestley to arrange for him to come to the house on Friday the 6th April, not before 7.30pm.'

'Yes, but on Susan's instructions, as I told your colleague yesterday.'

'But you had a motive for murder, didn't you.' said Straker. You stood to gain a considerable amount from Miss Linton's will; the house plus the remainder of her assets, such as they were.'

Kate Bellingham gave a derisive snort. 'If I believed that I was the sole beneficiary of Miss Linton's will, why would I want to murder her, Inspector? Answer me that.'

'Because, following the acrimonious meeting of the 2nd January, you feared she might change that will. Which is exactly what she did, as you now know.'

Kate Bellingham turned towards McBride. 'This is all pure conjecture. They have no evidence, none at all.'

Palefaced, McBride turned to Straker. 'I would appreciate it, Inspector if we could take a short adjournment while I consult with my client.'

'Of course,' said Straker reaching to switch off the video recorder. 'We'll take twenty minutes. Resume at 12.10pm.'

'Inspector...'

Straker had reached the door when Kate Bellingham called out.

'You do realise that I shall be lodging a complaint, don't you.'

286

He turned to face her. 'That's your prerogative, Miss Bellingham. Any complaint you wish to make will be thoroughly investigated I assure you.'

She turned to her solicitor. 'I haven't mentioned this to you before but on Wednesday of this week Inspector Straker called on me at home. I assumed he had come to ask me a few questions. But then he subjected me to considerable sexual harassment.'

McBride looked in surprise at Straker .

'Sexual harassment?' exclaimed Wakeman, returning to sit down opposite Kate Bellingham. 'That's a very serious allegation, Miss Bellingham. So serious that I'm surprised you didn't make a complaint straight away on Wednesday, when you say this happened to you.'

'I decided at the time there was no point. I know what you police are like, all closing ranks and sticking together. Besides I know how to take care of myself. I was able to fend him off.'

'It seems odd then,' said Wakeman, 'that only yesterday you were telling DC Reedman and myself what a gentlemen Inspector Straker was.'

'That's only compared with....'

'Listen darling.' Wakeman leaned forward menacingly.' As I'm sure Mr McBride will confirm, the police get complaints like this all the time. It's par for the course dealing with the sort of people we have to deal with. All I would say to you is you had better be absolutely sure of what you hope to achieve before you start making counter allegations. Because, as at this moment, you are in a lot of trouble.' He got up and followed Straker to the door. There, he turned. 'Talk it over with Mr McBride. I'm sure he'll give you good advice.'

'Thanks for that Kevyn,' said Straker as soon as they were out in the corridor.

287

'No problem boss. As it turns out you didn't need any assistance from me. Yes, it helps to be a gentleman. I could learn from that myself.'

Straker looked at his deputy. So far they hadn't discussed the news of Priestley's attempted suicide. 'Bad news about Priestley, Kevyn. But it sounds as if he'll pull through.'

'Until the next time.' replied Wakeman morosely.

'Do you want to take over with Bellingham?'

'Not unless you want me to. You're doing fine, Steve. Even if Bellingham walks free, we've still got the main one in the bag. That's not a bad result. Come on, let's get some coffee.'

iv.

Arriving home at 5.15pm Straker put the bottle of wine in the fridge and the bouquet of flowers in the sink while he looked for a vase. What a difference a day made. Twenty four hours ago, with the investigation stalled, he was preparing to come home and accuse his wife of having an affair. Now Bristow, at least, was in custody and his relationship with Emily was back on track. Crossing to the window he looked out at the garden. The shrubs had perked up no end with the overnight rain and the lawn looked greener than it had in months. With more rain forecast, the longest winter drought in years was over at last.

Last night, stumbling back down the hill with Emily shivering inside his jacket, he realised how close he was to losing her. By the time they got back to the house, she was no longer sobbing, but she would neither speak to him nor even look at him as he led her indoors and into the kitchen. As she stood there in her dripping clothes, he was in a panic of indecision. Wrap a blanket round her or help her undress? In the end he switched on the oven to its highest setting, then sat her down in front of the opened door while he went upstairs to run the bath.

For the next half hour, as he changed out of his own wet clothes and waited for her to come down, he had time to reflect on his behaviour since the consultation. If, in these last few months, she had sought comfort from Masterson, or any other man for that matter, he had only himself to blame. Ever since that meeting with Donaldson and maybe for a long time before , he had been nothing like the man she married. So preoccupied was he with the blow to his own self esteem, he had given giving barely a thought to how the consultant's verdict might have affected her.

At last she came down and in silence they sat at the table and ate the takeaway he had ordered. It was only when they moved into the lounge to sit in front of the fire that they began to talk. Yes, she had been drawn to Dan Masterson, she said, still sitting away from him at the end of the sofa. Not so much because she found him physically attractive, but because he was kind and funny and nice to be with. Above all, because he listened. She found she could talk to him in the way they had once been to be able to talk to one another, before his career and her obsession with getting pregnant had driven a wedge between them. But she wasn't in love with Dan. And nor was having a child more important to her than their marriage, although there had been times recently when she thought it might be.

By the time they got to bed, the storm had passed. Then, at around midnight, the skies opened again.

And with the rain lashing the windows in wave after angry wave, she reached out to him and they made love for the first time in weeks. Lying with Emily curled up against him, he no longer cared about what she had done or not done with Dan Masterson. He was just thankful that they were still together.

And even if the investigation hadn't produced the outcome he had been hoping for, they had achieved their main objective. Although they didn't have enough evidence to charge his co-conspirator, at least Michael Bristow was firmly under lock and key. On learning that Bristow had been charged with murder, Kate Bellingham lost no time in distancing herself from her lover. Twice since the big fall out, she said, Michael had expressed the wish that Susan Linton might die before she had an opportunity to change her will. She assumed both times that he was joking, but now she realised he wasn't. Michael was in deep financial difficulties, she said, so maybe he saw an early inheritance as the solution to his problems. Her big mistake, she said, had been to tell Bristow of Susan's decision to invite Priestley to the house on the evening of the 6th April. She could only conclude that he saw it as an opportunity to murder the actress and frame Priestley for the crime.

Hearing Emily's car in the drive he went to the door to greet her.

'Hi, Em.

'Has success finally crowned your efforts?' she said, kissing him.

'Not entirely. We've charged Bristow, but we've have to let Kate Bellingham go.'

'Even though she's guilty?'

'It's the way it goes. You win some. You lose some.'

'Never mind. At least you got the one who wielded the knife. Well done. This calls for a celebration.'

'It does. And I've booked the bistro. The taxi will be here at 7.00pm.'

v.

As Emily and Straker sat down at their favourite table in the corner, the waiter poured two glasses of champagne, returned the bottle to the ice bucket and quietly retreated.

'What shall we drink to?' said Straker as he and Emily clinked glasses.

'To our anniversary, I think,' she replied, smiling. 'With a resolution to try and celebrate on time in future. Work always permitting, of course.'

'And to the play, in which you will be a great success.'

And to your success with the investigation? It's a great achievement, Steve. I hope you get the recognition you deserve.'

Straker shrugged. 'Most of it was down to DCs Reedman and Taverner. Left to me, we'd probably still be floundering.'

'Nonsense. If it was a team effort, it was a team led by you. Do you think Paul Priestley will pull through?'

'The hospital seems to think so. He'll get substantial damages from the Daily Herald. His brother will make sure of that.'

She looked at him slyly. 'So, Kate Bellingham walks free. I should think you're quite relieved, aren't you?'

Straker looked at her sharply. 'Why do you say that?'

291

'Well, you did have a bit of a crush on her, didn't you?' She laughed. 'Come on, Steve. Don't deny it. I could tell by the way you were talking to her on the phone the other night. All breathless and strangulated like you were when we first met. I was half expecting you to drop everything there and then to drive over to see her.'

'Then, why didn't I?'

'What, you? Detective Inspector Steve Straker sleeping with a witness? Hardly. It could have cost you your job, couldn't it?'

Straker looked guiltily away. Five days ago he was given the career opportunity of a lifetime – an opportunity that many of his colleagues would have given their eye teeth for. And how did he respond to the trust that has been placed in him? At a time when his team appeared at last to be on the verge of a major breakthrough, he took the time out to go to bed with a key witness. He must have been mad, literally mad. It was a betrayal of everything he stood for, not just as a police officer, but also as a husband. And all for what? A few minutes of excited anticipation, followed by a sickening half hour of humiliation and a lifetime of regret.

Sitting with Kate Bellingham on that sofa, he was as sexually aroused as he could ever remember. So much so that when she pulled him to her in that sudden, unexpected embrace, he thought he might come there and then. But, from the moment she led him through to her bedroom, the spell was broken. Suddenly the insecurities that had been haunting him ever since the consultation, returned to unman him. His erection had subsided even before he was out of his clothes and from that moment, all he wanted was to be away from that cottage as soon as possible. For a few minutes he endured her attempts to rekindle his desire, but eventually could stand it no more. With a mumbled apology he got up from bed, gathered up his clothes and went to the bathroom to dress. Three minutes later, without another word exchanged between them, he was back in his car driving towards Aylesbury.

'Though I suppose you saw her on other occasions, didn't you? After all, she was a key witness'

'Of course.'

'On your own?'

Should he confess? Yesterday it seemed a possibility that Kate Bellingham might make trouble for him, but not any more.

'We didn't have sex, Em, if that's what you're thinking.'

She rested her hand on his. 'Really? It occurred to me that you might.'

'What? You mean, with Kate Bellingham?'

'Not necessarily with her. But with someone.' She smiled. 'I've been such a bitch, haven't I, Steve. My obsession with getting pregnant. It came close to destroying us, didn't it? For months, years even, it's been all I've been able to think about. I realise now how close I came to driving you away for good.'

He took her hand. 'I've been thinking, Em...'

'Yes?' She looked at him anxiously.

'You know Donaldson said something about going to a sperm bank.'

'Yes. But...'

'I know and I've decided, it's not a problem. After all, we don't have to meet the donor, do we? Or even know anything about him, if we don't want to. And if it's successful, well, the baby will still be ours, won't it?'

Emily's frowned. 'Actually...there may be no need.'

293

'Why?'

'I was going to tell you yesterday. I've missed my last two periods. I didn't build up any hopes, because it's happened before, of course. But when I was two weeks late again this month, I did a pregnancy test on Wednesday and it was positive. So I did another on Thursday and again this morning. I know it's still early days and it could all go wrong...'

'But wait a minute...... we haven't....'

She took his hand. 'Yes, we have. That weekend we went over to stay with Mum.'

'At your mother's? But I was hopeless. I barely made it..'

'I know. And I wasn't on my best form either? But maybe, between us, we weren't that hopeless after all.'

Straker looked into her clear blue eyes. Had she slept with Masterson? And if she had, would she admit it? Better not to go there, After all, who was he to sit in judgement? Lifting her hands to his lips he kissed them. 'Em. That's wonderful,'

She gripped his hands tightly in hers. 'I love you, Steve. You'll stay with me, wont you?'

'Of course.'

'Whatever the future holds?'

He drew her towards him. 'Whatever the future holds.'

At that moment his mobile rang. Releasing her, he put the phone to his ear. 'Steve Straker speaking.'

'Steve, its Jack Meredith.'

Reluctantly getting up from the table, he blew Emily a kiss and went into a quiet corner. 'Hello Jack. Not still at work are you?'

'Sorry to trouble you this late, Steve, but I think we may be able to charge Bellingham after all.'

'Tell me '

'When we went to search Bristow's property we also took his mobile phone. The voicemail was empty, but with a little help from our technical boys, we were able to retrieve recent messages. Take a listen to this.'

'YOU HAVE FOUR NEW MESSAGES. FIRST MESSAGE. RECEIVED ON SATURDAY THE 14TH APRIL AT 10.22AM.

MICHAEL, WHERE ARE YOU FOR GOD'S SAKE?... LISTEN. I'VE JUST HAD A VISIT FROM THE POLICE. THEY ARE ON TO US, MICHAEL. I DON'T KNOW HOW, BUT THEY ARE. I HAVEN'T TIME TO EXPLAIN RIGHT NOW, BUT WE BOTH HAVE TO BE EXTREMELY CAREFUL.

IF THEY CALL ON YOU, YOU KNOW NOTHING. DO YOU UNDERSTAND? NOTHING ABOUT THE LETTERS AND, PARTICULARLY, NOTHING ABOUT SUSAN'S WILL. WHATEVER THEY MAY TELL YOU, DON'T REACT. DON'T EVEN RAISE AN EYEBROW. THIS ISN'T GOOD NEWS, MICHAEL. YOU WERE RIGHT. WE SHOULD HAVE ACTED SOONER. BUT, IF YOU DO AS I SAY, AT LEAST IT WILL KEEP US BOTH OUT OF PRISON....'

THE END

If you have enjoyed reading **Seeds of Doubt** may we recommend James Parr's debut novel, **Deferral of Guilt.** Published in 2012, **Deferral of Guilt** went to number one in Amazon's Crime and General Fiction charts.

Deferral of Guilt

When a tramp is found with massive head wounds close to the property of wealthy retired carpet tycoon Frank Brownhills, the police have no reason to suspect him or his glamorous ex-model wife of involvement. But when they find a trail of blood leading into the garden and Carron Brownhills goes missing, the investigation begins to assume larger dimensions. As detectives Pat O'Donnell and Alex Paterson piece together a story of murder, rape, blackmail and revenge each is pursued by his own private demons. For both have guilty secrets which threaten to overwhelm them even before their investigation is completed.

13806269R00171

Printed in Poland
by Amazon Fulfillment
Poland Sp. z o.o., Wrocław